# Children
# of
# Blindness

'Hate and mistrust are the
children of blindness'

Sir  William Watson
(1858 – 1935)

# Children of Blindness

### A BRUTAL EXPOSÉ
### OF BIGOTRY AND PREJUDICE
### IN OUTBACK AUSTRALIA

## Trish Clark

IMPERIUM
HIgh Adventure PublIshIng.com
AUSTRALIA

First published 1976  by
Ure Smith, Sydney
© Trish Sheppard 1976

This 2010  edition designed in Australia and
published by
High Adventure Publishing/ Imperium Books
Tumbulgum, 2490 Australia
© Trish Clark 2010
ISBN10:    0-9807848-0-8
ISBN13:    978-0-9807848-0-0

*Acknowledgements*

For permission to reproduce portions of the lyrics from
'Black Superman' by Johnny Wakin, we thank Castle Music
Pty Ltd, Sydney

and

to reproduce portions of the lyrics from  'Country  Roads'
by John Denver, Bill Danoff and Taffy  Nivert, we thank
Cherry Lane Music.

Cover photograph: 'View of Urandangi, Queensland 2001'
by Ian Kenins.

*This book is dedicated to
my father,  Allan Clark*

*By the same author*
*ANDREA
*AUSTRALIAN ADVENTURERS
*MOTHERHOOD
AN IMMACULATE CONCEPTION

*with Iain Finlay*
*AFRICA OVERLAND
*SOUTH AMERICA OVERLAND
*ACROSS THE SOUTH PACIFIC
GOOD MORNING HANOI
THE SILK TRAIN

Titles marked with an asterisk were originally
published under Trish's previous name,
Trish Sheppard.

# CONTENTS

**CHAPTER**                                    **PAGE**

# INTRODUCTION TO THE 2010 EDITION

Why re-issue a book more than thirty years after it was first published? Because of the scorchingly shameful truth that the horror it portrays, far from diminishing, has in fact increased. I wrote this social documentary in what I realise now was the naïve hope that it could help change the situation for the better. It didn't. But that cannot be the end of the matter.

Early in 1975 I took off from Sydney and travelled for over four thousand kilometers around northern New South Wales. Up through Nyngan, across to Wilcannia and Broken Hill and up to Tibooburra. Back through Bourke, Brewarrina, Walgett and Collarenebri to Moree and then down through Coonamble, Coonabarabran and Gilgandra.

The space, the light, the colours and the feeling of physical freedom were all exhilarating. But best of all were the people. Everyone treated me with overwhelming generosity, kindness and hospitality.

The only blot on the whole trip was what I saw happening within the Aboriginal communities. I hadn't gone looking for stories, just simply to get away for a spell on my own, yet back in Sydney I was haunted by what I had seen and I knew I would have to go back and write about it.

What finally made me decide to return was that I was flabbergasted to discover when I told people in Sydney what I had seen, that they either hardly believed my stories, or dismissed the situation as incurable and of little consequence.

So I went back to live for a month in one of the small townships I had visited on my journey. It was during this period that the incidents depicted in this book occurred. Every major event is based on fact. Names have been changed and characters added to, or amalgamated with others, to make the story flow more easily, but it's important, as you read, to remember that all this is still happening in Australia today.

It is a violent, brutal and offensive book, and as I re-read it I am amazed that I could write in such a way. But it's the truth about a situation Australians cannot, in all humanity, continue to ignore.

Why does the fictional Woongarra and at least a score of other townships like it still exist? That is the question all Australians; those born here and those more recently arrived, must answer. We must apply ourselves, as individuals, to ensuring that no Australian lives under these sordid and deplorable conditions. Until we do, Sorry is just another word and we cannot call ourselves a civilized people.

Shortly after it first appeared, Children of Blindness was translated and published in Russian and a little later the film rights were signed over to Film Australia. For six months, through three drafts and several writers, attempts were made to produce a script considered acceptable to the general public. These failed. It appeared to be impossible to come up with a bums-on-seats, cheerful or even a mildly positive conclusion. Because there was and remains, as anyone who has spent time in these inhuman places knows: no happy ending.

Over the decades of a life lived to the full, Woongarra has been a heavy shadow on my heart. I've followed the bitter destiny of a blighted people in the seemingly fated settlement, habitualized to violence and ugliness by the harshness of their living conditions and the landscape. I've also made several short visits.

The last time I went it was to return the human bones of the victims of a still rarely discussed local massacre that occurred during the 19<sup>th</sup> century. They had been scooped from the earth and given to me by an Aboriginal Elder. But they had become a burdensome secret and I hoped that by placing them back where they fell, I would in some way be relieved of their pain. I was not. I find I cannot so easily cut adrift and free myself from our collective historical guilt and shame. The nation's public Apology to the Aboriginal people caused some easing of the load, but it was only minimal. The vicious crushing cycle of degradation continues to churn up and destroy innocent lives not just in Woongarra, but in numerous other similar townships around our nation.

Of course in the end, it is neither the politicians in Canberra, the police on the spot, nor even the people who live in these settlements who hold the ultimate responsibility. That rests with all of us. You and I have it within our capacity to make amends and to put right this terrible wrong. We cannot wait for or rely on our elected leaders.

It is an irrelevance that we, as individuals, did not create this horror. It remains our own personal responsibility. In another thirty years I'll be dead. Perhaps you will be too. Is this heritage of Hate and Mistrust what you want to pass on to your grandchildren? Is the fate of the indigenous people of Woongarra and all the other fringe Aboriginal townships in Australia to always remain a blot on our conscience.

Trish Clark
Tumbulgum 2010

# Chapter One

*Country roads, take me home*
*To the place I belong,*
*West Virginia, Mountain Mama,*
*Take me home, country roads.*

Doug shifted slightly, trying to make himself more comfortable as he sat with his back up against the cabin of the utility while it sped through the warm night. The music drifted back through the open cabin windows. Ever since the three whitefellows had picked him up on the road between Dubbo and Trangie they had played the same John Denver cassette over and over.

Not that I'm complaining, Doug thought, Christ no. He couldn't believe his luck when the utility had stopped and they'd told him to hop in the back. White blokes just don't pick up Aborigines, he thought. But perhaps things have changed while I've been inside. No. Not much hope of that. Be a long time before things change, if they ever do. The song ended and the tape clicked off. Perhaps they're going to try and roll me. Hard luck if they do 'cos I've only got a ten dollar bill. He felt the boner's knife stuck in his belt. And I'm not about to let three white bastards do me over anyway.

The low scrub stretched away from the edge of the road. It was too dark to see anything, but Doug knew they were driving through cotton country because he'd worked on a place down here once. Bloody backbreaking work it was too. But he'd stuck it out because the boss had been good to him. Whitefellow, but a good bloke just the same. He had been struggling to keep going and Doug had felt sorry for him so he had worked the whole season, even though it was a damn hard grind. The whites had called all the Aborigines Jackie and never got off our backs. Christ, maybe that's it. Maybe these white fellows are queers. Doug's grip tightened on his tired looking swag. Queers, poofs, homosexuals, like those bloody warders in Long Bay who always tried it on with the dark blokes because they knew they wouldn't squeal. Yeh, well just let the bastards try it on with me and I'll whip their balls out just like they were sheep. Doug felt the bile bitter in his mouth, swallowed hard and consciously relaxed his hold on his swag.

Whoa-up Dougo, what's the bloody matter with you? They're probably nothing more than a trio of city slickers up for a bit of pig shooting and they don't know any better than to give a bloody boong a lift. He smiled a little to himself. Anyway, what the hell does it matter, they're going all the way to Woongarra. They're going home!

Doug tilted his head back and stared up into the deep black night, at the millions upon millions of tiny stars. The sky stretched hugely from horizon to horizon. It was like being under an enormous upturned dish. Christ, it's great to be out. Out of Long Bay, out of Sydney, out beyond the cities, out in the bush. Six months trapped in that stinking hole, like a roo with

2

its paw caught and mangled in a steel trap. Six bloody months. Every day the same routine, the same walls, the same people, the same food. The same monotonous, useless existence. Doing time is right. I've done time and time has done me. By Christ I've had time. A moment longer, one second more and I'd have gone flaming mad. In all his twenty seven years never had six months gone so slowly.

Doug took a large breath of the soft warm night air. all the time he was inside he had held on to his feelings about Woongarra until they had become coagulated and sat like a warm thing deep inside him, where he could turn it over and over, like he used to play with interesting pieces of stone while he sat fishing by the Barwon River.

For Doug, Woongarra was a magic place. Marooned between Brewarrina and Walgett, with only a dirt road to either place, it was like a ship at sea or a time capsule.

Woongarra was Flo. Doug thought of his wife and felt good. She is beautiful. Bloody beautiful. Well black is beautiful, isn't it fella! And Flo sure is black. Blacker than me even. So black you can lose her in the dark.

He grinned as he remembered the first time they had made love, one evening down by the Barwon River. They had walked along the edge of the open sewer, which runs out from West Woongarra into the river. Flo had been very quiet. Afterwards she had said that she had been quiet because she was worried he would realize she wasn't a virgin. Well of course I knew she wasn't a virgin. She was bloody well fifteen wasn't she, and who the hell is a virgin at fifteen for Christ's sake!

Then, as they lay among the bindie-eyes and sharp grass beside the river, they heard the chatter of the people walking the half-mile home to the West from the picture theatre in Woongarra. The Marshalls and the Joneses came by together in a crowd. There must have been eighteen of them with all their kids. The adults first. Jack Marshall talking about the film as if he'd made it. What a bloody skite that man is. And no one else daring to put in a word. The kids straggling behind teasing one another. 'Ah, rack orf,' eight-year-old Billy Saunders had said. 'You got flaming tickets on yerself mate.' A scuffle started and Mrs. Marshall yelled back at them. 'If you kids don't cut it out I'll give you all a bloody good hiding.' There was more subdued scuffling and Billy Saunders seemed to be coming off rather badly until, in a sudden silence, Flo and he heard Billy mutter with a viciousness only eight-year olds can muster, 'I know what's the matter with you, Ann Marshall, you're too tight in the bloody crutch,' and then they heard him race to catch up with his parents, safe in their adult world, until tomorrow.

All the while Doug and Flo lay silent fifty feet away in the grass listening. Doug couldn't understand why, but overhearing these private conversations made him feel even closer to her than when they had made love. When the last straggler had gone home and even Gary Andrews, drunk as always, had staggered past, Doug had turned to speak to her and found himself unable to see her in the dark until she suddenly opened her eyes. It gave him such a fright, those two white marbles suddenly so close, but it was at that precise moment that he fell in love with Flo and decided that from now on she would be his woman.

4

Woongarra was Flo. Flo and the kids. Christ they will have grown in six months. He was gripped by a sudden fear that they wouldn't recognize him, but in the same instant he knew that was nonsense. Carol will be eight and a right little madam, just like her mother. He'd learnt a lot about women by having a daughter. Not that I'll ever really understand them, they are another people, altogether different from men. But then there was Steve. Seven now. We'll be able to go fishing together and I'll show him how to catch the big yellow-belly with his bare hands down at the weir. Flo and Carol and Steve. He thought too about his brothers and sisters, Allan, Bob, Dave, Marge and Irene. And then there's Mum. Wouldn't they all be pleased to see him. He hadn't told any of them he was coming home because he wanted to surprise them all. I hope these white fellows stop at Nyngan and I can duck into the pub and get a couple of flagons so we can do a bit of celebrating.

I'll join the football team again and go fishing with the blokes and get a job doing something or other. Not straight away, after all I've been working hard the past six months, but in a little while. Then I'll get a good regular job on the shire or something and start to build a place down on the reserve by the river. I don't want to stay in the West. It's no place to bring up kids. Down on the river there's no brawling or shouting. No electricity, sewerage or running water either, but we'll be independent and we'll manage.

The utility didn't stop in Nyngan, but it pulled up outside the pub in Coolibah. The driver and his mates asked Doug to have a beer with them, but when they headed for the lounge he said he'd be right thanks, and went into the public bar. He knew better than to walk into the whitefellows' lounge. Must be the first time those blokes have been up round here or they'd know better than to ask.

It was almost closing time and obviously the paddy wagon had already done its rounds because there was no one else in the bar. The publican handed over two flagons of cheap red wine, slapped the change on the counter and eyed him suspiciously. 'Okay, Jackie,' he said in dismissal. Back on the road, with only a hundred miles to go, Doug felt his stomach getting tighter and tighter and the nervous sweat making his shirt stick to him.

Home. Home. Home. I'm going home. The flat land raced away from them. Momentarily Doug worried about hitting a kangaroo or a wild pig, but then he remembered that he had heard from his mother, in the one letter he'd got from anyone during the whole of his six months in prison, that it hadn't rained for almost three months. That meant the pig and the roo would all be staying around the watercourses, well away from the road, so there was little risk of meeting any.

The fragrance of the coolibahs and the gums filled the air, together with the smell of dust and dry grass. The thin moon rode high above the Southern Cross.

> *Country roads, take me home*
> *To the place I belong*
> *West Virginia, Mountain Mama*
> *Take me home, country roads.*

No, not West Virginia, West Woongarra, that's it. West Woongarra, the West, that's my home. And as

Doug Foster sang his voice was carried back along the bitumen to be lost among the dry bush.

*Country roads, take me home*
*To the place I belong,*
*West Woongarra, New South Wales,*
*Take me home, country roads.*

The utility moved off down the road and Doug stood and watched as the tail lights turned into the back of the Imperial Hotel. The whitefellows had insisted on driving down the main street and past the pub to where the dirt track to the West took off from the road and meandered across the paddock to the settlement of twenty-six wooden houses. They had wanted to drive him right to his house but he had lied to them and said that there was no road in for cars. Christ, imagine what Mum would think if I drove up with three white blokes. She'd be sure it was the cops and like as not Allan would come out and pick a fight with them!

Now he stood at the junction of the asphalt and dirt, toying with an empty beer can with his foot, feeling his heart pounding in his throat and his stomach heave. Unable to get up the courage to start the last five hundred yards of his journey home.

Suddenly a fox broke cover not ten feet from him, dashed across the road, down the table-drain and off. Doug jumped with fright and automatically began to walk. The edge of the track was littered with beer cans and bottles, wine flagons, cigarette packets, lolly papers and broken glass. Every now and then the pale moonlight was caught and reflected, making one piece of the refuse gleam with subterranean menace.

Doug heard again for the first time in six months the dull roar of the water hurtling over the weir. Heavy rain further up the Barwon had sent floodwaters rushing down past Woongarra and on into the Darling, and the rivers were alive with fish and water rats.

The lights were on in every one of the homes in the West, even though it was almost midnight, and a loud hum of noise enveloped the settlement and spread out across the surrounding bush. As Doug came closer the voices separated and he could hear the strident tones of Jane Saunders and the equally loud replies from her cronies, Betty Flinders and Barbara Evans. He scuffed his sneakers through the dirt, sending up little billows of dust behind him. He felt drawn to and yet repulsed by what lay ahead.

Suddenly little Wally Evans, nasty snivelling brat, Doug thought, came racing down the track towards him; when he saw Doug, he skidded to a halt and stood rooted to the spot as if he'd seen a ghost. Doug grinned foolishly, and after a pause Wally screamed into his face, 'Mum, Mum, it's Dougo. Dougo's back.'

People came from everywhere. Laughing and smiling, they crowded round shaking his hand and thumping his back. There was a splendid noise. 'G'day Doug, how you been, mate?' 'How you going Dougo, all right? "Heyya Dougo, what d'you know? How's tricks?' Doug was pushed and punched and kissed and hugged.

And then spontaneously there was a lull, the little crowd broke apart and there was Mum. Doug tried, but couldn't speak. He couldn't move; he couldn't lift his arms to embrace her. All he could do was look, and the picture of her standing there etched itself into his brain to be carried with him for the rest of his short life.

She looked old, grey and gnarled. Her worn floral dress was held together at a tear on the shoulder with a large safety pin. The hem was coming down. Her arms and legs were thin and her boney feet stuffed into a pair of broken-backed shoes. Her breasts swung loose under the thin cotton frock and her stomach pushed out against the gathers at the waist. Her curly hair was knotted and she swayed ever so slightly from a Saturday night on the grog. But her eyes sat deep in their sockets above a wide-spread nose and full thick lips and she was magnificently self- possessed.

For the first time Doug saw his mother not simply as his mother but as another human being. He loved what he saw and yet at the same time he was afraid.

It was she who broke the spell. 'Douglas,' she sighed. 'Douglas. Douglas.'

'Mama,'he cried. 'Mama, Mama.'

The crowd of welcomers drifted away, the momentary diversion over, back to their wine and their games of bingo, leaving the son to sob in his mother's arms, as he smelt again that same strange, bittersweet odour that he had loved since his earliest memories.


'Drink up Doug,' Allan ordered.

Doug obeyed and Allan refilled his mug. They were sitting on the verandah floor surrounded by the clutter of communal living. Mattresses, rumpled blankets and even more rumpled clothes grew and sprouted in jumbled heaps, threatening to overwhelm them like some rapacious monster from outer space. It was two o'clock and Mum had at last gone to bed, but not before reassuring herself that her eldest son was glad to be home.

'This booze is going to my head Al. I'd better knock it off or I won't be any use to Flo tonight when she gets back.' Doug felt a wave of anxiety sweep over him. 'What time d'you think she'll come?'

'You'll be right mate. Drink up. She shouldn't be long. She usually gets in about now.'

Usually? What did Allan mean usually? How usually? Since when did his woman usually go to a party without him and get home after two o'clock? Allan went on talking, but Doug didn't listen. He knew he shouldn't have had all that wine. Drink always made him introspective, and he was so out of practice that it hit him harder than usual. And the kids, Steve and Carol? Off staying with some people, Mum had said. What people? Mum didn't really know. He'd have to wait till Flo told him. Flo told him what? It was all so bloody disappointing. No Flo. No kids. Not how he'd planned it. Not how he'd imagined it every night for six months on his bunk in Long Bay.

'What's up Doug?' Allan's voice penetrated his reverie. 'What's a bloke got to do to get a civil answer? Sitting there like a flaming goldfish with your mouth open. What did they do to you down there, cut half your brain out?'

'I was just thinking.'

'Yeh, well you'd think that you'd have had enough of that for a while, and that now you're home you'd quit thinking and start talking.'

'All right. All right, what was it you were on about?'

'I was asking about poor old Jerry Brown, that's what. I was asking what happened to the poor bastard. All we heard up here was that he took crook and died. Seems pretty odd to me. More likely they bashed him to death or perhaps let him starve. Old Jerry never had a day sick in his life except from the grog and sometimes a dose of 'flu. So what happened?'

Doug took another swig from his mug. The wine tasted of bitter coffee. 'It's true; he did just get sick and die. I wasn't in his cell block and I only saw him every now and again when we got put on the same rosters. But from the time he came in he began to fade away.'

'That's a damn funny thing to say about a big bloke like Jerry.'

'Well, it's true. He simply gave up. I talked to the blokes in his cellblock and they all said the same thing.'

'Whitefellows?'

'Yes, some of them, but some of ours too. Ricky from Gilgandra, you know, the one who went in for sticking up that bigmouth farmer and his wife. And Bob, the Walgett bloke, can't remember what he was in for. Assaulting a copper I suppose. Well, they were both good mates of Jerry and according to them he was leant on by the bent warders, but he never took a bashing.' Doug drained his mug and grimaced, 'He was off his tucker for most of the time, and they think that's what started it. But Ricky heard from one of the warders after Jerry had died, that Jerry lay awake at night and sobbed and sobbed for hours and hours.'

'Bullshit,' Allan thumped the flagon down on the

broken floorboards. 'I can't believe that of Jerry. He was a real dinkum bloke.'

'Sure he was, but I can believe it and so will you if you ever end up down there, mate. It's enough to turn a man inside out. Even the toughest. In fact they sometimes suffer the worst.'

Doug shifted some of his weight on to his other buttock and reaching up grabbed some more loose blankets and clothes, stuffing them behind himself. 'They tried to force feed him at the end,' he said. 'He was unconscious in hospital for several days before he finally died. I'd say that he just couldn't bear being shut up. Remember that cockatoo you caught and caged and it bashed itself to death overnight? Well that's what happened to Jerry. Being the hard-hearted bastard you are you'll probably think I've gone off my rocker when I tell you that I think Jerry died of a broken heart.'

Allan got up and leant against what was left of the fly screen. A mug in one hand, the almost empty flagon in the other. He stared across the gravel track at the house opposite. In most of the homes the lights were out. The West had settled down to a fitful sleep. The bare electric bulb in the hallway behind threw an indirect glow on to Allan's motionless form. An inch over six feet with broad shoulders, strong forearms and hands like hams, he always stood with his feet apart, lightly tensed like a prize fighter, his head slightly tilted to compensate for the vision in his left eye, which had been so badly damaged by a punch in the face that it was going blind. I wouldn't like to meet that bastard on a dark night, Doug thought, looking at his brother.

Allan was remembering the anguish of finding

his cockatoo bruised and bloodied and very dead. He remembered too the scream Molly Brown had given when she was told that her husband was dead. That scream went on inside him still. But he wasn't about to tell anyone, not even Doug, about the anguish or the scream. That sort of talk was best left to women and whites. Instead he drank the remains of the wine straight from the flagon, threw it out on the bare patch which in wetter places would have been a lawn, turned violently towards Doug and said, 'I hope to Christ that bastard Clancy gets his throat slit, bleeds slowly to death and is so stiff by the time they find him that they have to break every bone in his lousy body before they can stuff him into a bloody coffin.'

Doug winced. He had forgotten what an ugly anger boiled inside his brother. 'Christ Al. Fair go mate. Is Clancy enough of a bastard to deserve all that?' He grinned, hoping to find some response in his brother. There was none.

'A fair go for Father Clancy,' Allan sneered. 'Is that what you want? A fair go for that bastard would be a knife in the guts and even that would be too good for him. You know what he did to Jerry Brown, don't you?'

'Well, no. Not really, because I only heard bits and pieces from the other prisoners. Clancy caught him nabbing stuff from his house, didn't he?'

Allan came back inside, and shovelling some clothes and blankets out of the way he sat on the floor beside Doug and leant back against a stained mattress. 'Yeh. Well now I'll tell you what really happened. Jerry's missus got sick, real sick. They took her down the track to the hospital in Dubbo and they chopped off one of her tits.' 'Christ,' Doug muttered, but Allan ignored him and went on. 'Then they sent her back but she didn't get any better, so they had her in again, and all the while Jerry is having to look after the kids, all eleven of them. As well as working up at the roo factory, where you know he's been for over three years, he took on extra jobs. Odd jobs like cleaning up out the back of the Imperial, and helping a white bloke build an extra room on his house. All to earn extra money to pay the hospital bills. Then he came down with a bad dose of bloody' flu and couldn't work, not even his regular job, for about ten days. Real crook he was. So then he started to fall behind. He asked the bank manager for a loan of a couple of hundred, but that bastard Stevens wouldn't reach out his hand to help his dying mother, so what hope does a blackfellow stand?'

A couple of cats had set up a dismal wailing in the next-door yard. Allan leant forward and expertly aimed an empty beer can. The cats screeched, and bolted into the next barren patch where they began their caterwauling again, beyond Allan's reach. He leant back, resigned. 'Jerry never really got completely better because he was so worried about money and the kids. He'd try to get rides down to Dubbo to visit Molly and a few times he couldn't get a lift back so then he'd miss a day's work. Les Cullen would dock his wages and warn him that it couldn't go on, which is fair enough, but the poor bastard didn't know which way to turn. The finishing touch was when one of the kids, Meg it was, gashed her leg very badly on a rusty tin in their back yard. When they took her up to the hospital to have it stitched Jerry was told she'd have to be kept in because she was suffering from malnutrition. Well you know what a poor eater that one's always been. Anyway they threatened Jerry that they'd come and inspect the rest of the kids to see if they were getting enough to eat.'

Their mother tossed restlessly in her sleep in the room behind them and mumbled something incoherent. Allan lowered his voice. 'The poor bastard went off his brain and on the way back home from the hospital he called in on Father Clancy. Clancy wasn't there of course. He never is. He's too busy riding around in that big bloody Statesman to have any time to spend in that bloody house of his. It must be the biggest in town, and what's more there's at least two thousand dollars worth of grog in his bar. I know because I saw it there one day when he paid a few of us to give him a hand to move some cases around. There's enough grog there to keep the whole town pissed for a month. So Clancy wasn't there. I think at this stage that all Jerry wanted was to ask the bastard to help him out. He would seem the natural person to turn to, seeing as the Catholic Church is so stinking rich and sets itself up as saviour of the world. Knock and it shall be opened. Ask and ye shall be given, isn't that it?'

Allan rooted around among a mountain of clothing and came up with a can of beer. He pulled the ring, took a swig and then offered the can to Doug, who shook his head.

'Well,' Allan sneered, Jerry knocked and the door wasn't opened so as there was no one there to ask, he helped himself. He emptied out the suitcase that Clancy carries when he visits other towns. It has all the crap in it. Sacred wine, blessed bread, fancy tablecloth, all that muck, and he filled it with groceries from Clancy's cupboards. He left the smoked salmon, oysters in garlic sauce and caviar, and took the slightly more basic things. Baked beans, eggs, butter, sugar and stuff.'

Allan skillfully rolled a cigarette. 'The story does have its funny side I suppose, because what happened was that here was Jerry humping this flaming case down the lane at the back of the house, and who should drive up but the man himself. At this point the bloody case broke open, spilling the groceries every-where.' Allan half smiled. Jerry had the bloody nerve to ask the bastard for a box to repack the groceries, and Clancy not only got one from his back yard but bloody well helped Jerry pack all the food into it. Can you beat that!'

Doug chortled. 'That's bloody ripe that is. The hide on him!'

'Yes,' Allan agreed, 'the stupid bastard didn't even recognize the tins and what have you, but more than that, he didn't even recognize the case, which shows how often he used the thing.'

'I wish I'd seen his face when he went inside to make tea, probably feeling all virtuous at having helped a boong in distress, found his stuff gone and then realized what had happened. Jesus, what a fool he must have felt. He was down at the station in no time flat, and insisted on bringing charges, even though Vickers, he's the new cop here, suggested that they go and get the stuff back and forget all about it. Not bloody likely. Clancy was out for blood.'

Allan drew heavily on his cigarette. 'When the case came up before the magistrate, Clancy pushed for a trial in Dubbo. None of us could believe it when we heard that Jerry had got two years. Two bloody years for a bagful of groceries! Talk about thirty pieces of silver! Judas had nothing on that bastard Clancy.'

Allan gnawed at a broken fingernail and spat the bits on to the floor. 'When it got back that Jerry had died in Long Bay and Molly was left here with their eleven kids, by Christ it was just as well that Clancy was out of town. He stayed out for six bloody weeks. Oh yes, he's a smart bastard is our Father Clancy. He knows his boongs he does. He knows it's only in the passion of the grog that we act and that we piss all our determination up against a wall. He knows what snivelling, weak-willed, no-hopers we are.'

The bitterness in Allan's voice was too much for Doug to bear. He got up and walked out on to the porch. Behind him Allan ground his cigarette hard into the floorboard. 'Well, how's that for a bedtime story on your first night home Dougo?' he said lightly, and coming up behind his brother he grabbed his arm, twisting it up behind his back, forcing Doug to double over. Then he spun his brother round, and bobbed to and fro in front of him, his fists clenched and raised, his head lowered. 'Muhammad, the black superman,' he crooned, 'floats like a butterfly, stings like a bee,' and he jabbed playfully at Doug who responded willingly, happy to ease the tension.

As they were prancing among the litter in the yard a car came suddenly round the corner, and catching them in its headlights, skidded to a halt on the gravel. A back door opened and out climbed a very drunk Flo.

## SUNDAY

Doug eased himself out from under the rumpled sheets, careful not to disturb the still sleeping Flo. She lay on her back, her mouth slightly open. Her breath smelt of stale liquor and nicotine, but her face was smooth and she looked little different from the fifteen-year-old he had fallen in love with nine years ago.

Still just in his underpants, he went into the kitchen to make a cup of tea. The cool morning air revived him. He looked at his watch. Five-forty. Too many sleepless nights on hard bunks had made it impossible for him to lie in. He rinsed his mouth and spat the water through the broken window. He felt terrible. He had a headache, a ringing in his ears, and shooting pains up and down his spine. His eyes felt like hot lead balls and his mouth, Christ! His mouth tasted like a septic tank.

The kettle had no lid so he watched as the water came to the boil and when he'd made his tea, strong and black and very sweet, he walked noiselessly back through the house, and sat on the porch as the sun started to creep over the horizon, to review the events of the night before. Flo had been drunk. Very drunk. She didn't seem in the least surprised to see him. Neither pleased nor displeased. Just as if he'd only been away for six hours, not six months. She had slammed the car door shut and laughed loudly at something the other person in the back seat had called out. Doug had caught a brief glimpse of a sweating face grinning through the window before the car pulled away and skidded round the corner.

As she turned, Flo smoothed down her skirt. Doug's stomach lurched. Christ what great big beautiful tits. They were squeezed together by her blouse, the buttons undone so far that the flesh was straining to fall out. The next thing he noticed about his wife left him feeling as though he'd been punched in the solar plexus. Flo was pregnant. Unless she's put on weight. No, she couldn't have put on that much, not all in one place.

She staggered and dropped one of her shoes, which she had been carrying. He picked it up and gave it to her. "Lo Doug,' she lisped.

'Hello Flo.'

Doug took great gulps of scalding tea and looked out across the paddock to the town. Smoke was already rising from the back of the Imperial Hotel. Harry Fletcher must have started up the boilers to heat the water for his guests' morning showers. Doug wondered idly what the three whitefellows would be doing today. Sunday was a dead day in Woongarra. The pubs were shut.

Doug had turned around to get some reassurance from Allan, only to find that his brother had disappeared, leaving Flo and him alone in the dismal yard. He'd wanted to kiss her, put his arm around her, but he couldn't. Jesus Christ, it's a bastard. Why can't I show her how glad I am to see her? He felt let down by himself. Instead he said, 'Where've you been? I've been waiting for you for hours.'

He hadn't meant it to sound accusatory, but it did. She didn't answer, just stumbled up the steps and tripped over the clutter of clothes.

'Fuck off,' she muttered, fiercely, whether at him or the clothes he wasn't sure. Inside their room she flopped face down on the bed and was instantly asleep. Doug could feel the anger rising. He felt like slapping her awake and shouting, 'Aren't you glad to see me, you bloody bitch?' Then suddenly he began to cry. He sat on the end of the bed and sobbed, gasping for air as the cries were wrenched from him. He didn't know what he was crying about. He wasn't crying about any one thing, just everything. The sobs came from nowhere, rolled up and forced themselves out, all but choking him. His nose ran and he wiped the dribble away with his bare arm. Flo slept on. His mother became dimly conscious, but soon slipped back into the depths, and if Allan heard his brother's grief he never mentioned it.

Slowly the sobs subsided and Doug got up and wiped his face roughly with some of Flo's clothing which littered the room. Then he gently slipped down Flo's skirt and pants, turned her over, undid her blouse, took it off and tucked her under the sheet, all the while eyeing the distended belly.

She must be about to pop. Why didn't the stupid bitch write and tell me? Another child. It'll be a boy. Another son. He smoothed the sheet over the unborn child, touching the knot of flesh protruding from Flo's navel, feeling overwhelmed by the mystery of a new life. Another baby. Well, that'll be good. Now we'll have to move. We can't have any more kids in this house. There's already too many of us. It's bad enough sharing his room with Carol and Steve. We can't have a baby in here too. We'll have to start that place down by the river now.

Doug felt washed through. He slipped off his shirt and trousers and sat in his underpants smoothing Flo's stomach and remembering how Flo looked with a baby clamped to her breast. He smiled to himself. Flo grunted in her sleep and turned on to her side, the belly lying out in front of her, like an already separate being. He slipped under the state-smelling sheets.

The tea was beginning to make him feel better. He could hear it gurgling its way through his intestines. He threw the slops into the yard and as he did so noticed a small child standing behind a broken-down old wickerwork pram.

'G'day mister,' the child said. 'G'day.' The early morning light was still so soft that he couldn't see whether the child was a boy or a girl. He grabbed a blanket from behind him and wrapped it sarong-like around his waist. 'That's a beaut pram you've got there.'

The child, encouraged, pushed the pram slowly up the path to the porch.

'You got your doll in there, have you?' Doug inquired.

'Nah, what do you take me for, a sissy?' and as the child now stood close to him, Doug recognized him as one of Gary Andrews's children though he couldn't recall his name. A boy of perhaps five, he was wearing a pair of very tattered, dirty shorts. The rest of his dusky body was bare, except for the angrily inflamed and pus-filled impetigo sores covering his arms and legs. He had thick mucus hanging from his nose, but it didn't seem to bother him. He reached inside the pram and rearranged a bottle for a greedily sucking infant of about three months. The baby, a girl, was completely naked, and lay inside the grimy pram on a crumpled dirty piece of linen. The wickerwork was coming unravelled and pieces of it trailed in the dirt. 'It's me kid sister, she was born while you was away,' the boy told him. 'Dad told me to take her for a walk to shut her up. He couldn't stand the racket because he's got a headache.'

Doug gently tickled the baby's feet while the boy sat beside him on the porch and they talked. They must have been sitting engrossed in one another's company for half an hour because the sun had already made the rusting dumped vehicle outside the corner house too hot to touch, when there was a gentle swish and Flo, sleepy-eyed and tousled, stood behind them draped in a greying sheet.

'Well, I'd better be off,' the boy announced, sensing with a child's perception the delicate atmosphere. Flo sat beside Doug and they watched as the child trundled his burden back up the rubbish strewn gravel track.

Doug put his arm around her, pulling her head down on to his shoulder. 'Why didn't you tell me?' he asked, putting his hand on her stomach.

'Well, you know, I'm not too good at writing and I didn't like to ask someone else to write it for me, and anyway,' she paused, 'I knew you'd be home soon.'

He kissed the top of her head, and she put her mouth up to his ear and whispered, 'Come back to bed Dougo.'

The river was muddy and flowed swiftly between steep banks. In the scorching heat the birds were sensibly silent. The branches of a giant tree, washed down in the recent flood, protruded black and menacing in midstream like giant seasnakes. The water whirled and eddied round them, sending beautiful patterns downstream, where they were quickly swallowed up by the onrushing flow. Where the tree had lodged against the bank Flo crouched digging in the mass of roots to ferret out yabbies. A little way upstream Doug and Allan sat on the dry cracked bank and leaned forward resting their forearms on their knees, each holding a fishing line lightly in his hands. A sudden tensing and with a quick movement Allan flicked a big fish out on to the bank where it lay gasping for air, its mouth and gills opening and shutting in agony. 'Bloody carp,' Allan said in disgust. 'Stinking rubbish. Bloody river's full of them this year. No use to anybody.' He hurled the carp further up the bank where it bent itself almost double, gasping for air, and then slowly, very slowly and painfully, lost consciousness, its body giving a slow reflex kick every now and then until it finally died.

Allan stood up and rolled a cigarette and watched as Flo, made clumsy by her belly, patiently hunted down her prey.

'Glad to be home?'

Doug followed his gaze and smiled at Flo triumphantly waving a wiggling yabby at them. 'That's for sure. It's great. Tomorrow we're going to pick up the kids and as soon as I've got a job I'm going to start knocking up a place on the river.'

There was a silence, an awkward silence. Doug turned round from watching his line and found Allan staring at Flo with a look he didn't understand. It made him feel uneasy.

'It's not that Flo and I aren't happy living with all of you,' he said quickly.

I know mate,' Allan said, still staring at Flo. 'I understand.'

But Doug felt compelled to explain further. 'You know what a bloody racket babies make. Well it wouldn't be right for Marge and her kiddies and Mum doesn't get any younger. Anyway,' he finished lamely, 'it isn't as though we're moving to Sydney.'

Allan said nothing but just kept on watching Flo. The silence lengthened and Doug was about to go on chattering to fill in the void, when Allan asked abruptly, 'She tell you when the kid's due?'

'Flo isn't too sure, but it must be soon because she reckons she was two months gone when I got sent down.'

'Yeh, well,' Allan shrugged, sat down again beside Doug and re-baited his hook.

As he swung it out into the river Doug asked quietly, 'What happened with Liz?' The bait plopped into the water.

'It fell apart kiddo,' Allan said lightly. 'Just fell apart. Nothing dramatic. No scenes, no fights. Nothing. We wanted different things, that's all. You know. I was okay living at home but Liz fancied moving into town. You won't catch me being an uptown nigger, pretending to be a whitefellow. So I said no.'

Doug felt a jerk on his line and quickly pulled it in. The bait was gone. 'Shit.'

'Yeh, that's right, Dougo. Shit. All women are shit.' And before Doug could interrupt he went on, 'They say one thing. They mean another. They're never straight.' He slammed the heel of his boot into the broken earth. 'Liz said she was happy enough living with Mum, but she'd get mad at her over little things. Like the time Mum drank some orange juice she got from those bloody white nurses. Sticky-beak bitches. Liz went off her brain. Accused Mum of coming into our private room. Get that, private room, and pinching food from her children's mouths. Mum hadn't known it was special for the kids and Liz really upset her.'

Flo yelled, and Doug turned to see her waving another scrabbling yabby. Allan seemed not to notice. 'Then there were some kids Liz wouldn't let our lot play with. Said they were foul-mouthed and she'd rouse on our kids if they swore. High and bloody mighty. Fancied herself better than others. I think she wished she wasn't black. I told her straight there was no chance I'd ever move into town, and after that she gave me the bum's rush. Wouldn't let me touch her.'

He picked up a piece of flat stone and sent it skipping and jumping across the river. 'Well I wasn't about to let her put one over me like that, so I started playing up a bit. That wasn't right either, and she was beginning to get on everyone's tits, so in the end I told her to take the kids over to her sister's in Moree for a bit. She jumped at that. That was almost three months ago and I've heard from her once. Full of what a beaut place Moree is, "how civilized" is what she said. They're living uptown like a couple of white tarts. Her sister's bloke pissed off years ago. He couldn't stand it either.'

He aimed another flat stone, but it sank after the first jump.

'D'you miss the kids?' Doug asked.

Allan wheeled round on him, shouting, 'No. Of course I don't miss the bloody kids. It's great not seeing them at all. Not knowing what they're up to. Not knowing what they think about their old man. What d'you think, you stupid bastard?'

'All right. All right,' Doug shouted back into his face. And then more quietly, 'Do me a favour. Forget I asked.'

Their shouting must have covered Flo's approach because now they heard her coming up the bank toward them, walking splay-footed and leaning back to support the weight of the baby and cardboard box, which she plonked heavily between them.

'There,' she said triumphantly. 'Eleven of the bastards.' The grey yabbies, each one about five inches long, lay surprisingly quiet, only their feelers moving about cautiously testing the air. 'Thirsty work,' she said. 'Where's the drink?'

Allan slithered down the bank and rescued the flagon from where it lay on its side in the water, resting in a well worn niche-cut in the bank. He twisted open the seal. Flo grasped it with both her muddy hands and took a deep drink. Doug, not knowing what made him do it, but meaning it just the same, held the flagon by the neck and raised it towards Flo. 'Here's to the new kid,' he smiled, and drank only a little, not wanting a repeat of the morning's hangover.

Allan laughed, a harsh laugh, took the flagon from him, and in grim-faced parody of his brother, drank, 'To all your kids. Steve, Carol and the new one, whatever it might turn out to be.' Flo glowered at him with open dislike.

Doug looked swiftly from his wife to his brother and back, and said quickly, 'Time for some tucker.' He got to his feet, pulling Flo up after him. She went ahead up the steep bank, carrying her loot and laughing as Doug gave her an encouraging steady push in the back.

Allan gathered up the lines and shoved them in a sack with four fat yellow-belly. Half way up he came across the stiff carcass of the carp, mouth gaping, eyes popping. 'Stinking heap of shit, 'he snarled, and gave it a vicious kick, which sent it arcing out into the middle of the river. The smooth river, darkened now by the lengthening shadows, digested the corpse and flowed on.

'Anyway, where's Uncle Bill and Auntie Irene?' Doug mumbled through a mouthful of yellow-belly. 'I haven't seen either of them. Nor the kids.'

The family, Mum, Doug and Flo, Allan, Marge and Len and their three kids, and Bob, were sitting round the kitchen table finishing off the afternoon's catch and washing it down with three bottles of port and two flagons of rough red. The youngest boy, Dave, was off with his friends, and Irene, the baby of the family, had finished her meal and was lying on a mattress on the verandah, drinking beer from the can and playing her David Cassidy records.

'They've been down in Bloomfield for three months. Must be coming back soon,' Allan said. 'We had the kids here for a bit...' '...but it got too much for Marge,' Len interrupted. 'Five extra, so a couple are with Joan and Eddie over on the river and the other three are down in Dubbo with Bill's sister.'

'Came through Orange on my way up. If I'd known they were there, I could have gone into Bloomfield to see them.' Doug wiped his fishy fingers on his shirtfront.

'Wouldn't have been any good,' Marge told him. 'They wouldn't have let you in. It's just like being in prison. They say it's a funny farm but really it's a prison. I remember Bill talking about the last time he got put in. He said it was awful, but mind you, when he came back he'd put on that much weight no one recognized him. So it can't be that bloody bad.'

'Who put him in? 'Doug asked Allan, who was concentrating on leaning back as far as possible and still keeping his balance on the two back legs of his chair.

'We got a new CPS,' Allan answered. 'John Smith. No, don't laugh. That's his bloody name for real. He's a stupid bastard. Started out by giving a long sermon to everyone the pigs picked up, like they were bloody kids, and then giving them ten days. It was a joke. The bloody court was taking an hour a day and the lockup was so full they had to bring in camp beds. Sergeant Evans took Smith aside and he soon wised up. So now they're back to the regular forty-eight hours and ten dollars bit.'

Allan's chair came perilously close to overbalancing, but he was still clearheaded enough to keep control. Flo stretched across the debris of the meal to pick up Allan's tobacco tin and roller. His chair came down on all four legs with a thump, and he grabbed at the tin and roller, catching Flo's hand under his.

'Want a smoke Flo?' he asked her insolently. She slid her hand out from under his with difficulty. 'No, I'll get me own.' Allan watched her with an ugly look as she got up and walked unsteadily to her room. Then he took another mouthful of wine.

'What's up with you and Flo?' Doug asked his brother, feeling the anger beginning to rise.

'Nothing,' Allan replied. 'Why, should there be?'

'Yeh, well for Christ's sake be civil to her.'

'Come on you two,' Len interrupted. 'Cut that out, will you. There, Dougo,' Len passed him the flagon.

Flo returned, fumbling with the cigarette packet. Doug laughed and took it from her. 'Here, stupid, try opening the other end,' and he lit two cigarettes, giving one to her and keeping one for himself. The atmosphere relaxed slightly.

Mum said, 'It was bloody rough that John Smith sending Bill and Irene down together. He knew they had five kids. Mind you, Irene's been taking a bit lately. She never used to. Not as much anyway. Bill's always been the same, ever since I've known him. This is his fifth time in Bloomfield. Irene's only been in once before, and then she put herself in.'

'Makes me bloody sick,' Allan said angrily. 'Bastards like Smith and Evans being able to push anyone they like into a nuthouse and then to have the bloody nerve to say it's for their own good. Pricks.' The chair wavered, and Allan clutched at the table, coming down with a heavy thud.

Marge got up and picked up the baby, which had been whimpering for a while on the floor while it tried to chew off the corner of the cardboard box containing the now pink boiled yabbies. Jeesus! What a stink.' She pulled out the child's nappy at the back. 'Yuk! Come on Miss Shittypants,' and she went into the bathroom from where they could hear her softly chastising the baby above the noisy flushing of the lavatory.

Doug took another gulp of wine, and noticed that his mother had dropped off to sleep, her head lolling forward on to her chest, a shining piece of spittle trapped in one corner of her mouth. He was still angry with his brother, but his tongue was starting to feel too big for his mouth, and he couldn't be bothered to tell him. Everything in the grubby cluttered kitchen appeared very three-dimensional and full of reflected light from the uncovered bulb, which hung above their heads. Len, at the other end of the table seemed very, very far away. The two kids, quarrelling as always, seemed still further away, but even so their voices were dazzlingly loud. No one else spoke for what seemed to Doug to be a very long time, but was in fact only fifteen seconds.

All of a sudden, as if someone had pulled a switch, everything happened at once. The older child, a girl, pushed her brother, who fell against Allan's tilted chair. Allan hit his head on the corner of the stove as he fell. He shouted, the children both burst into tears. Allan staggered to his feet, trying to reach the kids to slap them, but was kept at bay by Len, who pinned him, struggling like a trapped moth, against the wall. Marge came in from the bathroom holding the bare-bottomed screaming child on her hip while she demanded, loudly, to know 'what the bloody hell is going on', and Irene came in from the verandah to stare sullenly at her elders. Mum stirred slightly but slept on.

Doug saw it all happening as though he were watching a movie. Then he felt a tug on his arm, and turned to find Flo pursing her lips at him. He stood up to follow her into the hall and was hit by a wave of nausea. By the time she reached their room she already had her blouse off. She turned round, and leaning back against the door began to unzip his trousers.

They didn't hear the others finish the quarrel and go to bed. But an hour later when Doug got up to vomit into the lavatory, he disturbed a couple of feral cats who bared their teeth and spat at him before continuing to rip open the soft under-bellies of Flo's yabbies.

# Chapter Two

## Sunday

'What'd you think of the movie?' Harry Fletcher asked Gordon Wright who was standing next to him at the bar in the RSL.

'Not bad. Parts of it were rather funny. But it wasn't as good as I anticipated,' Gordon replied, bringing out a handful of loose change from his pocket. 'I read a review in Time which described it as a classic spoof and the start of a whole new genre.

'Well, I wouldn't know about things like that, mate,' Harry said. 'I just go to the movies to be entertained.'

The barman pushed five schooners of frothing cold beer and one rum and coke across the counter.

'Thanks.' Harry picked the glasses up with expert ease. 'Bring your wife over and join us,' he invited Gordon. 'My brother and a couple of his mates are up from Sydney.' He elbowed his way back through the small crowd to his table. The screen had been rolled up, the rows of chairs disbanded and the weekly Sunday night ritual was over. Now the members could get down to the serious business of drinking and playing the poker machines.

'Where you been, Harry?' 'I could have brewed the beer myself in that time.' 'I know, he's been chatting up that sexy barmaid, haven't you Harry boy?' Harry distributed the drinks and sat down beside his wife. With no formalities or toasts, they drank.

'It's like a zoo over there,' Harry said. 'Worse than in the public bar at my place on a Saturday night.'

'Except there's no blacks,' his wife added.

'Too bloody right. Got to have one place in the town where we can get away from them.'

'Aren't they allowed in here?' Greg Fletcher asked his elder brother.

'We have a couple. Johnny Phillips. He's not a bad bloke. Works for the shire. There he is over there. Little squat bloke with ears.'

Greg looked in the direction Harry indicated. 'He's not aboriginal!' he laughed. 'He's as white as me.'

'Yeh,' Harry replied, 'that's what you think. You should see his brother. Blacker than the ace of spades. That's the way it goes.' Harry took a drink, automatically straightened his already perfectly tied tie, and smoothed down the lapels of his fashionably cut large-checked jacket.

Deidre, his wife, slim, immaculate and tense, sipped her rum and coke. 'It's not that they're not allowed in here,' she told Greg. 'But we need to have one place where you can go if you want to be a little dressy.' She crossed her legs, which even on this very warm night were discreetly stockinged, and swung a modish clog idly back and forth. 'It's so easy when you live in a town with only two thousand people to get sloppy, you know. We have dress rules in the club. No jeans or thongs on Saturday and Sunday nights.'

'Anyhow,' Harry added, 'they'd just get drunk and start to fight and shout and swear. You haven't seen that yet, but you will, that's for sure.'

'They can't all be like that,' Darren said, but seeing Harry's face added, 'can they?'

'They can and are,' Harry told him. 'All but a very few.'

'We gave a lift to one of them on the way up last night,' Greg told him. 'He didn't seem a bad bloke.'

Harry's glass stopped momentarily on the way to his mouth and then continued slowly on its way. He took a long drink, keeping his eyes on Greg, put the glass down carefully and said, 'You what? You gave a lift to a blackfellow! You must be out of your mind. Christ! D'you know what happened to a bloke up here last year? He gave a lift to a couple of them and they bloody rolled him. Took all his dough and left him to bleed to death in his car.'

Harry, sure that he could hold his audience, took another drink. 'It was out on the Goodooga Road. Just luck that someone came along. It was Les Cullen, bloke who runs the roo factory, good bloke, married to a black girl. Les got the fellow into the hospital here and they flew him down in the air-ambulance to Dubbo. He had fifteen stitches in his head where they'd clubbed him, and a broken arm and ribs where they'd kicked him. He was covered in bruises and they kept him in hospital for ten days. Cost him a fortune, because he didn't belong to the ambulance fund. They got the blokes. One from here and his mate from Bourke. They got five years for it, but that didn't help the bloke they'd done over. He didn't get a penny compensation, and he couldn't work for a couple of months. Had to employ people to run the property for him.'

Harry finished his beer. 'Doesn't matter what they say down in Sydney. They don't know what it's like up here. Things are very different. The blackfellows in Redfern are one thing, what we've got up here is something else. Makes me sick when I see these blokes on TV talking a lot of rubbish about white racists and how we should help the bloody blacks. All those university professors and other idiots. They want to come up here and see what it's really like. They don't have to live with them, but if they did they'd soon change their tune. Anyhow,' Harry straightened his tie again, suddenly aware that he'd been doing all the talking, 'drink up and it's the same all round.'

'My shout,' Ian said.

'No. No. Tonight's on me. They wouldn't let you buy drinks here anyway, you have to be a member.' Harry pushed back his chair, getting up and saying, 'but do us a favour, don't go giving lifts to any more blackfellows while you're up here. Mum would never forgive me if you got your brains smashed in. Ooops!'

Harry had stood up into Gordon Wright who had moved sideways, bumping into his wife and causing her to spill some brandy on to her majestic brown-jerseyed bosom. 'Sorry, mate. Sorry about that.' Harry's hand went out to brush off the drops of liquor, but it faltered and fell undecided by his side. 'Here, let me get you a refill.' He grabbed the glass from a protesting Mrs. Wright and propelled her into a chair, pulling up another one. 'Here, Gordon. This is my brother Greg and his mates Darren Jones and Ian Maconachie. They're up from Sydney for a month, want to do some shooting and see how the other half lives.' He laughed awkwardly. 'Gordon's the headmaster here.'

Mr. Wright shook hands all round, while his wife smiled brightly at everyone, pretending she didn't mind not being introduced.

'Now, what will you drink?' he asked them, and having got the order, pushed his way through the groups of people round the poker machines back to the bar. The grinning, gleaming, clanging machines went on mechanically, gorging twenty cent pieces, avidly watched by faces shiny with sweat, which every now and again, when the machine insolently threw back a few coins, broke into smiles full of childlike glee.

In the far end of an adjoining room, a group of shearers were playing poker, and nearer the lounge was a pool table surrounded by young schoolteachers. 'Mighty Wrighty's here,' one of them observed. 'Bit above his intellectual capacity isn't it?' another commented, and the game continued. In the corner, on the wall, a colour television with the sound turned down continued to flash images of a startlingly young John Wayne flexing his masculinity.

'Here we are,' Harry leant across his wife's head and placed the tray in the middle of the table. He distributed the drinks and bags of chips.

'Chips with everything,' Gordon Wright quipped, but no one noticed, and Harry pulled up a chair.

'Gordon's been giving you the local gossip?' he asked his brother. 'Woongarra's a great place for gossip.'

'Well, actually we've been talking about his work,' Gordon said.

'Yeh, he's got a good job. How much do you make now, Greg?' Two hundred a week isn't it? Not bad for chucking a few bolts in a few holes. Wouldn't mind getting that sort of money for filling a few holes myself.'

The young men laughed. Mr. Wright took a sip of his whiskey and the two women shifted uneasily in their chairs.

Later that night, as they lay in their single beds, Mr. Wright would remark to his wife that Harry Fletcher was an extremely crude little man, that he wished to God there was more mental stimulation in Woongarra, and that watching 'Blazing Saddles' followed by a conversation with a young man who spent his life bolting together Holden cars was hardly what one would describe as the nirvana of intellectual life. And Ina Wright would pretend solicitous agreement, then turn over to go to solitary sleep, wondering where her life had gone wrong, and why it seemed as long and empty as a garden hose which has been turned off at the tap.

'I hear you won at golf again,' Gordon said, giving a shallow smile and hoping to turn the conversation away from money.

'You can't scratch yourself in this town and everyone knows,' Harry said, his pride obvious to everyone.

'He fancies himself the Jack Nicklaus of the north-west,' Deidre put in with an edge to her voice, revealing bedroom fantasies and wielding the wifely knife. Harry adjusted his tie and lapels. Unrepentant, Deidre informed Greg and his friends, 'He's taken up bowls too.'

The fellows burst into loud laughter and there was a pause in the general conversation while everyone in the room turned expectantly towards their table.

'You haven't, really?' Greg asked his brother.

'Why not?' Harry was defensive. 'It's not a bad game. Damn sight harder than you imagine. I'll give you a game while you're up here and you'll see what I mean.'

'No thanks mate, you wouldn't catch me playing bowls. That's strictly over forties stuff.'

Deidre put in her final rapier thrust. 'He looks very good in his whites,' and the fellows broke up with loud guffaws.

'You wear a hat too, do you mate?' his brother managed to get out between belly laughs. The Wrights looked on politely. Deidre swung a slim leg, inspected her nail polish and when the boys finally laughed themselves into a lull she said, 'Well what else is there to do in a town like this?'

'We could have a massacre,' Harry volunteered, 'and wipe out the blackfellows.'

The boys laughed and John Wayne finally got his man. The West was won; Woongarra could sleep easy that night.

## MONDAY

Gary Andrews's head jerked forward as a nerve in his neck contracted in a spasm, and he became instantly awake. Or at least as awake as his befuddled brain would ever be. He blinked slowly, and shook his head. The dirty checked rug had slipped off his knees and was caught under one wheel of his chair. Slowly and with great effort he managed to free it and cover his useless legs. Ever since he had become paraplegic the lower half of his body constantly felt cold. Dr Hitchcock had told him that this was impossible, that it was just an illusion, but illusion or not his legs per-petually felt icy cold, even in this midsummer heat.

He coughed, a deep chest cough, and spat the greenish blood-speckled slime over the low wooden half-wall, which ran along the verandah. He wished to God that Fred Pepper would come. He wasn't at all sure, but guessed that it had been around three o'clock when he'd gulped down the dregs from the last bottle. He'd woken at about five with a fiery thirst and had wheeled himself out on to the verandah where he'd dozed on and off as he waited for the welcome sound of Fred Pepper's van.

Now he heard the baby wake in the back room and start to bawl. He mentally cursed it and hoped to Christ that one of the other kids would give it a feed so it would shut up. His skin was beginning to itch and he knew from too many past experiences that within fifteen minutes the itch would be unbearable, just as if his body was covered with red-hot, biting bull ants. He put his hand inside his soiled pyjama-top and be-gan to scratch at his chest and then forearms, so that the dry cracking skin, already worn paper thin from intermittent scraping, began to gently ooze blood and several sores started to suppurate. The sun was well and truly up, so where is that bastard Pepper? I'll give him hell when he turns up. I'll go someplace else for my stuff, he thought, knowing very well that there was nowhere else to go.

A young child appeared at the door to the house and pushed the creaking broken thing open on its one hinge with a battered wickerwork pram. Inside lay the baby greedily sucking at a bottle. Gary glowered at both the children. He couldn't recall what his son's name was, or the baby's. He wasn't even sure if they were his. The boy said, 'G'day, Dad.' So he must be, but he was damned if he could remember his name. Gary grunted a reply and moved irritably, trying to lose the sensation of being eaten alive by hundreds of ants. The boy didn't wait to be told, but carelessly shoved the pram down the sagging steps and off on what had become his routine morning walk.

With both hands Gary scratched off some scabs from behind his ears and had bent his head forward to attack some further up in his hair, when he heard the distant sound of a vehicle. He knew it was Fred Pepper's van, he could recognize it even though it was half a mile away. Sound carried for much further than that across this silent flat land. Every morning for seven years since the time West Woongarra was built and he'd been moved up here along with everyone else from the old mission, he'd waited for Fred Pepper.

No one seemed to know exactly where Pepper came from originally. He'd been in Woongarra for almost twenty years, and in that time there had been a lot of different stories about his past. One was that he'd been working up on the Ridge, had killed a bloke in a fight over some opal and had been told to get out of town. Another was that he'd got into similar trouble over at Mount Isa, and some said that the trouble had happened over in Western Australia. The one element all the stories had in common was that there had been some violence, which had forced Fred Pepper to move on. But in the two decades he'd been in Woongarra he'd been in no trouble with the police and he'd remained a silent shadowy figure on whom the townspeople had slowly come to depend as being able to provide anything anyone wanted. 'Ask Fred Pepper, he's sure to be able to help you' was a common answer to a request.

Three years ago Pepper had bought a new van, but it had taken Gary only a few days to adjust to the new engine tone. Now he estimated how much longer it would be before Pepper arrived. He prayed that he would come straight over to the West instead of stopping off, as he sometimes did, at the Imperial to pick up supplies from the storage room at the back of the hotel, to which he had his own key. No, he could hear him cruise past the pub and change down as he drove off the bitumen on to the dirt track. Gary pushed at the wheels on his chair, bringing himself perilously close to the edge of the top step, craning forward to catch the first glimpse of the van.

In the good days, before he'd lost the use of his legs, he'd been able to stroll down to meet Fred Pepper. But for just under a year he'd been confined to this wheel-chair. Dr Hitchcock had told him that it was due to what he drank that he'd become paraplegic, and that if he continued in the same way he would sooner or later become totally paralysed. But what do doctors know? Bloody nothing. He'd been down to Bloomfield more times than he could remember, sometimes on a court order, sometimes voluntarily. They'd dried him out and fed him up and then sent him back home, where within a month he was drinking just as much as before. What else is there to do in Woongarra?

Years and years ago when he was still at school he'd had dreams of becoming a qualified builder. His mother had encouraged him to finish his schooling and take up an apprenticeship, but all the whitefellows had scoffed at such an idea. Boongs were all right as labourers, they said, but who ever heard of one becoming a qualified builder? 'What you going to build then Jackie? Gunyahs?' and they'd laughed, Stronger-willed men might have ignored such jibes, pushed ahead, gone down the track, and taken up an apprenticeship in Dubbo or Sydney. But Gary Andrews was easily put off, so that by the time he'd finished school it seemed easier to sit around with his mates and boozily dream about what could have been, than to face up to actually making it happen. Anyway, he consoled himself; there wouldn't have been any future in Woongarra for a builder because there hadn't been a new place built in the area for over five years, apart from the teachers' homes.

Gary leaned forward in his chair, his tongue lolling out, the illusory ants biting the whole upper half of his torso so that it burnt and flamed while his legs ached with the cold. He shivered with anticipation as Fred Pepper's van drew up at the end of what an ambitiously idealistic city planner in Canberra had called Wattle Street, in commemoration of his country's national emblem. As Fred Pepper got out carrying a bulging brown paper bag and walked across the littered street, Gary smiled to himself.

'G'day Gary,' Fred Pepper said.

Gary nodded and stretched out his hand but the white man held on to the bag. Gary began to sweat and the itching rose to a terrifying crescendo.

'That'll be two dollars,' Fred Pepper said.

'The pensions come this week. I'll give it to you Tuesday.'

'That makes it fourteen dollars, altogether.'

'Tuesday.'

'Don't let me down Gary. Not like last time.'

'No. No. I promise. Tuesday.'

Gary suddenly lurched for-ward, grabbed the parcel, tore it open, and as one bottle fell into the rug across his lap, he fumbled with the screw cap on the other. With a look of complete contempt on his face Fred Pepper watched as, in his haste, Gary spilt some of the liquid over his chin from where it ran down on to his pyjama-top. Fred Pepper tightened his nostrils as not even the rose hip syrup base could cover the acrid smell of the methylated spirits.


'How many today?' Ed Vickers asked his ser-geant, Ron Evans. 'Just eleven. Mostly regulars. Rich-ard Brown's in again, picked him up myself at the Garra on the six o'clock run. Full as an old boot. I told Reg I'd book him too the next time I found anyone under age drinking on his premises, but he said that he can't tell the difference between Richard and his brother David. I believe him too, because I can't ei-ther, even though David's a good two years older.'

Vickers frowned. 'Poor Molly Brown must be going round the bend trying to keep tabs on that lot. Eleven kids is more than I'd like to manage, specially on my own. It'll be a miracle if she doesn't go under.'

The two policemen stood behind the counter in the small station, shuffling through the charge sheets for the eight men and three women who had been picked up the previous day. The wooden building was immaculate inside and out; the floors and windows kept polished and clean by the regular residents of the lockup. Tacked on the wall was a map of the area for which the six policemen posted to this outback township were responsible. Next to it were pinned photographs of children from all States listed as missing. All of them were country kids for whom the lure of the glamour and bright lights of the big cities had become irresistible. The shots, many of them slightly out of focus, no doubt supplied by anxious parents, showed smiling, carefree teenagers on a family picnic or clowning around with a friend. They were a strange contrast with the stark official facts printed below. 'Beverley Mathews, 14. Dark hair. 5'6", 130 lbs. Last seen in Narran Street, Collarenebri, 13/6/74, wearing yellow skivvy, denim trousers and thongs.'

Outside in the garden, small shrubs and flowers stood rigidly to attention in a regimented garden, weeded and watered by the prisoners, and in the street the paddy wagon and two police cars gleamed from the efforts of the same captive labour.

Sergeant Ron Evans stood the charge sheets on one end and banged them gently into a neat pile. Handing them to Constable Vickers, he said, 'I hear Dougo's back.'

'Dougo?'

'Oh, yes. I'd forgotten you don't know him. He went down before you came to us. But don't worry, you'll meet him soon enough. He's one of our regulars.'

'Dougo who?'

'Foster.'

'One of Stella Foster's boys?'

'Right.'

'Not Flo Foster's husband?'

'Right. Except that of course they aren't married.'

'Does he know about his kids yet?'

'Can't do, otherwise he'd have been in here.'

'Poor bastard.' Ed Vickers shuffled the charge sheets like an overgrown pack of cards.

'Poor bastard be damned,' Sergeant Evans said.

Ed didn't appear to hear him. 'What did he go down for?' 'Six months for assault and intent to cause grievous bodily harm. Lucky he didn't kill the bloke. Knocked him out and then kicked him in the head. The fellow was unconscious for several days and in hospital for weeks. He's never been right in the head since. They were both drunk of course. Neither of them could remember what it was they were fighting over.

Either that or they didn't want to tell us. Lucky for them that it was one of their mob. If it had been a whitefellow he'd have gone down for a hell of a lot longer. Jim Andrews it was he half-killed. The brother of that paraplegic, Gary. They're still over at the West. Should be an interesting reunion.'

'But didn't Stella Foster take Gary's kids in for a while when he went into hospital?' Ed asked.

'Yes. Just goes to show what mixed-up bastards they are. They're like kids, and like kids they need protecting from themselves.'

Ed reshuffled the sheets. 'Is he as militant as his brother?'

'Who?'

'Doug Foster.'

'No. Nothing like each other. Different as black and white.' He laughed at his own joke.'Probably got different fathers. Who'd know? Not Stella Foster, that's for sure.'

Ed looked up from the charge sheets. 'Stella Foster doesn't seem like that to me.'

'Like what?' the sergeant asked, and without waiting for a reply, went on. 'Ed my boy, you've been up here four months, just wait a while. Wait till you've been here five years like I have, and then you'll know these blackfellows like I know them. I'm telling you they're all the same.' He said it slowly and not in anger. 'They are bludgers, no-hopers. When they're sober you couldn't wish to meet a nicer bunch of people, except that they were born idle. But they can't hold their liquor, and drunk they're worse than useless. They're a bloody menace to themselves and everyone else. I don't treat them any differently than I treat anyone else. If a whitefellow was drunk and being offensive in a public place I would pick him up just the same as I pick up these blackfellows. To be honest, I feel sorry for them. They're the result of interbreeding between the scum of both races, black and white. The sooner they drink themselves to death the better.' He met Ed Vickers's accusing look with a level gaze and for a few seconds the two men stood like a tableau in a waxworks, portraying a police station in Outback Australia.

Then Ron Evans ran his fingers back through his thick wiry grey hair. 'Better get them in to John. 'He indicated the charge sheets. 'It's almost time for the run, The pension checks are in so I reckon it's going to be one hell of a day.'

Ed went out into the harsh mid-morning sun and round the back of the station to where his two smallest sons were playing in the shade between his house and the lockup. One of his boys was obviously winning a game of five-stones he was having with a prisoner, because when his father announced, 'Come on everyone. Time for court', the boy cried. 'Oh wait, wait. We'll just be a minute.'

The other boy who was sitting on the grass between a prisoner's knees put up his arms and Ed picked him up and swung him round to hoots of delight from the boy and the prisoners.

'I've won! I've won!' his brother announced and rushed inside to tell his mother.

'Off you go for a while.' Ed propelled the other child towards their house, and then walked ahead of the knot of prisoners, who shuffled and ambled round to the adjacent courthouse.They sat on the familiar bench on the cool flagstoned verandah running along the front of the courthouse, and talked quietly to one another. All of them looked drawn and haggard and pale beneath their brown skin. Most of them had distended stomachs where their livers, grossly swollen by cirrhosis, hung down below their rib cage and pushed aside the other organs, distorting their bodies.

Constable Edward Vickers, armoured in the cap and uniform of a constable serving the State of New South Wales, came out from consulting with John Smith, who as Clerk of PettySessions was the highest judicial authority in the town, and formally announced that the court was now open.

'Richard Brown,' he called, and the fifteen -year-old fatherless boy, already destined to be an incurable alcoholic, blushed and stood up, just as Doug and Flo drove along the main street and past the courthouse.


A brisk knock on the door. Gordon Wright looked up. 'Come in.'

Lesley Armstrong hurled herself into, rather than entered, the headmaster's room. Without waiting to be asked she sat down opposite him and, looking him straight in the eye, waited for him to oppose her.

Gordon tried again. 'It's about this visit to Sydney.' He dared not pause, he'd prepared this speech for a full half hour before sending for her, and he knew that once he hesitated he'd he finished. 'Most of the places you've suggested taking your class to are eminently suitable. Highly nutritious knowledge made more palatable with a sprinkling of entertainment and a dash of fun.' He smiled weakly, 'Haute education.'

Lesley tugged hard at a stray piece of her thick blonde hair.

Gordon continued. 'The Art Gallery, the Museum, the Harbour trip, the Shark Aquarium, even the ABC. But – ' he made the mistake of a moment's silence, during which he recapped his fountain pen.

'But,' Lesley threw herself back against the hard chair, stretched her arms along the curved sides, drumming her blunt fingernails on the stained wood. 'But,' she repeated, 'you don't approve of us visiting the Aboriginal Legal Service or the Aboriginal Medical

Centre or even spending time at the Leisure Centre in Redfern.'

Gordon Wright clipped his pen in his shirt pocket.

'That's it, isn't it?' Lesley insisted. 'You might as well come straight out with it.'

The headmaster leant forward and tried to smile. Lesley stared at him. He leant back. 'It's not that I don't, as you put it, approve, Lesley. It's just that as each secondary class only visitsSydney once a year, I feel there are other places of greater significance and educational value which should be included in your itinerary.'

'Like what?' she demanded.

'Well, there's Old Sydney Town and...'

'Old Sydney Town! You've got to be kidding.' She thumped her hands on the chair's arms. 'Have you been there? I have. Christ. It's supposed to show how this great country of ours was settled, and yet the solitary Aboriginal to be seen can be viewed on Friday, Saturday andSunday only, at which time he plays a tarted-up didgeridoo and wails a bit. He doesn't even speak any Aboriginal dialect, He lives in Sydney and can relate to my kids about as well as a galah can relate to a cage. The only other things they would see are the ritual hangings and floggings. Don't you think my kids get enough brutality in this town without taking them away on trips specially to see more?'

Gordon Wright swallowed hard. 'There are other aspects of early Australian life exhibited,'he said. 'Surely the girls would like to see the period costumes, and they'd all be interested in the construction of wattle and daub houses.'

48

Lesley glared at him. 'Perhaps it might give them a better idea of what poor quality their own present-day housing is, but I see dangers in it. They might just decide that they would be better off building their own wattle and daub houses right in the middle of 'Garra, rather than living in those rat-infested dumps in the West. They might even decide to build on that vacant land over the railway.' Mr. Wright's house, built by the Department of Education at a cost of $40,000 the previous year, was situated beyond the railway, which bisected the town, and was surrounded by empty building blocks.

Gordon Wright took the point, inclined his head, and tried another tack. 'Miss Armstrong,' he started. 'Lesley,' he deliberately softened his voice. She noticed and squirmed in her chair. 'I know, we all know, how much you care about the Aborigines, but you must not let your political motivations completely overwhelm your responsibilities as a teacher. Confronting those children with the Aboriginal movement in Sydney is pointless in the extreme. They are not city aborigines, they are small country town aborigines. What works in Sydney does not work up here. Firing their imagination with dreams and schemes for social revolution, and then bringing them back here is cruel and dangerous.' He paused before adding, 'and I cannot allow it.'

Lesley Armstrong put her eight years of teaching on the line, and said, 'Mr. Wright, it is you who are cruel and dangerous. Your petty snobbery and your minuscule intelligence I can live with. They don't harm the children. They are an education in themselves because kids have to learn to live with and accept all types of people. But your paternalism and patronage, your total lack of moral strength, empathy or even imagination, make you the worst type of man to be the headmaster of a school where seventy per cent of the pupils are dispossessed and de-cultured.'

In the silence that followed, the squeals and shouts of laughter emanating from the playground became unnaturally loud. Suddenly the siren screamed, sounding the end of morning recess. Lesley stood up.

'I am taking my kids to Sydney next week, Mr. Wright, and we are going to visit theAboriginal Legal and Medical Services and also the Redfern Leisure Centre. If you try to stop me I shall inform the department, and insist on an inquiry into your reasons. If necessary I shall even go to the lengths of approaching the press.'

She closed the door quietly behind her, and Gordon Wright leant back, gave a deep sigh and stared through the windows at the now empty playground, whose black bitumen soaked up the blistering sun.


'Wasn't that Richard Brown?' Doug asked Flo as he caught sight of the young boy stumbling along the courthouse verandah.

'Probably. He spends more than half his time in the lockup. If he's not careful he'll end up in Bloomfield, or take to metho and finish up like Gary.'

Doug winced at the mention of a member of the Andrews family. He wanted to ask how Jim was getting on, but not this morning, he decided. His head ached too much and his eyes stung.Though it wasn't as bad as the previous morning's hangover. I must be getting used to the stuff again, he thought, not without a twinge of regret. Anyway, Flo seems in a funny enough mood without bringing up Jim. Doug pursued his usual policy with the female of the species in general, and Flo in particular. Best let her go. She'll come right soon enough.

Flo's mind was indeed in a turmoil, but Doug could never have guessed at the reasons why,and she could never attempt to explain. The gap between them, there since the beginning, had been stretched to a chasm by Doug's six months absence.

'Which way now?' Doug asked as they came to the end of the main street.

'Over the river,' she told him, and Doug turned his brother's two-year-old red Ford Capri, happy to be behind the wheel again. He was so pleased to be spinning along the open road, the car responding to his movements, in charge and responsible again after six months of not being allowed to make even one decision for himself, that he turned off the road as Flo directed, without even questioning why. The flat dry bush on either side concealed the wildlife, which lay stupefied by the immense heat, waiting for the cool of evening. The blue cloudless sky was so clear that it seemed impossible that there were people in the world who were unhappy.

His head didn't feel the best, but he was home, he had Flo, and very soon he'd have his kids.Life was great and he began to whistle to himself. Flo turned to watch him, amazed that he could be so unaware, so cheerful. Momentarily she felt a flash of envy, which turned to anger.Not for long, Dougo, she thought bitterly, and before he realized it, Doug felt the car jolt and rattle across the cattle grid, as he drove into the yard of the old mission station.

The car skidded to a halt, sending up a screen of dust and a shower of stone chips. Two youths were sitting on the tailboard of a ute parked about fifty feet away. 'Bloody lair,' one of them muttered. Jesus, it's Dougo,' the other said, half rising and then sitting down as if stunned bya sudden blow. 'Jeeesus,' his friend whistled through his teeth, and then catapulted himself across the patchy grass, under the wisteria, which grew over a trellis, and up the unsteady wooden steps of the dilapidated old colonial-style farmhouse.

Doug snapped to, and realizing where he was, asked Flo, 'What we doing at George's? I thought we were going to pick up the kids.'

But Flo was already out of the car and waddling, as all heavily pregnant women do, quickly towards the house.

Why has she brought me here? She knows I hate the place. Ever since he was a small child it had filled him with fear and horror. From the time when his father had walked out on them, and his mother, desperate on some occasions and angry on others, had threatened her children by saying, 'If you don't behave I'll put you in George Davies' place.' The home for orphans and State wards. George Davies, the non-swearing, non-drinking, non-smoking, reformed alcoholic, religious fanatic. All of which would have made him unusual, had he been white.But, as a black man, it made George Davies unique in Woongarra. An Uncle Tom was how Allan described him; to Doug he was just an unfathomable oddity.

Doug suddenly felt very alone and was gripped with panic. He fumbled awkwardly with the handle of the car door, unable for a moment to open it, and when the door burst open he almost fell out, and not quite ran after his wife, calling, 'Flo. Flo.' She took no notice of him,and when George Davies appeared at the top of the steps, she walked up and past him so that the two men were left to face one another alone.

'G'day Doug.'

'G'day George.'

'I heard you were back,' the older man said, and in an instant Doug knew why he was here.

'Where's my kids?' he asked.

'They're at school, they'll be back later this afternoon,' George replied, and then added quietly, 'They're all right Dougo. They're fine.'

Doug Foster felt like a brown paper bag, which in fun has been blown up and then burst. He sat down heavily on the top step. 'How long you had them?'

'Six weeks,' George told him, and then realized. 'Didn't Flo tell you?'

'No.' Doug said flatly. 'No bastard told me.' He wrapped his arms around his knees and rocked to and fro, feeling the anger slowly forming and beginning to bubble up.

' They're fine, Dougo,' George said again.

The anger frothed out. 'Don't bloody tell me they're fine, you bastard!' He stood up quickly,coming to within six inches of George Davies, and spat the words out.

George neither flinched nor moved, but several small black faces appeared at the open windows of the verandah behind them.

'You pinch my kids and lock them up with a whole bunch of snivelling snotty-nosed bastards and you tell me they're fucking fine.'

A few more faces appeared cautiously peeping around the edge of the windows. Slowly and quietly George Davies said, 'Please do not use that language in front of my children.'

Doug raised his hand to strike him, and George continued to look levelly into his wild eyes.

'You fucking bastard,' Doug shouted and then his fist unclenched and fell unused. 'You fucking bastard,' he said once more, but quietly, and then he lurched down the steps and across the yard. As he threw his whole body face forward against the car he didn't feel the sharp edge of the small lip on the roof cut into his nose, or the scorched metal burn his bare outstretched arms as he flung them across the car top. But the rage went as suddenly as it came, dissipated by three generations of bitter experience as a half-caste.

The gravel scrunched behind him, and Doug turned to find George Davies with a look which offered male compassion. 'I'm sorry, Dougo,' he said.

Doug hung his head and then lifted it slowly, looking not at George but at the group of children gathered at the top of the steps. 'I won't let you keep them,' he promised. 'I'll get them back.' When George said nothing he turned his gaze towards him and asked, 'Tell me. Tell me how it happened.'

'Let's take a walk,' George suggested. And as Doug fell in beside him and they walked towards the river, George said, 'It was neglect. The court...'

'My God, they went to court?' Doug stood still.

'No, the children didn't go to court,' George answered, 'but Flo had to. She was charged with neglect. Gross neglect.'

54

Doug felt the tension return, but the two men resumed walking. 'Who brought the charge?' he asked.

'Bruce Stannard.'

'That bastard.' He registered George's distaste for his language, but he didn't feel like apologizing.

'He was only doing his job,' George continued. 'The children were in a terrible condition.'

'What d'you mean?' They had reached the riverbank and George, his dark skin perspiring freely, sat down, but when Doug continued to stand, he got up again. On the far bank the mission's cow grazed, raising its head every now and again to stare vacantly across at them. The banks were not so steep here, and there were only a few trees, most of them having been chopped down about eighty years previously, when the mission was in full operation.

'It started with them not turning up at school for days at a stretch,' George told him. 'They'd always been so regular that Bruce was genuinely worried that something was up. Of course he knew you were in Sydney, so he thought perhaps things had gone bad for Flo. He went over to your mum's place and couldn't get an answer. He kept knocking, and eventually Flo came to the door. She'd obviously been asleep and Bruce's knocking had woken her. She was also obviously very drunk, and when Bruce asked where her children were she told him . . .' George hesitated, 'in so many words, to go away.'

Despite himself, Doug smiled at the thought of Flo telling Bruce Stannard to 'fuck off.

'When Flo had gone back inside, Betty Flinders came out from next door and told Bruce that she knew where the children were, over at Jane Saunders' place. Bruce found them there. They were playing bingo along with about fifteen other kids. She's an evil woman, that Jane Saunders. She makes at least thirty dollars a day out of the bingo games she runs. Bad enough to do that with adults, but some of the kids are only four or five years old.'

Doug nodded, not just in agreement, but so that he wouldn't have to speak, to fill the silence. Steve and Carol playing bingo and wagging school and Flo drunk in bed in the middle of the day. It all seemed so unreal. There must be a mistake. But if there was, why was he standing by the river with George Davies, asking him why his kids had been taken into custody?

Looking at him, George realized Doug was dazed and in a state of shock. 'Come back to the house and have a cup of tea,' he offered.

Doug shook his head. 'Tell me the rest,' he ordered, and sat down on the grass.

George sat beside him and said, 'Well, that was only the first time. Soon Steve and Carol were missing from school three out of five days, and sometimes a whole week at a time. Bruce would go and look for them, but after that first time he couldn't ever find them. I suppose the kids would get wind of his visit and warn Steve and Carol and they'd hide.

'Then one day,' George continued, 'Sister Phyllis Hutchins was visiting Molly Brown. Molly's youngest baby is under a year old and poor Molly has been in such a state since Jerry died in prison that she thought the kid had scarlet fever, but it turned out to only be impetigo.'

Doug stared into the muddy water and George picked a long blade of grass and began chewing it, before saying, 'Phyllis ran into Steve and asked him where his sister was. He said she was sick and took her back to your mum's place. He asked her to creep in quietly through the back because his mother was sleeping, and they found Carol in your mum's room. Phyllis said she was horrified when she examined Carol.'

'Why? What was the matter with her? 'Doug felt his stomach beginning to leap and churn and the anger starting up again.

'She's all right now, Dougo.' George had sensed Doug's changing mood.

'What was the matter with her?' Doug insisted.

George waited a while before saying, 'She was huddled up on a blanket in a corner of the room with the blinds drawn. Phyllis put the blinds up so she could see Carol better, but Carol begged her to pull them down again because she said the light hurt her eyes. She was extremely dehydrated and suffering from malnutrition. Phyllis said she could hardly recognize her.'

Doug grimaced and clenched and unclenched his fists. 'That can't be true,' he accused. 'She's eight. Old enough to get her own food if she has to and to drink when she's thirsty.'

'That's right Dougo,' George agreed, 'and Phyllis couldn't understand why she should be in this condition. But she took her up to the hospital and when they examined her they found that both her eardrums were perforated.'

Doug stared at him, and George forced himself to meet his gaze as he said, 'They were flyblown, the maggots had eaten into the eardrums. Carol told them that the pain had got so bad that she'd helped herself to some of her mother's tablets. Valium. They were adult dosage of course, and had made Carol so dopey that she hadn't wanted to eat. She didn't feel hungry or even know she was thirsty. It was lucky she was still alive when Phyllis found her.'

Doug kept staring at George. He was trembling, his heart was pounding, his stomach churning, and there seemed to be a white-hot fire in his brain. He kept staring at George, but he didn't see him. Instead he saw his eight-year-old daughter lying maggot-ridden on the floor, while his wife slept in a drunken stupor.

Suddenly he was up and running. Running towards the house and Flo. And as he ran he yelled: 'Where are you, you fucking bitch? I'm coming to get you, you fucking bitch! You bitch. You lousy, no good, stinking, bitch.'

# CHAPTER THREE

## MONDAY

The grey paddy wagon cruised up Culgoa
Street past the small wooden frame shops that had
opened for business again after the dinner break. Ed
Vickers unconsciously counted the number of places
that were boarded up, the owners having gone south
in search of better prospects. The town hadn't yet
quite begun to decay, but it showed signs that this was
its inevitable future. It was like a middleaged yet
beautiful stripper. Men still came to gaze at her, but
while once they couldn't stop ogling long enough to
light a cigarette, now they both smoked and drank
and were even beginning to chat with fellow customers during her act. Her days were numbered.

Johnny Phillips was standing talking to Les
Cullen outside the shire hall, and both men waved as
the wagon rolled by. Outside the middle pub, The
Woongarra Hotel, leaning against the verandah posts
or sitting on the kerb, were small groups of Aborigines. Several of them were clustered round the door,
and as Sergeant Evans and Constable Vickers went
past a scuffle erupted and Billy Saunders staggered
backwards, dropping a wine flagon which showered
splinters of glass in all directions. They heard Ann

Marshall yell, 'Fuck off Billy, you stupid bastard,' and saw her lean forward into a battered pram to pick slivers of glass off the sleeping bodies of her twin daughters.

'Told you it was going to be a good day,' Ron Evans said.

'D'you want to do the Garra first or shall we go on up to the Imperial?' Ed Vickers asked.

'Imperial first. With any luck Billy Saunders will have shot through by the time we get back. I can't stand the little swine, and I don't fancy having to lock him up. Last time he stirred the others up so much we damn near had a riot on our hands.'

The paddy wagon pulled up in the gravel yard at the back of the Imperial Hotel, stopped, and the two men got out. Sergeant Evans pulled down his peaked cap. Vickers patted the truncheon which was stuck casually into his side pocket. Around him the noise was deafening.

> *Muhammad, Muhammad Ali,*
> *He floats like a butterfly and stings like a bee.*
> *Muhammad, the black superman*
> *Who calls to the other guys*
> *I'm Aaaaaaaali Catch me if you can.*

The record blared from the jukebox and the noise reverberated round the corrugated iron shed tacked on to the back of the hotel.

'Looks as though the sows 'pen is pretty full,' Evans shouted. 'Come on, let's go.'

They walked into the gloom and for a moment or two, after the strong sunlight outside, were unable to see anything. Bumped and jostled, they worked their way round the walls of the hut. Ed kept his hand on his truncheon. Sergeant Evans used his arms to force his way through the mass of bodies as if he were pushing aside thick scrub. He skidded on an empty beer can and came down heavily against the jukebox. The needle jumped.

*Muhammaddddd.......bbbbutterfly Stings like a bee.*

No one seemed to notice. They just kept on yelling the words.

*Muhammad the BLACK SUPERMAN...*

...they screamed. Everyone danced, not with a partner, but by themselves or with everyone else. Momentarily Ed was frightened. All he could see were series of white teeth gaping like the jaws of ferocious beasts and staring white eyeballs. The rest gradually came into focus as a heaving, seething mass of dark bodies.

'G'day Ed,' a voice shouted in his ear, He jumped and turned to see Len Foster dragging his wife away. She was gesturing back towards him, waving a flagon and shouting something, but he couldn't hear what. Her mouth opened and shut like a robot.

The two white men met at the jukebox and leant back against it to review the scene. An Aboriginal man in his early twenties staggered towards them, and when he was only five feet away, vomited down his shirtfront. He stood still for a second, as if in surprise at the thin vomit hanging from his chin.

'Oh Christ,' Ed heard Ron Evans sigh, 'take him out, Ed.'

Constable Vickers propelled the compliant drunk towards the door, noticing Stella Foster slouched on a collapsible metal chair. She looked at him, but he knew she didn't register him. A cigarette hung from one comer of her mouth with a piece of miraculously long ash clinging to it. On her lap, its head all but smothered in Stella's bosom, lay Gary Andrews' small baby, fast asleep. Ed wondered vaguely why the child was not at home.

A crowd of young Aborigines at the door dispersed as Ed came out pushing the drunk ahead of him. They took no notice of either man as Ed unlocked the wagon and helped the prisoner up the step. He all but fell on to the hard seat and sat bolt upright still holding a flagon. Ed took it from him, and was handing it to one of the young men by the door as Sergeant Evans emerged half clutching and half supporting on one side a middle aged woman, and on the other a young girl. The two were trying to scratch and tear at one another. The girl's blouse had a sleeve half ripped out, and there were deep bleeding gashes in her shoulder.

'Why don't you piss off you bloody bitch,' the mother yelled at her daughter. 'Leave him alone. You bloody well know he's mine.' The daughter spat full in her mother's face. Sergeant Evans pushed the young girl into the back of the wagon with the drunk, and took the older woman round to the cabin, shovelling her up on to the bench. 'You chuck up in there my lady,' he warned, 'and by Christ I'll have you lick it up.'

Harry Fletcher came down the outside stair-case ready to take over the afternoon shift behind the bar. He flexed his shoulders and ran his tongue round his teeth.

'What d'you know mate? Busy day eh?'

'You can say that again.'

Behind them the jukebox started up again and with it the chorus of drunken accompaniment...

*Now all you white men you've got to agree,*
*There ain't no flies on Muhammad Ali.*
*Muhammad, the BLACK SUPERMAN ...*

'Black superman my bloody arse,' Harry growled.

The two policemen got in with the now slightly calmer woman and started up for the Garra. Around the door of the tin shack a quarrel broke out over the unexpected gift of a half full flagon of wine.

Doug Foster walked into the front office of the Aboriginal Legal Service and stood at the counter. On the other side the typist stopped clacking away on her machine and stared at him. The silence made Allan look up from the sheaf of forms in his hands. The eyes of the two brothers met.

'I hit her,' Doug announced flatly. 'I hit her.' Blood had congealed over the deep cut in the bridge of his nose. His shirt pocket was half torn off and the material had come away from the collar where the men had held on to him and dragged him away from his wife.

In the silence the typist cleared her throat. Allan went to the end of the counter and lifted up the flap. Doug walked through and followed his brother into an inner office. The typist bruised her hip on the edge of the desk in her rush to get out and be the first to break the news.

'I hit her,' Doug repeated as he sat down in Allan's office.

'Of course you hit her, what man wouldn't?' His brother poured two large glasses of port. 'Drink this.' He thrust one into Doug's hand. Doug put the glass down on the desk.

'I wanted to kill her.' He looked beseechingly up at his younger brother.

'Drink the bloody stuff, will you.'

Doug drank. 'I did. I wanted to kill her. I wanted to go on bashing her head until I smashed it in. They dragged me off. I wanted to kill her.'

'For Christ's sake Dougo, lay off, will you? Stop saying it over and over.'

Doug was quiet for a while and took another drink. 'Why, Allan? Why did she let it happen? Couldn't you have stopped her?'

'Don't you think I bloody tried?' Allan flared. 'We all tried. When you first got sent down, Marge made Steve and Carol's breakfast along with her own kids' while Flo slept in. I'd drop them all off at the school on my way to the office.'

'You mean she went bad as soon as I was gone?' Doug asked.

Allan gestured with annoyance. 'What d'you mean, went bad? She's always been bad.'

'That's not true,' Doug said angrily.

'Of course it's true. She's a slut. She's always been a slut.'

Doug was out of the chair and grappling to get at his brother. 'Don't you bloody talk like that.'

But his brother was too quick and too strong for him. 'All right. All right. You don't want to face the truth. But look where that's got you.'

Doug collapsed back in the chair and thumped the sheet of glass on top of the government issue desk. Jesus. Jesus,' he moaned.

'Yeh. Well he ain't going to help you mate. You've got to help your bloody self. The trouble with you Dougo is that you're a bloody soft touch, and by Christ she knew it.' He looked down at his brother and his features softened. 'I tried, Dougo. Honest I did. I tried talking to her, but it was hopeless. Then when Auntie Irene and Uncle Bill got put into Bloomfield, Mum went down to try and visit them and stayed in Orange for a bit. 'Bout that time me and Liz were finishing up and when she decided to shove off I drove her over to Moree. See what bloody suckers we are? Imagine driving your bloody wife and kids to Moree when she's bloody leaving you.'

Allan poured another port. Doug kept his head down, resting it on his hands on the cluttered desktop.

'With all that going on, I sort of forgot about Flo and the kids. Then we had Irene and Bill's five move in and Marge almost went off her brain. Steve and Carol must have been missing school then, but no one had time to notice.'

Allan sat on the desk. 'I'm not saying it was right. I'm just telling you how it happened.'

'Maggots,' Doug mumbled into his hands. 'Maggots.' He shivered.

Allan looked away. Through the glass partition he could see that a few people had congregated at the counter and around the door. 'Jesus Christ! A man couldn't bloody die in private in this bloody town.'

Doug looked up, puzzled. Allan shook his head. 'It's nothing mate, nothing.'

After a pause, Allan started up again. 'When I saw them in hospital, Jesus, I wept, poor little bastards. I don't know how I stopped myself from beating the bloody bitch up.'

'Why didn't you tell me as soon as I got back?'

'I thought she would. I hoped she would. When she didn't, well, it was partly that I wanted you to realize what a bitch she is that she could let you go a whole day without telling you, and partly . . .' Allan got up, 'and partly that I couldn't bring myself to. So you see I'm as much of a bastard as she is a bitch.'

Allan wheeled round. 'But you were so happy, you dumb fool. Talking about building a house on the river and the new baby and all that shit. I couldn't believe that you wouldn't feel something was up.'

'Did you go to the court?'

'Yes, of course I did, what d'you take me for? I even gave evidence. Told them what a beaut bloke you are, and how it was a onetime lapse on Flo's part due to her being under such pressure, with having her loved one torn from her. Shit.' Allan wrenched at the venetian blind. 'What absolute shit.'

He sat down and leant towards his brother. 'And then the magistrate asked me where you were and I had to say Long Bay. What for? Six months for assault and causing grievous bodily harm. Next they produced Flo's record. Thirteen arrests in the last six months for drunkenness, using obscene language, resisting arrest and offensive behaviour. Didn't look too good I can tell you. Even the smartarse white lawyer the Legal Service got up from Sydney was a bit thrown by that lot. Then when Bruce Stannard gave evidence he let drop that you and Flo are not legally wedded. Well then you were cooked mate. Never mind that the magistrate is a bloody poofter and pays little boys to pull him off and that Bruce Stannard is a virgin at twentynine and probably isn't even sure what sex he is. The fact that you and Flo aren't married is what finished you. That's like thumbing your nose at the whitefellows' system. And they don't like that. The magistrate knew then that you had no legal leg to stand on.'

'Help me get them back,' Doug pleaded with his brother.

Allan looked at the man sitting opposite him, utterly crushed, and was trying to think of words which would allow him to avoid telling his brother the truth, when a large, fat, very black woman pushed her way importantly through the people at the door, and standing at the counter yelled, 'Doug Foster, you'd better get up the hospital. Quick. It's Flo!'


'Keeping you busy, are they Harry?' Michael Clancy asked as the publican set the glasses down on the counter. The beer foamed over the sides to be soaked up by the already drenched towel which ran along the full length of the bar.

'That's right Father, and judging by some of the things which are going on round here tonight, I think it'll be your turn to be busy on Sunday.'

'No, no, Harry,' the priest picked up the glasses. 'My people,' he threw his head back in a gesture which included the white men in the saloon bar behind him, 'my people know when they've had enough.'

'Yeh?' Harry said sceptically and stepped through the side door into the public bar to serve the noisy throng of Aborigines.

His wife Deidre had been busy for the past five hours filling and refilling schooners and middies with icecold beer. They met at the till. She was tired and tense. 'I can't take much more of this.' She counted the change.

'Just hold on a bit longer love. We're coining it here, and in another year we'll be in Surfers sitting on our backsides in the sun and we'll never have to work again. 'He ran his hand across her thin rump and felt her stiffen with distaste.

Father Clancy carried the beers outside into the hotel's back yard and gave one to Les Cullen and the other to Johnny Phillips.

'How's business, Les?' he asked.

'Picking up again.' The big blond man leant back against the wall and took a deep drink. Wiping his mouth with the back of his hand he said, 'That was good. Didn't touch the sides.'

'The Government lifting those export restrictions must have made a big difference.'

'That's for sure. I knew they would in the end. It was just a matter of sitting it out. Cost me a few bob though. They only brought them in under pressure from a few ratbags who call themselves animal lovers. They wanted to appear humanitarian and get on the ecology bandwagon. It's fashionable. It wins votes. But they soon realized what a moneyspinner roo is and that they can't afford to drop it. I told those government blokes they sent up from Canberra.' Les smiled and took another drink. 'But they always think they know better than we do up here. We're just a bunch of bloody idiots from back of Bourke as far as they're concerned. Just look what's happened since they got in. Bottom's dropped out of the cattle market, wool prices at an all time low. They don't give a damn about the man on the land. All they care about is the cities, where the votes are. The only thing left for us to do is either move down the line, and I'd rather end up in my own abattoirs than do that, or become a flaming peasant.'

'What happened with the Yank girl who came up here with them saying she wanted to save the roo from extinction?' Johnny Phillips asked.

'Oh, Jesus, don't let's talk about it,' Les answered. 'Pity she was a woman or I could have really told her what I thought of her. She came up here with her own ideas and nothing I showed her was going to change her mind. I was a bloody fool to try. Took her out on the Dargans' place and showed her hundreds of roos and the damage they've done. Took her round my factory and showed her how well run the place is. Showed her loads of facts and figures, and what happens?' Les finished his beer. 'She went back down south and was on every bloody television programme and in every newspaper saying how we are butchering our national emblem and how the roo is an endangered species. Jesus! Have another beer, Father?'

At the end of the counter stood Bruce Stannard trying to fit into the surroundings and failing miserably. He smiled stiffly at Les.

'How are you going?' he asked selfconsciously.

'I'm right. Have a beer?' It was a reflex question and gesture of friendliness because Les knew that Bruce never touched alcohol.

'No thanks. I'm all right. Can't have one tonight. I have some paper work to catch up on this evening.'

Les couldn't help feeling sorry for Bruce. His Pommy accent, his obvious sexual diffidence and his religious beliefs made him a sitting target for crude jokes by the young men in the town. But he felt he had to admire the man for the way he stuck to his guns. He must know about the jibes and yet he continued to play guitar and sing at George Davies's weekly street meetings. He also continued his thankless job as field officer for the Department of Youth, Ethnic and Community Affairs. A job which ensured him the dislike of blacks to whom he was a stickybeak, as well as the dislike of the whites for whom he was a boonglover. Les happened to know Bruce earned a mere five thousand a year, and he wondered at the motivation behind a university graduate, who could earn far more money in more pleasant circumstances, but who chose instead to come and work in the emotional jungle of Woongarra.

What Les didn't know was that Bruce's father had died when Bruce was eleven, and the only memories he left behind were of brutal drunken attacks on Bruce's mother and his two older sisters. His father's sudden and horrific death he had fallen in an alcoholic haze from a train and been crushed by a goods

engine   unhinged his mother more or less perma-
nently, and Bruce became the man of the house, making decisions which many men twice his age would
have agonized over. His belief in a force more powerful than any living being helped him considerably and
this assistance had strengthened his faith in an al-
mighty and yet personal god.

By the age of fifteen Bruce had decided that he
and his mother and sisters must go to Australia to try
to make a new life for themselves, and once there,
having experienced the suffering which excess drinking could cause, he decided to finish his education
and then use his degree in sociology to help people. It
was a vague ideal and this, his first field job, had not
proved to be quite what he had anticipated. But Bruce
Stannard was a sticker. The trouble was that years
and years of coping with three very clinging females
had made him nervous and wary of women.

'Father Clancy and Johnny Phillips are out the
back, come and join us,' Les offered, and Bruce followed him out into the yard. Seeing him coming, the
other two men sighed audibly. Both of them found
him a judgemental bore. They all exchanged g'days.
Bruce sipped his lemonade to cover his embarrassment. There was a slight tension.

'And how's things going with you then?' Les
asked the priest. The bull neck, shaved free of hair,
perspired freely, and the sweat ran down the hairless
chest and stained the pale blue sports shirt where it
pulled tight across the priest's large stomach.

'That grant to paint the outside of the convent
and the school came through at last, but like everything else with this Government, there are so many

strings attached I might just as well not collect the money.'

'How's that?'

'Well it's on this RED scheme. Regional Employment Development, isn't that what it stands for Johnny?' The Shire Clerk nodded.

'They've given me enough to pay three blokes a hundred and fifty a week each for six weeks.'

'Well, you'd have the whole place done in that time, wouldn't you?'

'Yes, sure. If I could do things my way. But there's a catch, you see, and the catch is that the men I employ must be taken from the local unemployed. So what's the bloody point? All I'd get is Richard Brown or Bill Flinders or some other no-hoper. I phoned up a bloke in the department in Canberra and told him that all the unemployed up here are unemployable and that even if I employed them I wouldn't get any more than a couple of hours' work a day out of them, and that it was like chucking money down the drain. What's the bloody point in that? After all, it's taxpayers' money I'd be wasting.'

Bruce took another sip of lemonade, and Johnny said' G'day' to a couple of men who were making their way to the bar. From the other end of the pub the paean of praise to the world heavyweight boxing champion still reverberated round the iron shed.

'What did he say to that?' Les asked.

'He got smart with me. Asked me how many white blokes were unemployed up here. I said I didn't know but that there were probably one or two. Then he asked how many blackfellows were out of work, 'cept that of course he didn't say blackfellows, he called them Aborigines, and the way he pronounced the word made it sound as though it was written in bloody capitals. I told him I didn't know that either, but that it was probably a hundred. Then he told me it was 214, so I asked him why, if he was so bloody smart, did he ask me. Then he went on with a lot of garbage about how we have to assist them to become full members of our society. In the end I told him straight, I said, look mate, the blackfellows we've got up here are bludgers who sit around waiting for government handouts and when they get the money, all they do is drink it.'

Father Clancy threw his head back, and Bruce Stannard watched as the priest's adam's apple bobbed up and down.

'It finished with him telling me that I was a racist bastard, and that if I was so opposed to government handouts why had I applied for one myself, and me telling him that instead of sitting on his fat backside with a safe job in Canberra, he should come up here and see what it's really like. It's all very well for you mate, I said, but you don't have to live with them.'

Bruce wondered again, as he had wondered many, many times in the fifteen months he had been in Woongarra, why Johnny Phillips, whose brother lived in the West, and was as black as night, and Les, who was white but whose wife and children were part Aboriginal, didn't get angry at such comments from men like Father Michael Clancy.

Instead Johnny Phillips shook his head, not in disagreement, but in sympathy, and Les said, 'These Canberra wallahs give me a pain in the whatnots. So what you going to do with the money?'

'I suppose I'll use it to get the place painted. It's badly in need of it, and I haven't any other money to use. But I feel very tempted to get some blokes up from Sydney to do the job. There's men down there who need the money and who'd be prepared to work for it.'

'Oh Christ, don't do that mate, 'Johnny said quickly, 'or I'll have Allan Foster down my throat accusing me of allowing in scab labour and we'll have the press and everyone else up here.'

The priest sighed. 'Don't worry Johnny, I won't do it, I'll let the government waste your money instead, and mine too.'

Despite himself, Bruce Stannard heard himself say, 'Well it's a good idea, isn't it? I mean, using the money to employ locals who are out of work, I mean, someone has tried to come up with something constructive to bring down unemployment in small towns, to stop the drift of country people to the big cities, I mean, . . .' he tapered off as he felt the priest regarding him with absolute contempt.

'That's right mate. It's a good idea. But like so many good ideas, it's only good on paper. If you want your tax thrown away on these bludgers, good on you. But I don't. There's no good idea which is good enough to solve the problem of what to do with the blackfellows. All we can do is pray for a miracle.' The priest smiled cynically.

Bruce said nothing.

Johnny and Les shifted uncomfortably, and then with obvious relief and pleasure, Les said, 'Hello, hello,' as a young Aboriginal woman came out through the bar door. She was wearing brief towelling shorts and a halternecked top and as she turned and stood up on her toes to kiss Les on the neck, the three white men were presented with a large expanse of dark supple skin, and a single thick braid of black hair.

Bruce Stannard swallowed hard, and examined his well polished shoes. Johnny Phillips and Michael Clancy looked at one another.

'I thought it was one quick one you were having,' Dianne punched her husband playfully in the stomach. He responded by pretending to double up in agony. 'You nut,' she put her small hand in his big one.

'What'll you drink, Mrs. Cullen?' Father Clancy asked.

'Not for me thanks Father, the kids want Les to take them for a swim. They're waiting outside in the car, that is if they haven't driven off in it.' She laughed, and they saw her pink tongue nestling behind regular teeth.

'OK love, let's go.' Les put his arm around his wife's shoulder. 'See you later, fellas,' and the three men watched as the couple crossed the yard, Dianne talking animatedly, her slim body glowing in the sunlight.

'Not bad for a gin,' one of the other drinkers remarked.

'Be the same as all the rest of them by the time she's thirty,' his friend added. 'Fat gut and skinny legs.'


Flo breathed heavily, her face showing blacker than ever against the crisp white sheets and the pads of cotton wool stuck over her right ear and eye. Deep bruising round her right temple showed purple beneath her dark skin, and above, little pieces of congealed blood were stuck in her hair. On the same side of her face the upper lip was swollen and stitched almost up to her nose. The wound was not covered and the nylon thread sprouted like some gruesome misshapen moustache.

She lay flat on her back, her distended stomach pushing up the bedclothes, with one arm stretched alongside her body outside the cover. A large needle had been forced into her vein at the elbow, and was held there with strips of sticking plaster. From the needle a tube ran up into a bag suspended above the bed. Every now and then the bag shuddered a little.

Doug stood beside the screens surrounding the bed and looked down at his wife, registering no emotion. Instead he felt hollow and empty. It had taken him almost two hours to get to see her and now he felt let down.

'Flo! Flo! Where's Flo?' he had babbled at Phyllis Hutchins who was on duty at the little hospital reception desk. Phyllis, smelling the alcohol on his breath, said coolly, 'Flo? Flo who?'

'My wife,' he shouted. 'You've got her in here. Where is she?'

Phyllis stood up and crossed to another desk beside a metal filing cabinet. She pretended to shuffle through papers as a cover for edging round to the far side of the desk and pressing the emergency button which would summon Dr Hitchcock, if he was still in the hospital, and the two nurses on duty.

'Sit down, please,' Sister Hutchins indicated the hard bench, 'and I'll take some particulars.'

Doug had never actually spoken to Phyllis Hutchins, but he knew who she was, and he knew that she knew who he was. But he felt intimidated by her uniform, the smell of disinfectant, the neatly typed notices on the desk, the long white corridor stretching off into the distance and the general feeling that he didn't belong here. So he sat down.

Sister Hutchins took her time. She put carbon paper between three sheets of paper, rolled it carefully into her typewriter, settled her starched uniform into the chair, pushed her glasses up her nose and said, 'Right, now. Name please?'

Doug answered all her questions and Sister Hutchins thought up a few more while she stalled for time. She sighed with relief when she heard Dr Hitchcock's footsteps coming along the corridor; thank God he hasn't gone home.

'What's the trouble, sister?' The doctor ignored Doug's presence.

'This is Doug Foster, doctor. He's Flo Foster's husband and he's asking to see her.'

'Impossible,' the doctor stated, turning to Doug. 'She is not well enough to receive any visitors, apart from which Flo Foster is registered here as an unmarried woman.'

'What d'you mean?' Doug jumped up. 'I'm her husband. How can she be unmarried?' he shouted.

Dr Hitchcock came out of the reception area. 'Sit down, Mr. Foster,' he said forcefully, 'and don't shout. This is a hospital. There are people in here who are very sick. If you start to cause any trouble we shall be obliged to send for the police.' The doctor had a stiff white coat, carefully manicured and scrubbed hands, smooth, shaved skin and short, groomed hair.

Doug obeyed. 'She's my wife,' he tried again. 'You know that doctor. You delivered our kids.'

'I did, and I know where they are now. I also know that you and Flo are not legally married because that came out at the court case in which I gave evidence.'

Doug glanced up at the doctor. He wanted to ask him about Steve and Carol, but he hadn't the courage to ask this man in the white uniform anything.

'Mr. Foster,' the doctor continued, 'the last time I heard of you, you were in prison for assault. Your children, who had been brought to my hospital in a deplorable condition, had been taken into state care. Then your wife, whose pregnancy is almost full term, is brought in suffering from shock, severe lacerations, abrasions, bruising and possible internal injuries, and I am informed by reliable people that it is you who have inflicted these injuries. Now you arrive, smelling of alcohol, obviously highly inebriated, insisting on seeing your wife.' The doctor paused for emphasis. 'Mr. Foster, it would be gravely irresponsible for me as medical superintendent of this hospital to allow you, in your present condition, to visit any one of my patients, least of all one who is in need of medical attention due to your actions.'

Two nurses had joined Sister Hutchins behind the reception desk and were surveying Doug with open dislike.

'I just want to see her,' Doug mumbled. 'I won't touch her. I just want to see her.'

The doctor was silent for a moment and then, 'Nurse,' he ordered, and one of the girls came out to stand beside him, 'bring some coffee for this man.' And to Doug, 'I shall come back in a while, and if I find you are sufficiently sober and calm you will be allowed to see your wife, but only for a moment or two. I should warn you that she is under heavy sedation, so that there is actually very little point in visiting her, but if that is what you wish, and you can satisfy me that you are going to behave, then a short visit will be allowed.'

'Is she going to be all right?' Doug ventured.

'We don't know yet.' Dr Hitchcock turned on his heel and left.

The next hour passed very slowly for Doug. Sister Hutchins went on with her work and said not a word to him. He drank the bitter coffee the nurse brought him, and watched the minute hand circle the institutional face of the clock. He thought about Steve and Carol, about Flo and the new baby. But his thoughts were jumbled and confused. He couldn't make any pattern from them, all they did was leap around in his brain like a sack full of freshly hooked fish.

He had never felt more sober in his life. By the time the doctor returned at 9.15 p.m. he felt so oppressed by the tiled walls, harsh fluorescent lights and tomblike silence, that he couldn't even look up to face the authority of that uniform again. Having assured himself that Doug Foster was in a suitable condition, Dr Hitchcock summoned a nurse to escort Doug to his wife's bedside.

So now he gazed down at her sleeping form and felt nothing. After a couple of minutes the nurse touched him on the elbow, and he turned away and wandered dazed down the long corridor and out into the hot night.

Out the back of the Garra Betty Flinders lay on her back on the dry hard dirt among the refuse of the night's drinking. Her breasts, made unnaturally firm and wellshaped by being pulled out of the top of her dress, quivered and shook as Billy Saunders thrust himself hard into her receptive body. With the skirt of her dress rolled up round her waist, she held her own legs back and clung to his buttocks with her heels driving him further into her. Her arms were thrown wide, and in one hand she clutched a can of beer, the contents of which spurted up through the hole in the top, each time Billy pushed into her.

'Fuck me. Fuck me harder. Bang me. Ride me. Hard. Hard.' Betty Flinders yelled. Her shouts were drowned by the music blaring from the jukebox in the back room of the hotel fifty feet away, where her husband slumped in a corner sleeping off his pension cheque.

Billy pulled away from her. 'You have another go Harry,' he ordered one of the halfdozen young men standing round the prostrate middleaged woman. 'Stuff it right up her, that's what you like isn't it, you old tart?' He ripped the bodice of her dress so that her breasts collapsed, and then he pinched and squeezed her dark nipples as he pushed his penis into her mouth. She let go of the beer can and the remaining contents spilled out, to be quickly soaked up by the parched earth. Now she clutched his penis with her hand and pulled it into her mouth, kneading his thighs and scrotum with the other hand.

'Careful, you old bitch,' he yelled, and she moaned with delight as Harry Evans ejaculated.

'More, more,' she begged, and Harry's fourteenyearold brother George took his place.

When George finished, Billy yelled to Peter Jenkins to take his turn. 'No more for me, mate,' Peter said. 'Can't get it up again. Worn the fucking thing out.'

'Jesus, what a bloody piker. Come and let her suck you up,' and as Peter took his place, Billy mounted her once more. Betty moaned again.

'You're a fucking beauty, Billy. A great big fucking beauty.'

George belched, and caught the vomit in his mouth. One of the other boys broke wind loudly.

'Beauty,' his mate said, and took another swig from his flagon.

The lights from the pub threw grotesque shadows of the group into the yard, but beyond everything was black, and any noise was drowned by the full sound of the music, so that none of them were aware of Ann Marshall's approach.

The first they heard was the smash as she broke the bottom off a bottle of port, and in the next instant charged with it into Billy Saunders's face. Billy screamed and fell backwards with Ann on top of him. Blood spurted from his face, and as he covered it with his hands, it poured through his fingers and ran down his bare arms.

Ann raised the jagged bottle again, 'You fucking bastard,' she screamed. 'You bastard! You fucking bastard!' As her arm swung down, Harry Evans broke from his trance and clutched her wrist, forcing her arm back. She screamed louder.

Billy struggled out from under and staggered to his feet, holding his head, while the blood kept on spurting, spraying the thirsty earth like a garden sprinkler. Rocking to and fro on his feet, he bellowed like a beast in labour. Ann Marshall, still struggling and screaming, tried to bite Harry's hand. He slapped her hard across the face, splitting her lip so that she too began to bleed.

'Pull his fucking trousers up,' Harry shouted, but the other young men were all too horrified to move. 'You,' Harry lashed out at one of them with his foot, 'pull his fucking strides up for Christ's sake.'

The boy moved cautiously towards Billy, but when he was only three feet away, Billy suddenly lurched forward into him and lost consciousness. Screaming, the terrified young man pushed the slack body off him and ran towards the pub. Billy fell between Betty Flinders's widespread legs where the earth, already slippery and moist, was immediately drenched with his blood.

'Fuck me. Fuck me,' the woman yelled. 'Some bastard fuck me.'

'Jesus bloody Christ,' Harry breathed as he stared down at his friend.

Billy's face was split from cheek to hairline, the raw white bone burst through the jagged scar, and across the rest of his face was smeared the smashed remains of his left eye.

# CHAPTER FOUR

## MONDAY

'**I**'m glad you came by.' Lesley opened the door to Allan Foster, and he followed her through into the room on the side of the house which she rented from old Mrs. Taylor. 'Have you eaten?' she asked.

'No. But I'm not hungry.'

'I'll just whip you up an omelette. It won't take a minute.'

'For Christ's sake, I told you I'm not hungry!'

'OK. Sorry.'

'And for Christ's sake don't start apologizing.'

Lesley sat down in a big beanbag chair and lit a cigarette. She was wearing just a sarong wrapped around under her arms.

'What a way to start a conversation,' she said. 'Why do we always get off on the wrong foot?'

Allan said nothing, but looked around the big room at the walls laden with her woven hangings and her paintings. A loom in one corner, an easel in another and leaning beside it, a decorated didgeridoo. Behind a Chinese lacquered screen was the sink and portable stove. The huge ricepaper lampshade, decorated with Chinese funeral symbols, hung low over the mattress on the floor, which was covered with a heavy, intricately patterned Indian bedspread and masses of huge pillows in various batik designs. On a desk was her typewriter and a clutter of papers and next to that a bench covered with cameras, lenses, film, negatives, contact prints and enlargements.

Every direction Allan looked there were things which fascinated him. A piece of patterned trunk from an Indonesian pakis tree, a green ceramic balustrade post from colonial Malacca, the stone head of a Vietnamese god and a Thai incense burner, masks from New Guinea and, everywhere, books: on shelves, in separate piles under and on every piece of furniture. Allan recalled the first time he had come into this room three months ago. It had been like walking into another world, an exciting Aladdin's cave. He had immediately felt that he wanted to stay for a very long time, to lie on that opulent bed, read all the books, play the records, and not so much examine each treasure individually, but rather wallow in the fantasy world they created.

He had come to challenge her with a report that one of her white pupils had been to the police and told them that she had been raped by three young blacks. He had been surprised by the way she had shouted back at him, not as a white shouting at a black, but simply as a woman may shout at a man who has insulted her. It was the first time he had been treated by a white as just another human being. It was a startling sensation, and it had deflated his anger a little.

After that he found himself making excuses to visit her. She didn't seem to mind. In fact he began to realize that she wanted him to come. Gradually he started to depend on these visits and to tell her about his family and his life. If he saw her elsewhere he never acknowledged her, and even though this hurt her, she played the game his way.

'Dougo's found out,' he said, still looking around the room.

'She told him?'

'No, she just took him over to George Davies' place and let him find out for himself.'

'The bitch.'

'That's what I told him and he tried to punch me.'

'You've seen him then?'

'Yes. He came into the office and carried on about how he'd tried to kill her.'

'Christ. Did he hit her?'

'Too bloody right he did! George Davies came in later and told me they had to drag him off her. They're worried it might start the baby off.'

'Was she badly hurt?'

'Bashed her in the head a bit. Gave her a black eye. Cut her lip. Half tore her ear off. They're worried he might have injured something inside. He's slow to rouse, old Dougo, but when he goes, by Christ he goes. That's why she was too frightened to tell him I suppose. Perhaps it was just as well to wait till there were plenty of people around.'

'Where is he now?,

'He went up to the hospital, but when I went to look for him he'd gone and he isn't back at Mum's place.'

'So you came here?'

Allan looked at her for the first time that evening, and pushed his hands further into his pockets.

'Last resort?' she asked.

He didn't answer.

She got up and from behind the lacquered screen he could hear her grinding coffee. He studied the ibis on the screen, its neck outstretched as it flew low over the reeds, which sheltered a family of brilliantly-coloured waterfowl. From the far edge a dwarf magnolia tree spread its branches. He looked again at the waxy bloom, which was forever falling into the overflowing stream, and remembered the first time he had heard the coffee grinder. He had wondered what the hell it was and, sensing this, she had without any condescension or patronage said, 'I'm just grinding some fresh coffee.' It was ready now and she brought out the mugs on a beaten brass tray with a plate of cheese and biscuits. He sat on the bed and after she'd put on a record, she sat down beside him and lay back into the cushions.

They ate and drank in silence, neither of them sure what the other was thinking, both of them unwilling to make the first move towards the other. In the end it was Lesley, as it always would be, who broke the barrier by putting her hand in his.

'It'll be all right Allan. We'll find a way round it all. Now that Dougo's back we can start things moving.'

He didn't respond, except not to take his hand away.

'Does he know how Pete feels?' she asked. Peter Mathews was Allan's offsider at the Legal Service.

'No. Pete left on the Sunday plane and doesn't get back till tomorrow afternoon. There's still a chance that the Minister will have turned down his request and then he won't have anything to lose, and perhaps something to gain by sticking to us.'

'Bloody megalomaniac. You bred a right little monster there.' Lesley lit another cigarette.

'Pete's a good bloke.'

'How can you say that when he refused to help over your brother's kids, just because it might have jeopardized a bloody government grant?'

Allan dropped her hand and stood up. Lesley cursed to herself.

'I trained Peter to be like that,' he said. 'If we can't be brutally hard then we have no protection against you whites.'

'I wish you wouldn't include me in that comment. I'm not even Australian. I'm a bloody Pom.'

He ignored her interruption. 'We've got to be tough, cold, hard and rude. That's the only way we won't be broken.'

'Even when it comes to helping your own family?'

'That's something you'll never understand. How could you? You're white.' He was shouting and she shouted back. In the back room old Mrs. Taylor pretended she didn't hear, but her granddaughter Jeanna turned down her record player so as to hear better.

'I don't want to understand. If to gain your selfrespect and dignity you have to lose your humanity, it's not bloody worth it. It's not worth it,' he sneered. 'How do you bloody well know what's worth what? You white bitch.'

She'd heard it all before, many times, and she'd learnt to cut out at this point. Not to listen, but to think of other things. To conjure up pictures of favourite places. Tonight she went back to the tiny out-island in the Bahamas where she had lived for a couple of months in a stone hut with no electricity and no running water. The mail boat had called in once a fortnight with provisions and she had spent glorious hot days on the deserted white beaches. In the evenings she'd read by kerosene light to groups of black children, all of whom had one desire when they grew up: to leave their idyllic island and move to the mainland.

Allan continued to shout, and even Mrs. Taylor couldn't pretend not to hear what he said.

'You can afford to say it's not worth it because you've got everything and at no bloody cost. You've never had to pay for any bloody thing. It's all been handed to you on a plate, and why, because you've got a fucking white skin, that's why. How would you know what it's like to walk into a bank and be refused a loan and know that it's not because you're not a good risk, but just because you've got a black skin. Not to be able to drink in the clubs or the whitefellows' bars. To be dismissed as a fucking bludger, a nohoper, an alcoholic. Or to be patronized by people who want to win themselves a place in heaven. The white man's heaven, run by a white god. How do you know what it's like to have people look at you in the streets and without even speaking to you, or knowing anything about you, dismiss you as a bloody boong, an abo. A dead bloody loss.'

Allan didn't have to pause for breath or to think what else he had to say. He had lived with these feelings for so long, scarcely concealed beneath the surface, that they tumbled out with no effort at all.

'You know bloody well that all the white bastards in this town know about the trouble between Pete and me. And they're saying. "They can't even stick together to get things done. All they can do is quarrel and do nothing." And they're right. That's the fucking trouble. They're right.

'And now Liz has gone and they're all saying, "Look at him, even his wife and kids can't stand him and see how he's drinking now. He'll end up just like the rest." They hated me because I was powerful and organized others into resisting them, and now they despise me all the more. "Lo, how the mighty have fallen." You see, I can even quote from your bloody Bible. So don't tell me what's worth what. If Pete can squeeze a few thousand out of that bloody white government to buy land for our people, then no price is too great. Including having to sacrifice the possibility of getting my brother's kids back. You can't understand that now, or ever. You're too bloody protected. You think you understand us. You want to bloody help. But you're just white cunt as far as I'm concerned. White cunt and all you're good for is fucking. We don't want your help. We'll do it ourselves.'

Shaking with exhausted emotion, Allan turned his back on her and stared out through the window into the blackness. An ambulance drove by heading in the direction of the main street and the West, but Allan didn't even register it.

Lesley got up from the Bahamian beach and slipped off her sarong. She walked softly up behind him and put her arms around his waist. The first time, she thought, as always, you'll be raping every white bitch and getting quits with every white bastard. But the second time we'll just be a man and a woman.

## TUESDAY

'You'll have to do something about her,' Pat Vickers told her husband. 'Almost ten hours she's been at it now, and she's not stopped for more than fifteen minutes at a stretch. If you don't do something soon to shut her up I shan't be responsible for my actions. I'm going mad. I have four small boys in this house, and I won't have them subjected to that woman's language, let alone her noise!'

'They're my kids too you know, love.' Constable Vickers said affably.

'Well, from the way you behave you'd never know they were yours too. You don't seem to care what happens to them at all. Look Ed, when you took this job on as lockup keeper I agreed to leave Sydney and come up here. You promised me that we'd be able to live a normal happy life. I took the children out of school, away from their friends, away from their grandparents, because you promised me it would be all right up here. Is this what you call all right? My boys having to listen to that woman screaming filthy language all night. Is it? You tell me, is it?'

Constable Vickers reached across the breakfast clutter on the kitchen table to hold his wife's hand. She had tears in her eyes and he knew that she was tired and overwrought. Even at the best of times when things were running smoothly Pat Vickers found life difficult. She was never really ill, but then she was never completely well either. Being married to a policeman, even though she loved Ed, and having four small boys, put so much mental and physical strain on her that when things got difficult she couldn't cope at all. She had been awake all night pacifying one frightened child after another, each woken by Ann Marshall's continual screaming abuse coming from the lockup next door. Even when Ed had finally come to bed at 4 a.m. after getting Billy Saunders to the hospital and locking up Betty Flinders, the six young men and Ann Marshall, she had still been unable to sleep.

'It won't be for much longer, love,' Ed held her hand. 'I'm sure she'll have to be taken across to Bourke to be held. They won't keep her here for fear of Billy Saunders' family turning nasty. So it'll soon be over, and you know that after we've done our twoyear stint here we'll be able to ask for any posting in the State and get it, and I tell you what, you can choose.'

'You know Ed,' Pat gripped his hand, 'I do love you.' She gave a watery smile. 'I suppose I should have known what to expect when they told us this place is listed as a hardship posting, and I know we took it because it meant we could choose to go wherever we wanted after this, but I couldn't have believed that a place as awful as this existed anywhere in Australia. You know I used to feel sorry for the Aborigines before we came here. I thought we'd done the wrong thing by them, and that they hadn't had a fair go. But it's different when you live with them. I can feel my views are changing. You know what depresses me more than anything else, Ed? It's that I can't see any answers to the problem. I don't want to end up hating them like the rest of the whites in this town do, but I can't help feeling disgusted and angry with them a lot of the time.'

'I know, love. But what we have to keep telling ourselves is that the ones we get in here are the worst and that we'd feel the same about them if they were white, and that they aren't all like that.'

'Oh Ed,' she said, the tears starting in her eyes again, 'sometimes I wonder what's going to happen to the people in this town and then I get so frightened.'

He pulled her head towards him and kissed her eyes, tasting the salt, and as he did so Ann Marshall started up her screaming again. Pat flinched. 'I'll go and get Ron to hurry it up a bit,' Ed said. 'And promise me one thing, that when we take her over to Bourke you'll go round and ask Mrs. Taylor to mind the two young ones, so that you can hop back into bed yourself. I'll be back at two and I'll ask for the afternoon off so we can take the boys for a picnic down by the river. How's that?'

She promised.

Round in the station Sergeant Ron Evans was talking into the telephone when Ed arrived.

'Yes, that is correct. The alleged assailant was a woman but I am not at liberty to disclose her name until she has been formally charged.' He paused. 'Later this morning.' Another pause. 'No. I can't tell you anything further. Police Headquarters in Sydney have taken over the case, and any further information for the press will have to be got from them. Thank you. Good morning.' He put the phone down and sighed. 'Jesus.'

'Morning, boss.'

'G'day Ed, except that it isn't a good day.' Ron ran his fingers wearily back through his hair. 'I've got John coming up straight away so we can get that screaming madwoman off the premises. I've fixed it with him that he'll refuse bail and send her across to Bourke. Hitchcock is coming down to give her a shot which should quieten her down and I'm afraid you'll have to drive her across singlehanded because now we've got another little problem.'

'What now?'

'It's Gary Andrews. Dead.'

'Jesus Christ!'

'You can say that again.'

'How did it happen?'

'Misadventure. No suspicious circumstances. Yet. I got a call at home about an hour ago and went over. He was still in his wheelchair. Stiff.'

'What the hell was it?'

'Metho. Whole place reeked of it. Hitchcock came while I was there, and he said it was just the final straw. He's taken him up the morgue to do a PM.'

'I thought he'd sworn off the stuff since it had crippled him. Anyway where the hell did he get it? None of the shops would sell it to him, so someone must have given it to him.'

'That's right. Some kind friend.'

'When did it happen?'

'No one's sure what time. I suppose the PM will show that.

He'd been off colour all day. His wife had to go off and clean up at the school like she always does every afternoon, and as he was too sick to mind the kids she farmed them out around the place.'

'That explains why I saw the youngest one with Stella Foster in the Imperial.'

'What time was that?'

'On the afternoon run, when we picked up the bloke who vomited, and that mother and daughter.'

'That'd be right. Mrs. Andrews said that when she got home at seven Gary was pretty far gone, but she didn't realize just how bad he was. Poor bitch blames herself, thinks she could have saved him if she'd got the doctor sooner, but I told her that he'd have had to die sooner or later, so he might as well go now.

Ed winced inwardly at his Sergeant's insensitivity. Bloody Mick, he said to himself, and immediately felt guilty.

The phone rang again. Sergeant Evans told the post office operator that he wasn't taking any more press calls and to direct them to police headquarters in Sydney.

'Have the press got on to Gary as well?' Ed asked.

'No. Not yet. But they will, don't worry. If things don't quieten down soon they'll base a permanent bloke up here!' He grimaced. 'It's not Gary I feel sorry for. It was the only end in sight. He took a damn long time to die. Eight years he's been on the metho, and he must have been drinking heavily for at least fifteen years before that. Slow bloody agony, not so much for him, because the metho had destroyed that much of his brain he didn't know whether he was dead or alive, but for his poor bloody wife and kids. Six of them he's got.' Sergeant Evans slammed his pen down on the desk. 'May the good Lord forgive me, but I sometimes think that castration is the only answer.

Ed brushed a piece of imaginary fluff off his uniform jacket. 'Well,' he said, 'I think I'll go round and see if John's arrived yet. The quicker we get Ann Marshall over to Bourke the better.' As he turned to go he asked, 'How's Billy Saunders?'

'He'll be right. The air ambulance picked him up at first light. He'll be in Sydney now. Free ride all the way for the blackfellows. They'll stitch him up. Give him a false eye and no doubt he'll be back here and in trouble in no time flat. Just imagine how he'll be able to skite about the scar he'll have. I've no time for the bastard. Something like this was bound to happen to him. Just a pity that it was Ann Marshall who did it. She's not a bad kid, and you know Betty Flinders is her bloody auntie, so I can see why she did it. It's the kids that worry me again. Ann's still feeding her twins herself. She's demanding to have them brought in, but by Christ we've got enough problems without trying to run a baby home. Like I said, they should all be castrated at birth, that would solve all their problems.'

Ed looked down at his shoes and gave each of them a little bit of extra polishing on the back of alternate trouser legs. 'I'll be off,' he said.

Sergeant Evans sensed that he had gone too far. 'Sorry Ed,' he said. 'I'm not myself this morning. Think the game's getting to be too much for me. I'll be glad to get out of it next year. I'm not looking forward to going over to the West either and trying to get information out of them about Gary.'

Ed said nothing, and Ron continued. 'Why don't you take the rest of the day off when you get back from Bourke?'


'You right?' Harry Fletcher yelled. 'OK then. Here we go.' He slammed the throttle forward and the speedboat took off up the river, the waves from its wake slapping up the muddy banks. Greg leant back, keeping the rope between himself and his brother's boat taut, his knees slightly bent and his feet neatly aligned one behind the other on the one ski. Gum trees, coolibahs, wattles and boxtrees all raced by in a greygreen blur. Some wild goats, taken by surprise, scampered surefooted up the slippery steep bank. The sunlight flashed on the water, blinding Greg for seconds at a time and creating a stroboscopic sensation.

Bursting out of a blind spot, Greg saw his brother gesticulating wildly, and knew that the time had come. His heart, already thumping, felt as though it would burst through his chest. He had a vivid split-second vision of himself exploding into a bloody mess, with parts of his body scattered all over the river and the speedboat roaring off, the rope dangling loosely in the water with his amputated hands still clenched to the guide bar.

He knew then just how frightened he must be, because he only had those hideous miniature daydreams when he was really terrified, and always at a time when he was under pressure to show his paces. He might tease his brother about fancying himself as the Jack Nicklaus of the northwest, but he sympathized completely with him. How many times on the football field with his father on the sidelines yelling at him, had his mind been filled with horrific imaginings, which he could only conquer by telling himself that he was Bobby Fulton playing for Australia.

He recalled the excruciating postmortems after every match when his father, wheezing asthmatically, had always abused him for faults in his play, and never congratulated him on his good points.

Greg hadn't spoken to his father since he had left school without matriculating and started work in the Holden assembly plant. Both sons had been a disappointment to the father, who had never forgiven them for not going on to university. His mother now had to pay clandestine visits to her sons or she too would suffer the same punishment of silence.

Greg considered the miserably constrained life his parents lived. His father working from eightthirty to five every day at the accountant's office for the past thirtytwo years, and his mother running her immaculate home. He was quite sure that he was going to do things differently. You're only here once, and in too short a time I'll be pushing up daisies, he thought, so I'm going to have a ball while there's still time, and for starters I'm going to lay that Jeanna chick.

The fibreglass speedboat turned in a wide circle to go back down river. It sat stern heavy as it roared through the water. Greg followed the circle and watched as Harry began signalling again to him. He smiled, because Harry was shouting too, even though he must know that there was no chance at all that Greg could hear him. A flock of brilliantly coloured parrots scattered from a treetop.

The boat sped on, trailing its passenger past the makeshift jetty. His Sydney mates, Darren and Ian, had brought borrowed trailbikes down to the water's edge and were sitting astride them watching his every move. Greg didn't care if he made a fool of himself in front of them, but he wasn't going to do so when he knew the girls were looking.

Jeanna Taylor and a couple of her girlfriends had wagged school for the afternoon and were sitting by a huge fallen tree that had been dragged up out of the river. Jeanna had made no secret of her delight when Greg and his mates had arrived in town. It wasn't often that three new, attractive young men presented themselves all at one time to provide a diversion from the stultifying boredom of smalltown life. Jeanna had hung around the hotel for the last two days, making sure they knew she was available. She was available all right, but at fifteen she was already determined to always get the pick of the bunch. Even in the instant which it took to skim by, Greg registered the manner in which Jeanna lounged against the tree. Although he knew she was four years younger than he, he recognized in her an air of sexual authority and expertise. And if she's going to practise on someone, he thought, that someone's going to be me.

To win Jeanna, Greg knew he had to be the best. Darren and Ian had already managed to stay up on one ski. Now he had to go one better and do it barefoot.

His brother turned the wheel and the boat circled to start up river towards the jetty again. The two boys leant forward on their bikes. They also knew what the stakes were. Twenty yards before the jetty the fear left him. He was no longer Greg Fletcher, he was the barefoot champion of the world. He eased one foot and then the other out of the ski which swirled away and was quickly left behind.

'He's done it! He's done it!' the two girls chorused. 'Good on you mate, 'Darren said, and the two young men looked at each other and laughed just a little ruefully. Only Jeanna said nothing. She just sized up the receding figure.

'I'm Jesus bloody Christ. I'm walking on the water,' Greg shouted triumphantly and Harry saw his brother throw back his head and laugh with delight.

A large black crow cruised low among the branches, cawing disdainfully, before sweeping down to pluck the eye out of an old sheep that had dropped fifteen minutes earlier from heat exhaustion.

'Look mate, I'd like to help you, but I can't.' Pete Mathews watched as Allan scored over the lines of the complicated doodle he was constructing on the official application form for unemployment benefits. 'And you know I can't,' Pete added. Allan still made no comment.

The two men made a strange physical contrast. Against Allan's athletic build, Pete looked even thinner and paler. In any of the southern Australian towns he could have passed himself off as the son of an Italian immigrant. After one school trip to Sydney and the Snowy when he was fourteen, Pete had weighed the possibilities of doing just that.

It had been this dream which had spurred him on to finish his schooling, even though the local school didn't have a fifth or sixth form, which meant going down to Dubbo and boarding with relations for a couple of years. His father was sure that the only reason any child of his would want to continue his education was to avoid going to work. His mother was equally baffled. So Pete supported himself through those years by delivering newspapers before school and cleaning offices after.

Every time he came home to visit his family they seemed increasingly foreign to him. The West was no longer home, it was a ramshackle smelly slum, and he had to restrain himself from complaining about the filth in which his family seemed content to live. He saw his father as boozing, bullying and ignorant, and his mother as merely another Aboriginal alcoholic. He realized that his three brothers and five sisters were going to end up the same way, and he wondered what it was that set him apart. Surely it couldn't only be that he had the palest skin of them all. Sometimes he wondered if his father, and even his mother, were his real parents. His alienation was almost complete. But then the Freedom Ride came through Dubbo and Pete met Allan.

Pete looked down at his mentor, and recalled their first meeting and the days which followed and his complete conversion to the Aboriginal cause. Allan had been strong then. Forceful and sure. He had so scorned and verbally lacerated Pete for wanting to become a white man, a gub, as he sneeringly referred to them, that Pete had begun to despise himself for turning his back on his own people. When he had absorbed enough self-hatred to feel that he really was worth nothing more than the pile of rotting faeces Allan likened him to, Allan told him that this was nothing more than another whitefellows' trick. That white society expected, and indeed demanded, that all Aboriginals, in particular part Aboriginals, should feel they were worth less than the dirt on the white man's boot. That even when they tried to live the whitefellow's way, they were still less than them.

'Now,' Allan had told him, 'you must learn to be proud of being what you are. Proud to be black.' And with the pride Allan taught him hatred. Hatred of all white men. 'Never trust one of them,' he had said. 'Even those who say they want to help you, Trust them even less. Because if you ever let yourself trust or like a whitefellow you will begin to see them as individuals. You can't win a war against a group of individuals, only against a faceless army.'

Allan was right. They were engaged in a war. If they lost they'd be annihilated. Not in the sort of bloody massacres the first settlers had carried out, but rather more slowly, though just as surely. And if they won? Well for a start there would be no more fifteen yearold Pete Mathews ashamed of their family and their colour.

Pete watched as the doodle grew, and consciously stopped himself from feeling sorry that Allan was turning soft. Another rule of the war, and one which Allan himself had always stressed, was that you must remain ruthless and angry and show no sympathy even for those of your own who couldn't take the pace. You couldn't allow them to slow down the movement or to give it a soft vulnerable underbelly. There were always those ready and able to take over the leadership. Pete felt a surge of excitement run through him as he realized that his time had come.

'That's the deal I made with the department,' Pete said. 'We get sixty thousand dollars to do up the West. A hundred and fifty thousand to buy up that land in the town and another hundred thousand next year. Jesus Christ, Allan, that's over a quarter of a bloody million dollars. Imagine what we can do with that lot.'

Allan went on with his drawing. 'Look, for Christ's sake Allan, your brother's case is hopeless. The facts show there was total neglect and that Flo is an unfit mother. With the father in prison for assault, what else could the courts do but take the kids into care?'

Allan's silence was beginning to irritate him. 'Shit, man, you didn't even tell us Doug and Flo aren't

101

married, and see what bloody fools that made us all look in court.'

Allan looked up slowly and then eased himself out from behind his desk. The back office of the Aboriginal Legal Service suddenly seemed very small. 'Since when,' Allan spaced his words carefully and quietly, 'since when have you set yourself up as a judge of other people's morals? Since you got that little white slut pregnant and sent her down to Sydney to have it swilled down a lavatory? Eh?'

'Steady on, Allan.' Pete flushed.

'Or was it,' Allan continued, his voice becoming louder and his words coming faster, 'or was it since you screwed poor old Molly Brown, who was half demented over her husband's death when you put the hard word on her and hinted that you'd be able to get a special grant for her if she came across? Eh?'

Allan was shouting at the top of his voice now, and he came so close that Pete looked not much more than an extra arm on the bigger man. 'Or was it when you fucked my thirteen-year-old sister in the back of your flash car? Eh?' He pushed his face even closer and it took all of Pete's will power not to pull back. 'You didn't think she'd tell me, did you, you underweight weedy little runt? But she did, and perhaps you'd also like to know that she said you were the worst fuck she'd ever had and that you have a prick like a limp handshake. A small, limp handshake.'

There was a long silence before Allan went back to his desk and sat down. He fiddled with his ballpoint pen while Pete waited for his breathing to return to normal. Then Allan looked up.

'All I asked was that the Legal Service should push for an appeal of Doug's case.'

'The Minister said...'

'I know what the fucking Minister said,' Allan interrupted, shouting again. 'I don't have to have been there to know what the Minister said. I knew what he'd say before you even went down to Canberra. Shall I tell you what the Minister said to Peter Mathews? Yes, I shall tell you. The Minister said, "Peter you have been a good boy, pat, pat, so I am going to give you sixty thousand dollars to clean up West Woongarra and a quarter of a million dollars to buy up land in the town on which your people can build their own homes." And after you had stopped licking his boots and no doubt his arse too, he told you what the catch was, and the catch was that there must be no further trouble in Woongarra. Nothing the media boys can latch on to and beat the government with. No stories of braindamaged black babies due to malnutrition in pregnant women, no news about our hospital being full of kids suffering from trachoma, worms, scabies, malnutrition and dehydration, and young girls who have been pressured into being sterilized. No stories about seventy per cent of the population living on welfare and pissing their pension cheques up against hotel walls. No stories about the illiteracy rate among children and adults, about the Catholic school having only one black pupil, about the banning of blacks in the RSL or even about the impossibility of those who really want to work being able to get a bloody job. They know it's cheaper to pay out a couple of hundred million dollars in social service cheques to the boongs over the next ten years than it is to try to really find answers to the problems.'

Allan stopped, but Pete knew better than to say anything. He'd seen Allan in this mood before, though only in confrontations with white people.

'The Minister,' Allan began again, 'wants it to be all quiet on the western front, so that it appears as though his government has solved the Aboriginal Problem.' Allan said it in capitals. 'They want it like this, not only to keep their armchair small "I" liberal voters in Australia happy, but also to improve their image abroad. Cultural minorities have become useful coinage in the international diplomacy game.

'And in exchange the Minister gives you sixty thousand dollars to prop up buildings which should be torn down and burnt. Did you perhaps remind the Minister that when those shacks were thrown together seven years ago, they were erected on nineinch foundations instead of the minimum requirement on that sort of ground of four feet, so the fact that they have fallen apart can hardly be blamed on the bloody boongs who live in them? No, of course you didn't. You were too bloody busy conjuring up in your tiny mind what you could do with the quarter of a million dollars he had promised you to buy land and build houses for people like you, who fancy themselves as uptown niggers,' Allan sneered.

'You've never changed, Pete Mathews. Beneath that shallow radical veneer there beats a whitefellow's heart. Small and mean. Why didn't you ask for the money to be given to those who want to build a home down on the river where we come from and where we belong? I'll tell you why. It's because you still fancy living in the whitefellows' way in a whitefellows' town.'

Allan snapped the pen in half and flung the pieces into the wastepaper basket where they lay among the heap of crumpled documents. 'Well, you might have won the battle,' he said, 'but you've lost the bloody war, mate. It's too late now to put in an appeal for my brother's kids, but what about Betty Flinders and Gary Andrews? I can just see the headlines in tomorrow's Sun. "Aboriginal Woman in Pack Rape", and "Black Cripple Suicides on Metho". What will the Minister think of that little lot? Not much, I should say, and bang goes your quarter million. You'll be lucky if you even get the sixty thousand.

'And that's not all you've lost, Pete.' Allan pushed back the chair hard and got up again. 'You've lost your fucking humanity.' Allan heard himself repeat Lesley's words and inwardly cringed. Violently he crumpled up the doodle and threw the paper after the shattered pen. Then he pushed his way past Pete and out of the Aboriginal Legal Service.

After a while Pete Mathews walked over to Allan's chair and sat down, trying it out for size. Then he leant forward and opening the second drawer down, got out the halfbottle of port and took a long swig. Next he put his feet up on the desk. To the victor the spoils. Uptown bloody nigger, am I? he thought, who's lost his humanity. Well at least I'm not making myself the joke of the town by fucking that white whore teacher.

The sun glowed with pleasure across a huge horizon, pulsing with thick orange light. Doug stood for a moment longer, thigh deep in the cool water where it foamed and frothed over a small natural weir. He had walked into the water with the 'intention of catching a fish or two, but even when he saw them charging towards him, boggle-eyed, over the rough stones, and felt them thump against his shins, he didn't try to scoop them up, but let them wiggle past and glide on downstream. Instead he simply stood, slightly tensed against the rush of water, letting it play around his legs. He wasn't so much looking at the scene as being part of it. He wasn't thinking. He wasn't even feeling. He was just existing. Existing in the same way as the water which made up the river, and as the dull ochre earth which formed the steep banks.

Further downstream, where the river curved eastward, a little crowd of ducks waded at the water's edge or floated in tight circles. Suddenly round the bend came a big bird flying low over the middle of the river. Its large wings flapped a few times and Doug heard them beat the wind before it glided up towards him. He stood completely motionless and it wasn't until it was almost on to him that the black swan recognized the man as an alien and in a magnificent display of aerobatics, gained instant height. Doug felt the rush of air on his upturned face as the beautiful bird swept above him, and he eased round to watch as it went on upstream, losing height again to fly back low over the water in search of food.

Doug waded barefoot across on the sharp stones to the bank, and digging his toes into the squelching mud, clambered splayfooted up into the dry grass at the top, to be met by the full force of the sun setting across the nineteen-mile flat. He lay down. It seemed the natural thing to do in the face of such awesome beauty.

Ever since leaving Flo at the hospital the night before, he had wandered beside the river. Unconsciously he found solace in it. Quite unknowingly he had slept on the same high ground where his people had slept for centuries before the white man came. He had slept better on the bare, hard ground than at any time during the past six months. Kangaroo, emu, wallaby, wild pig and goats had all come down to drink at the river, and smelling the man had moved downwind of him.

Doug spent the next day moving slowly and seemingly aimlessly in wide circles, which always brought him back to the river. Not at any time did he consciously think of Flo or his children, but now as he lay on his stomach, staring into the sunset, he knew without knowing, what he would do. That everything would come right. It was as if by a process of osmosis, the river had cleansed him.

He had forgiven Flo. Not the sort of calculating forgiveness which comes from totting up the score for and against and then finding it in the heart to accept and forget. Nothing so external. Doug had forgiven his wife with simplicity. They'd get their children back, the baby would be born, and they'd all come down and live by the river.

As Doug watched, the earth seemed to lurch on its axis, and the sun slipped out of sight leaving trails of fiery remembrance. The air was purple and the velvet particles so intense as to be palpable. He turned over on to his back and his body fused with the atmosphere so that Doug Foster was no longer a singular man.

For a further hour, until the sky had blackened and stars had begun to show in the infinity above him, Doug lay in the parched, stiff grass. Then he got up and, still without thinking, moved off towards Joan and Eddie's place downriver, where he would be as welcomed by his people as he had been by his land.

# CHAPTER FIVE

## WEDNESDAY

The brilliant morning sunlight flooded on to Flo's bed as the nurse pushed aside the screens. Flo kept here eyes closed. The right one, covered with a thick cottonwool pad, felt swollen, but numb rather than painful. As the nurse checked the drip bag and took her temperature and pulse, Flo mentally examined her injured body.

The worst thing was that her whole head felt immense, far too large for her body. It was as though she had been travelling at fifty miles an hour and had suddenly slammed into a brick wall, after which a steamroller had come along and ironed her out. Apart from that it was a bit like having a gigantic hangover. Every muscle and joint ached and she decided that the best thing to do was to lie completely still. The trouble was she was so uncomfortable. The baby pressed down on her kidneys and up into her chest cavity. There seemed to be far more of it than there was of herself, though at least it had stopped kicking and was now lying quiet. She longed to roll over on to her side, but the anticipation of the pain which would accompany such a move made her decide to stay where she was.

'And how are we this morning?' Sister Hutchins asked briskly.

Flo opened her good eye, and seeing the white face above the starched white uniform, topped by what looked like a child's white paper party hat, she replied, surprised by how muffled her voice was, 'I'll be right thanks.' But she winced spontaneously as the slight movement of her jaw sent shooting pains through her damaged right ear.

It was Sister Hutchins who, two months previously, had found Flo's maltreated children and brought them to the hospital. Many years of marriage had disappointingly left Sister Hutchins childless. Noticing Flo's pain, she said coldly, 'Yes, well I think we'll give you another little injection to help with the discomfort. Over on your side now.' She pulled back the covers and began pushing Flo, none too gently, over on to her left hip. It wasn't that she did anything to actively hurt Flo, but long years of nursing, mostly Aborigines, had left their mark.

Even though Flo felt her body would disintegrate from the pain, she forced herself not to give even a hint of this to the white woman.

The sister pinched up a piece of Flo's brown bottom and jabbed the needle home. 'There now,' she said. 'D'you want to stay on your side?'

Flo was afraid that if she tried to say anything at all she'd burst into tears, so she stayed mute and Sister Hutchins, interpreting this as Aboriginal apathy and indifference, left her where she was and replaced the screens round the bed.

Gradually the bruised bones and muscles settled into tremulous quiescence, and Flo began to think about her children. In her sober moments over the last six weeks she had done little else, and it was the nightmarish quality of these thoughts which had spurred her on to drink even more. Over and over again the picture of Steve and Carol, lying in those institutional iron beds looking at her with puzzlement and hurt, had filled her entire being and made her feel physically sick and very, very frightened. She had wanted to grab them and make a run for it, but Dr Hitchcock and Sister Hutchins stood behind her, passing judgement, so she had left and been unable to face visiting them again. In the court case this fact came out as another example of her callous indifference to her children.

I'm sorry Carol, she thought, and automatically the tears started in her eyes, the right one burning with bruised ferocity. Imagining in her pethedrined brain that she was actually talking to her daughter, she went on, I'm sorry. I'll make it up to you. I promise. I just didn't know you were so ill. I know it was all my fault, but I don't understand how it happened so quickly. She almost lost consciousness, but the drug couldn't quite control her yet. There didn't seem to be anything else to do when they took Daddy away, except drink. I knew I shouldn't, but I couldn't stop myself. What's wrong with me that I let it all happen? I didn't give a stuff about any of those other blokes. I love Daddy. I do. Like I love you and Steve. I know it sounds stupid and no one would believe me if I told them, but I do love Daddy and I just don't know why I go with other blokes or drink so much. I think I must be no good. I must have been born rotten. Dougo's such a good bloke. I know that, and I wish I was a good wife to him, but I'm not, am I? No. He was right to hit me. If Mum had had someone to hit her when she played up, perhaps she wouldn't have gone bad either.

Flo recalled the numerous white men who had come down to their shack on the river when she was a small child, and the celebrations after they'd left when the neighbours would come in and help drink up the gifts. She remembered the girl at school announcing to the entire class that Flo's mother was known as 'the best fuck in town'. Flo had hit her in the face with a brick, even though she was secretly rather proud of her mother's accomplishment, which at least set her apart from other mothers.

When she had finally and thankfully left school at fourteen, unable to either read or write, Flo had none of the usual visions which teenage girls cherish. She had no idea of wanting to become a model, an air hostess or even a nurse or teacher. It wasn't that she dreamed about these jobs and rejected them as impossibilities. They were just so far outside the ambit of any expectations she might ever have had, that they never once entered her mind.

Consciously since she was eight and probably unconsciously long before that, Flo had been bleached clean of any motivation. She had no dreams or ambitions whatsoever.

Now as the pethedrin sent her zooming down a narrowing black tunnel into unconsciousness she took with her the inescapable image of Carol and Steven, while the other child lay dormant in her womb, gathering all its strength in preparation for its entry into a new world.

Jim Dargan jumped down from the race which led up into the sheep pens, heaved the saddle and stirrups off the back of his Japanese motorcycle and flung them over the wooden rail running up the side of the race. Then he joined his father who was pushing his worn old felt hat on to the back of his head. Wiping his face with his calloused hand, Mr. Dargan flipped the wetness on to the dirt. The two men said nothing to each other as they each rolled and lit a cigarette.

For a hundred and four years the Dargans had owned land in this area. James Dargan had come out from what was then a great Britain in 1850 at the age of twenty, and as a guest of Her Majesty, Queen Victoria. After serving only six of his fourteen years sentence in the penal colony of Norfolk Island, he was given a ticket of leave in recognition of his good behaviour, and had at first tried his luck in Sydney. But spurred on by stories of great wealth and dreams of independence, he had packed everything he possessed into a cart and, crossing the Great Dividing Range, struck out on his own.

He had to travel further inland than he had anticipated before he reached land which wasn't already being worked, but eventually in 1861 he settled on the Barwon River and staked out a hundred and eighty thousand acres about thirty miles southeast of a tiny settlement called Woongarra, an Aboriginal name meaning 'sleeping place'.

James Dargan worked hard. Very hard. Clearing land, fencing, keeping the natural predators at bay and raising European animals on unnatural and unfriendly terrain. By 1866 he was running 20,000 sheep on his property and his word carried considerable weight in the area.

He played hard too, but the Aboriginal men who hunted and fished on what was now classified, under white man's law, as Dargan's land didn't object to sharing what they had with him. Their women had always been held communally, and any resultant children were cared for as members, not of a single family, but of the whole tribe.

They didn't even object when James Dargan took one of their most beautiful young lubras to live with him, though they didn't understand why he then made it a strict rule that the resultant children should not be allowed to play with the other children of the tribe. But, being the polite, gentle people they were, they accepted his behaviour as simply another example of the strange ways of white men.

It wasn't until the settlement at Woongarra grew and more white people came on to their land, with their own rules and regulations which they insisted the Aboriginal people should abide by also, that these peaceable people began to realize that their land was being taken from them. That the white man wasn't going to share it with them in their centuries-old way, but wanted it all for himself.

After many discussions round the campfires above the river, a large number of them decided that the best thing to do was to move further north. There the country was even dryer and sometimes it was difficult to find game, and of course there was always the danger of other, probably hostile, Aboriginal tribes, but at least there were not white men, yet. So they moved off, though they left behind a considerable number of their people who had decided to stay on the river where they had been for countless generations, to take their luck with the white man.

Life went on more or less as before, except for a few outbursts of violence between the two communities, until the start of the big drought in 1868. There was not a single drop of rain for the next thirteen months, and then only a few tantalizing showers over the next eight, which did nothing except madden the desire for more.

The Aborigines, their systems honed by thousands of years of living through such periodic hard times, knew which leaves to suck for liquid sustenance, and where and how to catch and find nourishing grubs and insects.

James Dargan, whose childhood had been spent in the industrial towns of northern England, had no such skills and his sheep, imported into an alien land, had no such resources. So they died by the hundreds, their bodies so wasted before death that they gave off remarkably little odour as they lay where they fell on the dry earth, under the vivid blue and cloudless sky.

Seeing seven years of incredibly hard work withering to nothing, James Dargan came very close to throwing in the towel and going back to Sydney. But already the harsh red land was so much a part of him that he couldn't leave it, any more than the wilting gum trees could. Not even after the terrifying evening when a band of marauding Aborigines stole one of the few remaining cattle he was managing to keep alive to eventually feed his wife and small children. He had chased them off and shot and killed five outright, wounding six others, all of whom had died slowly and horribly back with their families.

The Aborigines had retaliated by attacking the homestead and killing his wife and one of their five children. Still he stayed on, more determined than ever not to be beaten by the land or its inhabitants.

Then, in November 1870 the rains came and the river, swollen further upstream by heavy falls, rushed down over the weir and flooded the township of Woongarra. In the closest thing to a miracle which James Dargan ever saw, when the waters receded, the land turned green almost overnight. The gum trees revived, the river was full of fish and the grass was thick and lush.

So he began all over again and in less than eighteen months he was doing better than ever before. Hundreds of bales of wool from his sheeps' backs were being carted south and already there were definite plans to put a railhead in at Woongarra. The town flourished, and in gratitude James Dargan had an Anglican church built entirely at his own expense, with the Bishop coming from Sydney to lay the foundation stone.

He became a member of the shire council and eventually Shire President. He opened a general store in town, and then another and later on another. By 1880 he was one of the wealthiest, best-known and most respected men in the whole of the northwest region of New South Wales.

The only slightly less than reputable aspect of his life was now past history, for after the vengeful Aborigines had killed his wife and baby daughter, James Dargan had lost interest in the four other part-Aboriginal young children he had fathered, and they were relegated to the kitchen and then to the outhouses where they were taken in by the Aboriginal families who helped Dargan work his property. The more respected he became, the more he forgot about his four dark-skinned sons.

Several years later he took a trip to Sydney and there married a freshfaced young English girl recently arrived in the colony, who was very impressed with his obvious wealth and the idea of being the lady of a house, which rested on 180,000 acres. He brought her up to live in his by then magnificent homestead, and there she gave birth, in quick succession, to two boys, before dying in the process of producing another.

James Dargan himself lived on to the turn of the century and was finally buried beside his young wife in an elaborate vault on the family property on the same day as the Queen, to whom he had proved himself a loyal subject, was buried in Westminster Abbey. Buried with him, this fine example of a successful colonist, was all knowledge of the parentage of the four part-Aboriginal stockmen who lived with his other hands, and who themselves never dreamed that they had a right to share, with his two white sons in the old man's inheritance. So it was that James Dargan was great grandfather to both Jim Dargan and Doug Foster.

'You right son?' Jim Dargan's father flicked the soggy cigarette butt towards the pens full of noisily bleating sheep, and the boy pulled himself up after his father into the holding pen to join the three other young white men sitting on the top rail of the fence, the heels of their brown elastic-sided boots hooked over a lower rung, their hats pulled down to keep the bright sunlight out of their eyes.

Jim Dargan summoned a band of half a dozen or so Aborigines all perched on the top rail of an inner pen, looking like gaily plumed birds. 'I hope this bloody crowd's better than the last lot of bludgers we got,' Jim Dargan commented to his father, 'or we'll never get this job done.'

'And this is where I sleep.' Carol leapt on to the iron bedstead which creaked and groaned. Doug sat on the end, and as she showed him her teddybear and how his clothes came on and off, he looked around at the makeshift dormitory. There were fifteen other beds lining the walls of what had once been the verandah, before sheets of thin masonite had been tacked up. All right for now, Doug thought, but what about winter? There were cracks between the sheets through which he could see the clear blue sky. But they won't be here in winter, he reminded himself, because I'm going to get them out.

The other beds all had soft toys propped up on the pillows, but instead of making the atmosphere more homely, the assorted array of other children's castoffs gave the place an air of desolate hopelessness. The beds were all neatly made and the floors swept. The room was cleaner than their room in his mother's house ever was, and George Davies had obviously gone to a lot of trouble to make the children as comfortable as his limited resources would allow. Perhaps it was this feeling that someone had tried so hard, which gave the whole homestead an atmosphere of earnest endeavour, and made Doug feel uncomfortable.

Carol, noticing that her father was only half listening to her stories about what had been happening at school, suddenly leapt up and giving a big bounce, fell on to his back. Throwing her arms around his neck and smothering the side of his face with kisses, she said, 'I'm glad you're home Daddy.'

He pulled her round on to his knee and reached over to Steve, who having tied a golliwog to the end of his neighbouring bedstead, was intent on gagging him with a grubby handkerchief. With them both on his lap he leant back against the wall and hugged them to him.

'How is it here?' he asked them both.

'S'all right,' Steve said, 'but they haven't got a telly.'

'They can't, silly,' his sister said, 'they don't have any electricity.'

'What about the lights then?' Doug asked.

'We have kerosene,' she told him, amazed that he should need to ask.

'Oh, I see. And what's the food like?'

'OK,' Steve told him.

'And the other kids?'

'OK, but Bright snores and keeps me awake.'

'Well you cry and keep me awake,' Carol said.

'What d'you cry for?' Doug's stomach tightened.

Steve shot his sister a venomous look. 'Nothing. Well. Not much anyway.'

Doug squeezed him tight. 'Well it'll be all right now I'm back. You'll be able to come home soon. Very soon.'

Steve brightened visibly. 'Yeh? True?'

'True.'

'S'all right here, 'he said, 'but, well . .

'I know what you mean. I was glad to get home too.'

119

'What was it like? In prison I mean. Were they real mean to you?'

Doug frowned. His son's ingenuous directness startled him. This was the first time he had seen his children alone since the night he had left them at home and gone with Flo over to the Imperial. The fight between him and Jim Andrews had happened in the street outside the hotel, and they'd still been at it when Sergeant Evans arrived. The children hadn't been allowed to visit him in the lockup, so he had been sentenced and gone down to Sydney with no chance of explaining anything to them. In all the imaginary conversations he'd had with his children over the past six months, the subject of his imprisonment had not come up. He had glossed over the subject and expected them to do the same. But in doing so he had not taken into account young children's complete lack of tact or social manners.

He glanced down at Steve who was waiting expectantly for lurid details of his father's confinement. 'It wasn't too bad,' he said, and then added a parental warning, 'but you wouldn't want to ever go there. It's much worse than being here, that's why I'm so glad to be home.' He squeezed them both again, 'And it'll be even better when I have you two home as well.'

'Will we have to wait till Mummy comes out of hospital?'

Caught off guard again, Doug looked quickly at his daughter, 'Who told you she was in hospital?' Already sure that it must have been George Davies, he could feel the anger beginning to rise.

'One of the girls in my class,' she said, and he felt deflated.

'She said you'd hit Mum and hurt her baby.'

'Bloody rubbish,' he said quickly. 'The baby's fine.'

'What'd you hit her for? Don't you love her any more?' Steve asked with the outrageous audacity of a sevenyearold. Doug was faced with the impossibility of explaining adult emotions to children. The argument and the fight between Flo and himself immediately appeared futile and stupid.

'Of course I still love Mummy,' he said. 'Very much. I just got cross with her, that's all. But it's all right now. I've been to see her in hospital, and she's going to be fine and so will the baby.'

'We were in hospital too,' Carol said importantly. Doug, rendered momentarily speechless again, was fumbling around for something adequate to say when she added, 'I had maggots in my ears,' and Steve, not to be outdone, said, 'I almost died,' and then Carol assured him, 'but we're all right now.'

George Davies appearing at that moment to announce, 'Dinner's ready', was struck by the harmony of the scene. The father sitting with his two young children on his lap. He didn't register the silent way in which Doug followed him and the children into the big communal room where the table was set for the midday meal.

Even on these sweltering hot February days George Davies insisted on a hot dinner for the children who were too young to go to school. Steve and Carol had been allowed to stay home today in honour of their father's visit. This evening when George picked the other children up from school and brought them back, there would be another hot meal for the older ones.

Mrs. Davies, flushed from cooking over the open wood-burning range, joined them at the table. The meat, potatoes and vegetables were piled on to plates and George and his wife cut the younger children's food into more manageable pieces.

Doug had picked up his knife and fork, and was about to start eating, when he received a sharp kick on the shins from Carol sitting opposite him. About to ask, 'What the hell was that for?' he was checked by the way she rolled her eyes in warning at him. She bowed her head, clasped her hands, and then glanced up at him, ordering him to do the same. As he did so George Davies intoned, 'For what we are about to receive may the Lord make us truly thankful.' The Amen resounded round the table in childish tones, and Doug found himself sheepishly joining in.

Throughout the meal Doug inwardly marvelled at the way George kept control of the thirteen children without once shouting or getting cross, but with patience and affection. The youngest baby, a girl, was only four months old. George told him he had been given the baby in the West by the mother, who already had five children and couldn't cope with this new one, born braindamaged. The rest of George's wards ranged up to five years old, and the noise at the table was incredible.

When the meat and vegetables were gone, the fruit and icecream arrived and were quickly demolished. Then, after a closing grace, Steve and Carol helped Mrs. Davies wash up while George and Doug sat on the porch overseeing the older children, who raced around in the dirt outside on tricycles, scooters and homemade gocarts, while the young ones went off for their afternoon naps.

There was an uneasy truce between the two men. Neither of them had mentioned Doug's previous visit, but now George said, 'Well Dougo. What d'you think?'

A nonspecific question requiring the sort of specific answer which Doug felt unsure about giving. At length he said, 'I'm going to get them back, George.'

'That's all right by me mate.'

Doug was surprised.

'Yes, I mean that. I hope you can get them back. But it's going to be more difficult than you think.'

Doug waited for him to explain.

'The court found Flo to be an unfit mother, so until that decision is reversed, the children remain wards of the State.'

'What about me? Why can't they come with me? After all I'm their father.'

'Sure, but you're not Flo's husband, legally, and that makes for problems.'

'I'll marry her. I'll do anything they want. I'm going to get them back.'

'Look Dougo,' the older man eased back in his chair so as to look more directly at him, 'I want you to have them back. You and Flo were doing a pretty good job of bringing them up until you got sent down. But it's going to take time. Can I give you some advice?'

Doug said nothing, so George continued.

'Get a job. Start building that place down on the river you've always been talking about. Stay off the drink. Show that you could be counted on to be a good father, and they'll let you have them back. It's not that I want to keep them away from you. I have plenty enough without them and I expect I'll get a couple more soon now that Gary Andrews has gone.'

George had told Doug when he first arrived that morning about Gary's death, but it wasn't news to Doug who'd already heard about it the night before down on the river from Joan and Eddie. He still said nothing, but watched as George got up to brush the dirt off a small boy who had turned a tricycle over on top of himself. Doug again marvelled at the man's obvious affection for all these children, and when he sat down again Doug said, 'I used to be frightened of this place, you know. My mum used to tell us that she'd give us to you if we mucked up.'

George smiled a little sadly. 'The bogey man, that's me.'

There was a short silence and then Doug asked, 'How many kids have you raised, George?'

'Thirtyseven, plus our own four, and with no money from anyone to help us. We've done it on our own,' he said with pride.

'Why'd you do it?'

'For the Lord,' George said simply and without embarrassment, and then he laughed. 'But if you and I don't get going the Lord will not forgive us for missing Gary's funeral.'

Doug went into the kitchen to say goodbye to his children.

Steve clung to him. 'Come tomorrow,' he demanded.

'Yes,' Doug promised, 'after school.'

'And tell me about prison because I said I'd tell the boys at school what it's like.'

The Cullens' house stood at the end of a quiet culdesac on the edge of town. At the back of the house was a paddock where the two Cullen boys kept their horses, and after that came the bush. Built on stilts, it was a modem home with a well kept garden. The large garage was filled with the symbols of success: a powerful speedboat and waterskiing equipment, expensive golf clubs, two almost new cars, and in addition to the adult toys, a wide variety of children's playthings scattered casually about the place.

Inside the house it was the same story. The Cullens had been the first people in Woongarra, after the two hotels, to get a colour television set. It squatted in the comer of the lounge defying anyone to ignore it. Expensive stereo equipment ranged along one wall, and the room was divided by a wellstocked bar complete with Swedish glasses still wearing their manufacturer's labels. The furniture was tasteful, expensive and comfortable, the carpets thick and plentiful. The house purred loudly with selfcongratulatory confidence.

Dianne Cullen, wearing a long cotton caftan, lay along the sofa with her feet tucked up. Opposite, her sister, Sylvia, hunched on the edge of her chair and leant forward.

'Please, Di, please.'

'I can't help you. Not again. Not this time.'

Sylvia slumped back.

Dianne uncurled, got up, walked over to the bar and mixed herself a gin and tonic. She didn't offer her sister a drink before she sat down again. The physical differences between the two women were very marked. Even though Sylvia was only eighteen months older than Dianne, she looked ten years her senior. Dianne, despite two rather difficult pregnancies, was trim and lithe. No one would have guessed that she had a tendency to gain weight, because she made very sure she never did. Attention to diet, a strenuous game of tennis on Wednesdays and an eighteen-hole game of golf on Sundays saw to that. Her skin, which had a natural tendency to flake, was kept welloiled. Her nails, long and beautifully manicured, were painted a pale pink. Twice a year she went down to Sydney to have her patchy, brown, crinkly hair dyed and straightened.

Sylvia was fat. Her pendulous breasts almost reached her stomach, which was distended even further by a cirrhosis-enlarged liver. Her large, knuckly fingers were stained with nicotine, the skin drooped baggy under her forearms and her frizzy hair was knotted and tangled like a Medusa's head. Her stained teeth were chipped, and one was missing altogether, her eyes were puffy and bloodshot and today she had a big bruise on her left cheekbone.

Yet strangely enough, it wasn't the differences which were most apparent, but the similarities. It was as if Sylvia were a grotesque reminder to Dianne of what fate she had saved herself from, and as if Dianne were a shining example to Sylvia of what she could have been. Under Sylvia's haggard, bruised skin were Dianne's high cheekbones and underneath Dianne's glossy black hair was Sylvia's dull matted mop.

Dianne took a sip of her gin. 'Look Syl,' she said, 'I can't help you. I don't have any money of my own, only what I manage to save out of the weekly housekeeping Les gives me.'

Sylvia stared dully round the room, and Dianne guiltily imagined that she was comparing it with her filthy communal room in the West. In reality the other woman wasn't registering any of the things about her, she was churning over in her mind where she was going to raise a hundred and fifty dollars.

'And I spent all that I had saved on Christmas,' Dianne continued. 'Actually, I still owe a bit to Maison Marie's for a little dress I bought. I couldn't resist it.'

Sylvia said nothing and her sister added, not very convincingly, 'If I had the money I'd loan it to you, even though I know I shouldn't. You'd only drink it up and I'd never see it again, like the last lot.'

Sylvia, ignoring her sister's final remark, leant forward again, and kneading the knuckles of one hand into the palm of the other, said, 'Couldn't you ask Les to loan it to you?'

'No. 'Dianne was emphatic. 'I couldn't. I've never asked Les for money. Look what he's given me. Everything.' She gestured round the room. 'I'm not going to ruin it all by asking him for money. Especially when it's for my family. Les married me, not my family. It's good enough that he provides so much for me and the kids. Once I started to let you sponge on him there would be no end to it. We'd have the whole family queuing at the door. Les works damn hard for his money. He came up here with nothing. Now he has fifteen men working under him at the roo factory. He's offered Johnny and Reg jobs because they're my brothers and he's had Col working up there because he's your husband, but they didn't want to work. They thought he owed them a living just because he's their brotherinlaw. That made the other men dissatisfied, so he had to let them go. You're all a lot of lazy bludgers. Why should I feel sorry for you? I got off my backside and got out, you could have done the same if you'd wanted to. But all you want to do is gamble and drink, and when you run out of money you think I'll be a soft touch. Well that's the blackfellow's ways and they aren't my ways any more. I've married a white man and I'm glad. I don't want to live like blackfellows live. They disgust me, all of them, including my family, including you.'

Throughout this tirade Sylvia had sat still on the edge of the easy chair, waiting for a pause, and when it came, just as if she hadn't heard anything of what Dianne had been saying, she said, 'I need the money bad.'

'Badly,' her sister corrected, and then feeling ashamed of herself, she asked, though she didn't really want to know, 'What d'you want it for?'

'I'm pregnant.'

'Christ, not again,' Dianne was exasperated. 'Isn't seven enough? You don't even look after them properly. I saw two of them round the back of the Imperial ferreting through the garbage yesterday afternoon when they should have been at school. And Constable Vickers told me that if they pick Brendon up again they'll have to charge him. Last time it was taking Johnny Phillips' car for a joy ride. just as well it wasn't a whitefellow's car or he wouldn't have got away with it. Why don't you have your tubes tied? It's obviously the only answer for you, seeing as you can't be taking the pill, not even after I went to the trouble of getting you a prescription. You're hopeless. Anyway, why do you need the money now? It can't be due for ages yet and no doubt by that time the government will be picking up your tab at the hospital. Not like Les and me, ours cost eight hundred a piece even though I'm black.'

Again Sylvia hadn't been listening, but just waiting to be able to break in to Dianne's monologue.

'I've got to go down to Sydney. I've got to get rid of it.'

'What?' At last Dianne was astonished. 'Why don't you think of these things before they happen?'

This time Sylvia didn't leave space enough for her sister to continue. 'I'm three months gone. I've tried to get rid of it myself. I bled a lot, but it wouldn't come out.'

Dianne closed her eyes. She felt sick. 'For Christ's sake Syl,' she said. 'You can kill yourself doing things like that. And if you're so far gone you'll just have to go through with it.'

'I can't.' Desperate now, Sylvia didn't even hesitate before adding, 'It isn't Col's.'

'Jesus Christ!' Dianne uncurled and leant forward, her head in her hands, unconsciously adopting the same position as her sister. She was silent for a while. Digging back through the past twelve years of white thinking and discarding it as irrelevant and useless, she mouthed her first black thought in many years.

The two sisters looked at each other across the low stainless steel and glass coffee table.

'Just don't tell him. Col will never know.'

'Oh yes he will,' her sister replied, 'because it's going to be a white one.'

'Jesus bloody Christ.'


The little tinroofed gospel hall was crammed to the doors by the time they arrived and people spilled out and down the steps into the crowd outside. Doug felt very conspicuous driving up with George Davies in the big mission van, and was relieved to see his mother and brothers and sisters in the crowd. George, who had led the congregation at this hall for twenty-one years, ever since his conversion, left him and went inside, and Doug wove his way towards Allan, who stood out head and shoulders above those around him.

There were a lot of people in the crowd whom he hadn't seen since his return, and Doug, realizing that they must almost all know about his fight with Flo, felt extremely embarrassed and flushed beneath his dark skin. Despite this, and the solemnity of the occasion, everyone greeted him with jocular affection, but it was still a relief to reach his mother. They only had time for a very cursory greeting before George Davies's deep voice boomed out and the service began.

'Brothers and sisters we have gathered here today in sadness and in sorrow. . .'

Doug looked about him at the sea of faces. Over half the two hundred and forty people were related to him, either directly, or indirectly, by marriage. The rest were all wellknown to him. He was surprised to see that the entire Lane family had come down from Goodooga and that the Goodridges had come over from Wee Waa. Apart from these, all the rest were locals. He wondered where Barbara Evans had found the huge black picture hat, decorated with wilting red flowers, which she wore slightly askew and pulled down so far that her face was completely obscured by its slightly torn veil. Even Doug, who would normally never notice such things, was struck by its wild incongruity. Beside her stood her pimply snivelling son, Wally.

'For in the twinkling of an eye He created us. . .

He saw the back of Bill Flinders's head, highly recognizable because of the livid scar, which ran up from his neck and over which the hair refused to grow. Bill had a couple of his kids with him, but Betty was absent, still cooling her heels in the lockup.

Charlie Saunders was standing slightly apart from the crowd with his four daughters. His wife had gone down to Sydney the morning before in the air ambulance which took her only son Billy to hospital.

'Yea, though we walk through the valley of the shadow of darkness. . .'

Mrs. Marshall, with her head bent, stood on the steps, the sun reflecting off her shiny black skin. Her husband had gone over to Bourke to visit their daughter Anne in prison. It was then that Doug noticed Molly Brown, thin and haggard, also standing on the steps. He hadn't seen her since his return, and now he was immediately struck by how much weight she had lost and how much she had aged. He remembered her as a goodlooking, wellbuilt woman, and now he tried not to notice how she held a worn black cardigan over the damaged side of her body where the breast had been removed. He couldn't help registeringthe way she craned her scrawny neck to get a better look inside the church. With her mouth slightly ajar, she listened voraciously to George Davies's sermon, remembering the slow prison death of her own husband, whose coldly official funeral she hadn't been able to attend.

'He is our Saviour and our Redeemer.. .'

On the very edge of the crowd, trying to efface himself, but failing completely because of his white skin, stood Bruce Stannard on a little patch of brown grass, separate from the rest of the crowd. He wore a neat black suit and black tie and with his head slightly bowed, the balding patch on the top of his head showed quite conspicuously. Even at this distance, Doug could sense the man's discomfort.

A child cried, and looking in the direction of the sound, Doug saw the only other white face in the crowd. Lesley Armstrong's thick blonde hair sprang away from her face. She was quite obviously not listening to George Davies's appeals to his Lord. Instead she was staring across the tops of the bowed heads around her. Doug followed her gaze and found Pete Mathews levelly returning her look. Misinterpreting the visual confrontation entirely, Doug thought, Jesus, don't tell me he's knocking her off too. Don't know when the bastard finds the time. And then, as if they sensed his intrusion, they both simultaneously looked at him, Doug lowered his head to avoid them, and as he did so the keening broke out.

The women on the steps, led by Molly Brown, took up the moan which mounted to a crescendo as the coffin appeared at the doorway, carried by the dead man's brothers. Momentarily Doug caught the eye of Jim Andrews and his stomach leapt as he remembered the sound his foot had made when it had crunched into Jim's head, as he lay in the gutter outside the Imperial. But if Jim recognized him, he gave no sign, and the moment passed, drowned by the wails of the women.

Gary's wife, supported on both sides by blank-faced men, followed the coffin out and was helped into the large hire car driven by the third white person at the funeral, Graham Coddlington, manager of the bowling club and part time undertaker. Their car followed the hearse out over the rough track and turned on to the road leading to town.

Doug squeezed into Allan's car along with his mother, Marge and Les and their kids, and his young sister Irene, who sat squashed between his knees. No one spoke as they fell in with the long line of cars, which headed off towards the cemetery. In the car in front he could see Molly Brown with her sons and through the open car windows he could hear her continuous low moan.

The long unbroken string of cars spread out over two miles of bitumen, soft from the intense afternoon sun. Slowly they followed the hearse along the main street of the town where the white people paused to watch the procession go by.

Outside the Winchcombe Carson office, Fred Pepper was helping Les Cullen pack the fish he had just sold him into the boot of his car. The two men straightened. 'Poor bastard,' Les said. 'Rough way to go.' Fred Pepper stared at the coffin in the hearse, pursed his lips, but said nothing.

Inside his cool, airconditioned presbytery, Father Michael Clancy put his feet up on his coffee table and took another mouthful of beer from the can as he watched the test match being played in Brisbane.

Greg Fletcher, fixing the spotlight on the top of his utility in readiness for a night's roo shooting, heard the wailing and came out from the back of the Imperial. Harry, leaning on the sill of the open hotel window, said to his brother, 'One more down, only one thousand three hundred and sixtytwo to go.'

One block over, in the school, the Aboriginal children were restless, especially in Lesley Armstrong's class, and Gordon Wright, who had forbidden her to take her children to the funeral, tried unsuccessfully to gain their attention.

The Foster family arrived at the cemetery having not said a word to each other, and, still in silence, they got out and joined the crowd which threaded its way past old graves with their dejected floral offerings, to where the shiny new coffin lay beside a freshly dug hole.

The women were silent now, under the oppressive sun. The heat which it radiated was so intense that the particles of air seemed to hang motionless and exhausted. The spiky, dry grass scratched Lesley's bare legs as she stood a litle apart from the crowd. To prevent herself from seeking out Allan's broad shoulders, she looked instead across the flat land which spread off in all directions. The township appeared tiny and vulnerable even at this small distance, and she was struck by the impudence of people thinking that they could conquer a country where the huge horizons were lost in a dry heat haze.

George Davies, waiting until everyone arrived, was as surprised as he always was at funerals by the number of people, men and women, who had appropriately sombre clothing. It was as if funeral clothes were an essential part of their wardrobe. Almost all of these people he never saw except at funerals. Much to his chagrin, they didn't even come to him to have their marriages solemnized. Because of this, he took the opportunity of preaching a sermon which he hoped would stir them to do more than just wait for the next funeral.

Immediately he began, his voice was almost drowned out by renewed wailing from the women. Mrs. Andrews leant against Jim and her sorrow poured out in great, festering sobs. Gary's mother fell to the ground, beating it with her fists and her head. To Lesley it appeared that these Aborigines knew their sorrowing needed to be dramatic in order to be in keeping with the demanding landscape, which had surrounded them for centuries, and that they weren't grieving just for Gary Andrews, but for their whole lost race.

George shouted, determined for his warning to be heard. 'And don't you forget, my brothers and sisters, that nothing is surer than the fact that one day every one of you will be as dead as our brother Gary Andrews is today.'

The keening, vibrant with power, threatened to overwhelm him, but George kept going. 'Death, the great leveller, comes to us all, black and white, and on the Day of Judgement, when every person buried on this earth will be raised up to meet their Lord, on that day, brothers and sisters, we will stand naked before our Lord and receive His judgement. If we have lived good honest lives; if we have worked hard and obeyed our Lord's laws, then we need have no fear, for He will take us with Him into heaven where we shall dwell with the angels and sit at His right hand. But, if...' George paused, looked around the crowd, and the women, sensing the tension in the moment, paused too in their sorrowing, 'but if you have lived evil wicked lives, if you have broken His holy laws, if you have indulged in the sins of the flesh. . .' The silence was intense, even Mrs. Andrews stopped her sobbing. George lowered his voice and so that it had more impact he spaced his words. 'If you have taken intoxicating liquor or committed the sins of fornication or adultery, if you have taken the name of our Lord God in vain, then,' his voice cracked as he shouted, 'then, my brothers and sisters, you will burn forever in the fiery pit of everlasting hell fire and damnation.'

Lesley winced involuntarily at such rabid faith, and noticed that Allan flexed his shoulders and moved uncomfortably. In the still hot air the silence was more suffocating than the piercing lamentations.

As the coffin was lowered into the crumbly dry earth it was a relief when the keening started again.

'Dust to dust, ashes to ashes,' George Davies intoned, and Gary Andrews's ruined body, eaten away by methylated spirits, was covered with the red uncaring soil.

That night it was announced on the national news that the northwest of New South Wales had experienced its highest temperatures since records were begun in 1875.

# CHAPTER SIX

## WEDNESDAY - THURSDAY

**G**reg squeezed the trigger. A bullet burst out of the rifle muzzle and found its mark. The soft doe-like eyes of the grey kangaroo froze in amazement for a split second before disintegrating in a bloody mass of fur, flesh and shattered bone. The impact threw her body against a coolibah and her warm blood oozed down the mottled tree trunk.

'Bullseye!' Greg yelled with delight. 'You bloody beauty.' He dropped the spent cartridge on the ground and reloaded the clip with bullets from a small carton on the utility's bonnet. As he did so he looked straight at Jeanna Taylor who lounged against the car. 'What d'you think of that?' he demanded, his face frankly full of pride and pleasure.

'Not bad,' she replied, and with a small grin added, 'for a city slicker.'

He grinned back, realizing that she was more impressed than she was going to let on. And he was right too, for Jeanna was thinking, This one's a good one. Knows what he wants and goes about getting it, like me. Not a bad looker, either. Wonder how he goes.

Greg narrowed his eyes at her, and then turned in the full glare of the spotlight and walked the two hundred yards to where the almost decapitated carcass of the doe was slumped.

This was the second time he had been out shooting. Last night his brother had taken him and his friends and he had been secretly anxious, with the same sort of miniature daymares he'd had on the river when he forced himself to ski barefoot. Only this time he was worried he would let himself down in front of his friends, either by vomiting at the sight of blood, or by being unable, in the final instant, to pull the trigger and kill another living thing.

Instead, he had found himself so caught up in the thrill of the chase that when they had spotted the small herd of kangaroo drinking peacefully by the river, and Harry had slammed on the brakes, turned on the spotlight to blind the animals and yelled, 'Fire!' almost in the same instant, he had fired unthinkingly. He had scored with his first shot. 'Beginner's luck,' Harry had said, and Greg, determined to prove to them that it was more than that, had made them stay out for almost five hours, tiring them out so completely that when he had suggested another night's shooting tonight, they had cried off. Greg had been glad really, because he was sure that if in addition to barefoot skiing, he could repeat last night's performance then he was sure to win Jeanna, and that had become another goal he'd set himself.

Last night he'd shot sixteen kangaroos, two reds and fourteen greys. Much to his surprise he found that his prowess gave him a feeling of power, and he swaggered now as he approached this last corpse. The one occurrence, which had upset him on the previous evening, was when he'd found a small joey in the pouch of one of the does he'd shot. The tiny, almost hairless thing had lain fearless in his hands and he had thought he might take it back to Sydney and raise it as a pet. Put when he'd shown it to his brother, Harry had simply picked it up by its long hind legs, swung it back and smashed its head to pieces against a tree trunk. Sickened and angry, Greg had said, 'What'd you bloody do that for?'

'There's a law against shooting does with young,' Harry had told him, 'though how the bloody hell you're supposed to pick them, Christ only knows. Still it's best to get rid of the evidence.'

Greg tried to push the memory of the incident away by reminding himself of what all the townspeople had told him, that kangaroos are a pest, they ruin property, they eat the crops and the feed, and that they need to be kept down. But still he prayed to some unspecified god that he wouldn't find another joey in this one's pouch. He didn't.

He dragged the body back to the ute, and aware that Jeanna was watching him, flung it casually into the back where it landed with a dull thump among the four other carcasses. As he was wiping the blood off his hands on to his jeans, Jeanna came up beside him and putting her hands on top of his, pressed hard and moved them down his thighs. Without a word he undid the thin ties on her shoulders, letting the dress down. She was naked beneath the cotton smock and she grabbed him round the neck, pulling his head on to her adolescent breasts. He smelt of sweat mixed with fresh blood and a heavy animal odour. The pungency excited her and she spread herself welcomingly against the utility.

Over her shoulder, as he took her, pressing her between himself and the metallic bodywork, he caught a glimpse of soft, furry, dead bodies, disturbed by his own and Jeanna's motions, moving gently over one another, as if they too were making love.

Later he spread the thick blanket, which she had considerately brought with her, under the tall flowering gums. He wondered briefly how many other men she had pulled down on to this blanket. Then the sight of her, lying naked and demanding to be taken, swept all such thoughts aside. Later still they talked quietly, the gentle noise of the rushing river forming a continuous backdrop to their conversation, and she revealed more of her feelings than she had in a long time.

'It's bloody boring here, that's all. I've got to get out. Everyone's so small-minded and they know everyone else's business. You only have to be seen with the same fellow twice and they've got you engaged.'

Lying on his side, Greg traced the outline of her nipple with a dry gum leaf, which he then crumpled in his hand and put up to his nose to breathe the aromatic perfume. The chase over and the prey captured, Greg found his interest waning, though out of politeness he tried to look as if he were still listening.

'I've got a name around town as an easy lay,' she was saying, 'but actually I'm not.' She looked quickly at him and he tried to appear noncommittal. 'I've had a few blokes, that's for sure,' she shrugged her shoulders, 'but what else is there to do? Most times I just do it to give them a thrill, because they sure as hell don't give me one. All my girlfriends want to do is get married. Not me. I've seen what's happened to my two older sisters. Both of them were pregnant when they got married, all because they were bored and couldn't think of anything else to do.

Now they're still bored. That's not going to happen to me. I'm getting out.' She sat up, drew her knees up and hugged them to her. Her body gleamed in the pale moonlight.

'I want to go down to Dubbo to finish school. Lesley Armstrong thinks I should. She's the only decent teacher in the school. Have you met her?' She turned to Greg who shook his head. 'No,' Jeanna said, 'I don't suppose you would have. She doesn't seem very interested in whitefellows. But she's wrapped in Allan Foster, that's for sure.'

'Is he black?'

Blackest in town, fair dinkum. He visits her at her place. She boards with Gran and me. Lesley thinks I should go down to Dubbo, but unless Mighty Wrighty, he's the headmaster, gives me a good reference I won't get a place, and that's not likely because he hates me.' She stared reflectively in front of her at the blackness. 'Bet he hasn't screwed his wife in twenty years, and can't bear to think of anyone else getting a bit. I've got to get out.'

'It's not such a bad place.'

'You say that because you don't live here. But it's like a rat-trap. What is there for me to do here? Nothing. There's no jobs except nursing or teaching.'

'Well, what d'you want to do?'

'I don't know yet. But something more than that.' She was silent for a while and then, as if she had come to a different decision, she said, 'D'you really want to know what I'm going to be?'

'Yeh. Tell me.'

'I'm going to be 'rich and famous.'

His derisive laughter startled a couple of grazing wild pig, which scampered off through the spinifex as he pulled her down on top of him.

## THURSDAY

'I'm thinking of moving down to Sydney.' Allan's remark fell like a stone into a quiet pool and took a while to lodge in Doug's consciousness. The two men were sitting on the porch of their mother's house, just as they had five nights ago. It was early in the morning, but Fred Pepper was already making his second visit of the day to the West. The two brothers watched as he parked his van outside Molly Brown's place, got out, opened up the back doors, let down the little set of iron steps and climbed inside, where he began rearranging boxes of groceries.

'What d'you mean, Sydney?' Doug asked at last. 'What for?'

'Well, it would make a bit of a change from this dump, wouldn't it mate?'

'Yeh, change for the worse. What's the matter with Garra? And anyhow what about your job?'

'I've quit.'

This time Doug registered his brother's remark immediately.

'What? What for?'

'Well, the time came, you know. Time for a change, that's all. 'Allan lit a cigarette and watched as Molly Brown came out and bought a box of dry biscuits and some potatoes from Fred Pepper.

'Bloody funny time to choose, just when I get back.'

'Yeh, well, that's it. Now that you're back here to keep an eye on things, I thought I might be able to take a bit of a holiday myself and go down to Sydney.'

Doug moved irritably. There was something different about Allan, but he couldn't quite put his finger on it. 'It was no bloody holiday I had, mate.'

Molly Brown took her parcels and Fred Pepper wrote the prices down in his little book. That made thirty three dollars she owed him, plus the five per cent interest he charged on all debts over a month old. Thirtyfour sixtyfive. He'd have to start leaning on her a bit.

'Anyhow,' Doug began again, 'I was hoping the Legal Service would be able to help me.'

Even though Allan had anticipated this remark, he still hadn't been able to formulate any plan to cope with it other than to remain silent.

Doug went on, 'I thought the Legal Service would be able to help me get the kids back.'

Bill Flinders came out from next-door and shuffled across his littered yard. He lifted his hand at them. 'G'day.' and went on down towards Fred Pepper's van.

'Well, that's the way it goes, mate,' Allan said flatly. 'Fact is I don't think you stand much chance.'

Doug could feel the anger starting up. 'And you don't bloody care, do you? You don't give a stuff about anyone except your bloody self. As far as you're concerned Flo's a whore and we can all of us go to hell.'

Doug was shouting by now, and Fred Pepper came out from his van, still crouching, to get a better look at who was arguing.

Allan felt he was losing control of this conversation, and that it wasn't going as he had planned it at

143

all. He recalled that this often happened in his conversations with his older brother. They seemed to approach matters from totally opposite angles. He tried again. 'Yes. Well. I do think Flo's a hopeless bitch. I've always thought that, even before you started going round with her, and you must agree that she's not done anything to help me change my mind. But I'm not preaching, mate. How could I, when I can't even hold my own marriage together?'

Doug cooled down a little. Allan had always been able to slow him down with talk. He could express himself so much better that the older man found that by the time he'd tried to follow what was being said, his anger had dissipated.

Suddenly Allan was on his feet. 'That fucking white bastard,' he said. He went down the porch steps in one leap, came to an abrupt standstill in the yard and watched as Fred Pepper put three unlabelled bottles into a plain, brown paper bag which Bill Flinders held out to him. 'You'd think after he killed Gary, that he'd give those tricks away, wouldn't you?'

'Was it him Gary got the metho from then?'

'Of course it was. Same as always. Gets that rose hip syrup free from the child care nurses, chucks half of it out and fills the bottle up with metho and then flogs it to poor bastards like Gary. Now he's got Bill on the stuff.' Allan shrugged his shoulders, turned and came back up on to the verandah. 'What's the bloody use? The white pigs won't ever pick him up. I've been telling that bastard Evans about it for years.'

'Why don't you get the Legal Service on to it?'

'They wouldn't do anything about it, any more than they'll do anything for you, and Evans knows they won't that's why he can afford to let Pepper get away with it. The bastard is the only source of sly grog in the West and what would people here do on Sundays without him? The whites can get their grog round the back of the hotel any time, but not our lot, they have to rely on shits like Pepper. So what if he flogs metho to poor bastards like Gary and Bill? Too bad if it kills them. Jesus!' Allan kicked the stuffing which was spilling like grey brains out of a mouldering mattress.

Then Doug understood what Allan had been trying to avoid telling him. 'So you asked the Legal Service to help me and they knocked you back?' he said.

Allan sighed. 'Yeh, that's right. Something like that. It's a fair cow, isn't it?'

'So that's why you've quit?'

'Ummm.'

'Why didn't you tell me?'

'Well, I don't want to look like a bloody martyr, do I?'

'Was it Pete Mathews hit the idea on the head?'

Allan nodded.

'Yeh. That explains why he gave me a funny look when I saw him at Gary's funeral. He was busy making passes at that white teacher. He'd be better off spending time on his own people rather than screwing white women.'

Allan swallowed hard, moved uncomfortably and had almost made up his mind to tell his brother about Lesley when Bill Flinders shuffled past them clutching his paper bag. Neither man looked at him.

'I'm sorry about that, Allan,' Doug said, and for one wild moment Allan thought his brother had guessed his secret, then he realized that Doug was referring to him giving up his job.

'Well, it would have had to happen sooner or later. Should have left long ago. They've become part of the system. Political pawns. The Department of Aboriginal Affairs is like every other government department, full of people who are busy trying to stab everyone else in the back. And meanwhile nothing gets done. We're a bloody hopeless bunch. The whites are right, we can't even help our bloody selves.'

He scuffed a small pile of garbage out on to the top step. Doug noticed a young child pushing a pram down the street towards Fred Pepper's van, and realized that it was Gary Andrews's boy who had sat on the porch with him early on Sunday morning.

'G'day,' he called, and the child, pleased to be noticed, called back a cheerful 'G'day.'

'What'll you do then?' Doug asked.

'Oh, I don't know. Something'll turn up. I can always find things to do, even up here. The Dargans want some blokes out on their place, they're mulesing and marking. I might go out there this afternoon and get back into training. But whatever happens I won't stick around here for long, that's for bloody sure. The place depresses me too much, and I need a break from the politics. Sometimes I get bloody sick of being black, and then I get sick of being sick. Shit.'

Allan looked down at his brother, who was disconsolately flattening a CocaCola tin, and gave him a playful dig in the bottom with the toe of his shoe. 'Tell you what,' he said. 'I'll stick around till you get the kids back. What about that? Might even help you start that place down on the river you're always babbling about. OK?'

Doug jumped up with obvious pleasure and slapped his brother on the back. 'Beauty!' he said.

At that moment the police car slid around the corner and drew up outside the Flinders' place. Betty got out, escorted by Constable Vickers. Bill Flinders stood on the porch, still holding the brown paper bag, and Fred Pepper quickly shut up his van, got in behind the wheel and drove off, leaving Gary's young son standing in the dust.

'Hey,' yelled the child, 'come back here, you bastard. I want some bloody lollies.'


The headmaster's office was stuffy with stale recirculated air. Gordon Wright silently cursed the inefficiency of the department, which allowed him to freeze in winter, because they didn't fix the central heating, and boil in summer, because the airconditioner never worked properly. He wanted to shut the noisy machine off and throw open the windows, but he couldn't because Lesley Armstrong sat opposite him demanding an answer. He wondered again why he let this young woman intimidate him. She always made it appear as though she were cross-examining him, even when, as on this occasion, it was he who had sent for her and asked her to explain why she had gone over his head and written to the department, praising Jeanna Taylor and suggesting they find a place for her at the high school in Dubbo.

Lesley said nothing, just raised her eyebrows in query, and Gordon Wright felt compelled to say, 'No. I wouldn't have recommended that Jeanna should go down to Dubbo.'

'Well,' Lesley said, 'so I knew that, and that's why I did what I did.'

Gordon Wright's mind drew a blank.

'I'm not going to see that kid suffer because of your personal prejudices.'

Stung to reaction at last, Gordon Wright got up, snapped off the airconditioning and flung open the windows. 'Miss Armstrong,' he said, 'in the short time you have been in this school you have done more to disobey my instructions and undermine my authority than every other member of my staff put together.'

'That's easy to explain.'

'I didn't ask for an explanation. What...'

'No, that's your trouble. You never ask for explanations. All you require is that everyone should obey your orders and never question them.'

'Miss Armstrong, will you please be quiet!'

'No, I won't. Not until you listen to my explanation. It's simple. The reason why the rest of your staff don't disobey your instructions or undermine your authority is that they are gutless.' She paused, but Gordon Wright could think of nothing adequate to say.

'All of them took teaching positions in Woongarra because it's listed as a hardship posting. It improves their gradings. Once they've completed two years here they can choose to go anywhere they like in the State, just like the police; which is a comment in itself. The teachers you've got left college and decided to go straight for their ratings. They are the smart ones, the tough ones, who decided to get the nasty bit over with as soon as possible. They'll take anything from you, because they know that they only have to put up with it for two years. Like a jail sentence. They

aren't teachers. They're public servants, climbing lad-
ders and serving time in return for long service leave
and superannuation. They couldn't give a stuff about
the kids. Teaching is just a respectable way of earning
a living and a way to fill in time between birth and
death. So that's why they don't find it worthwhile to
disobey your instructions or undermine your authority. As for why I do,' she paused, expecting him to interrupt, but Gordon Wright simply stood by the window and waited for her to continue. 'Well, it's equally
simple. I chose to come to Garra because I wanted to
work with black children.'

She left unsaid the fact that she had first come
to Woongarra a year before when she'd been hitchhik-
ing round Australia. She'd had no intention of staying
in the country, in fact she'd only come down from In-
donesia where she'd been teaching for three years because a close girlfriend, with whom she'd been at
boarding school in England, had married an Australian and was living in Sydney. With what she now realized was inexcusable English snobbery, she had previously dismissed Australia as a cultural wasteland.
The only Australians she'd met before were the loud-
mouthed men who'd turned the pubs near her home
in London into stand-up-and-swill joints. And the
heavy-jawed women built like Amazons, wearing brief
shorts and boots and carrying knapsacks covered with
Southern Cross flags, as they hiked their way round
Europe. After that introduction, Sydney and her people had come as a pleasant surprise, and once she got
out into the bush and began travelling, she fell in love
with the country, though she still reserved judgement
on the people, mostly because she was irritated by be-

ing made continuously aware of being specifically a woman, rather than a human being.

It wasn't until she stopped off in Woongarra that the idea of staying in this country even occurred to her. It wasn't just the plight of the Aborigines; by then she'd seen plenty, and many of them in other Aboriginal townships in Queensland and New South Wales were worse than Woongarra. She'd thought vaguely about what could be done and how she, as a teacher, could do something positive herself. It was just something about the town itself, the aura of Woongarra, which made these thoughts gel, and she went back down to Sydney to apply for a teaching position in the town. With her special qualifications in teaching what the department euphemistically called 'educationally and socially disadvantaged children', she was made very welcome. Now, as she sat opposite Gordon Wright, she cursed herself for getting offside with him, but knew that it couldn't have been avoided.

'I'm sorry, Gordon,' she said, becoming the first member of his staff ever to address him by his first name. 'We seem to rub each other up the wrong way, don't we?' She said it in self-deprecating tones, hoping to encourage him to make a remark.

Slightly mollified, he sat down behind his large desk and straightened the array of ballpoint pens beside his obsolete blotter. The silence continued, until at last he said, 'I've had a report that Jeanna Taylor was seen down at the river with a party of young men who were water-skiing. This is the fifth time this term that she has missed school, and we've only been back for three weeks. Added to which I have a report here,' he tapped a form in front of him, 'from the school counsellor, in which she says she finds Jeanna, who perhaps I should remind you is only fifteen years old, to be highly anti-social and of questionable moral standing.'

Lesley thumped the desk so hard that one of the headmaster's pens rolled off the edge.

'Jesus bloody Christ! How dare that frustrated bitch file reports like that. Who the hell does she think she is to sit in judgement on young people?'

'She's a highly qualified social worker, and may I point out to you that your references to her are highly judgemental. I would also appreciate it if you would control your language.'

Gordon Wright's very correct English accent irritated Lesley. The phrase 'phoney Pom' came to her mind, and she might have used it if there hadn't been a deferential knock on the door. At Gordon Wright's request Bruce Stannard entered, and Lesley couldn't help remarking,

'Bringing in the heavies, eh?'

The young man stood uneasily waiting to be asked to sit down. Gordon Wright didn't give the order, so instead Bruce passed him a manila file. Gordon opened it and fingered its contents.

'These are reports on Jeanna going right back to when she was in primary. I've discussed her case with Bruce and he agrees.

'Of course he agrees, what else does he ever do?' Lesley retorted. 'No doubt he also thinks Jeanna's morals leave a great deal to be desired, but how would he know? He wouldn't know what sex was if it got up and bit him on the leg. You're like something out of a comic opera, the three of you. The Headmaster, the Field Officer and the School Counsellor. The Snob, the Virgin and the jealous Bitch. Jesus, what a trio!'

Bruce had the distinct impression that he'd walked on to the wrong stage and without a script.

'Have a seat, Bruce.' Lesley got up. 'You look as though you need it.'

Bruce glanced towards the headmaster. As he received no sign, he remained standing.

'Miss Armstrong,' Gordon Wright began.

'Jesus, Gordon, don't Miss Armstrong me, you're not heading a bloody army.' Gordon Wright's mouth stayed open. 'You've got it in for Jeanna, all of you, for your own reasons. But the facts are that whatever her social behaviour she is still a bright kid. An exceptionally bright kid. And given the right guidance and support, she'll go a long way. I intend to see she gets that support. Jesus, what does it matter if she races off a few blokes? Don't we all? Well, present company excepted. What else is there for her to do here, except jump at any young fellow who comes through? Yes, I know who she was down on the river with. I've heard from at least a dozen other people who have nothing better to do than gossip. I've even talked to Jeanna about it and made sure that at least she knows how not to get pregnant.'

Both men stared.

'Well, you don't want her to end up like her two sisters, do you?'

They didn't answer. Bruce was still standing, so Lesley sat down again and leant towards Gordon Wright.

'Look, Gordon, all this is so unimportant. What we should be worrying and talking about is not students like Jeanna Taylor; no matter what she does, she's a hundred times better off than the other pupils in her class. She's more intelligent and what's more important, she's white. What we should be planning is how to assist the rest, the seventy per cent of Aboriginal kids. We should be working out what sort of education they require. What is most suitable to their needs. How to keep them motivated. At the moment what are we educating them for? To be alcoholic bludgers, like most of their parents are? It's here, right here in this school, that we have the opportunity to make changes for a better future. That's what we should be working together to achieve. Not worrying about school counsellors who use tests which are dreamed up by white academics and which have no relevance whatsoever to the way most Aboriginals live.'

She turned to include Bruce. 'Both of you know that by the time they reach eight, virtually none of our Aboriginal pupils have any motivation left for finishing school, let alone trying to go further. That's why they all leave as soon as possible. What's the point in them going on? How many Aboriginal lawyers, doctors, teachers, politicians or even bank managers are there? You know all this, so why do I have to say it? Why can't we work together to help these people make something of themselves?'

'And create a few more Allan Fosters for you to fuck?'

Lesley reached across the desk and slapped Gordon Wright full on the face.

Constable Ed Vickers leapt up the three steps outside the police station in one bound and came to rest hard against the counter behind which Sergeant Ron Evans was perched on a stool typing up a report.

'What the hell are you up to?' he demanded. 'Why'd you let Fred Pepper go?'

Sergeant Evans had been in the New South Wales police force for too long to be fazed by an angry young constable. He continued to type to the end of the line and pushed the carriage back along the machine before looking up to say blandly, 'What's up, Ed?'

But the young man was not to be put off so easily. 'Why'd you let Fred Pepper go?' he repeated.

'Well, now.' The sergeant got down from his stool and unwound the report out of the machine.

'Well, I guess I just didn't see any point in keeping him in.'

'What d'you mean, no point? Did you read the charge sheet I made out against him?'

'Yes, I read it.'

'Then how can you say there's no point in keeping him?'

'Well, he wasn't really up to much.'

'Not up to much? He'd just sold Bill Flinders three bottles of metho mixed with rose hip syrup when I picked him up. He even admitted as much. It's all down there in his statement, didn't you read it? He also had gallons of cheap wine, port and beer stashed away amongst the groceries in his van, which he also admitted to selling in the West.' Sergeant Evans rolled a blank report sheet into his typewriter while Ed Vickers continued.

'He says he's been doing it for years. Don't you realize that this means he's more or less responsible for Gary Andrews's death? What a bastard the man is. What I can't fathom out is why he's so open about it all. It's as if he has nothing to hide. As if there was no point in trying to cover up because everyone already knew about it.'

Sergeant Ron Evans looked up slowly and the eyes of the two men in uniform met across the government issue typewriter.

'You did know?' Ed asked, though it was more of a statement than a question.

'Of course I knew, boyo,' the older man replied harshly. 'What d'you take me for, a fool?'

'No,' Ed replied, 'not a fool,' intimating that there were worse things to be.

Ron Evans bridled. 'I'd like to remind you that I'm your superior officer and as such, I make the final decisions. In this case I have decided not to press the charge against Fred Pepper, and so the case is dropped.'

Ed Vickers had been a constable for seven years, two years in Parramatta and five in the inner city areas of Sydney. It had not been an easy job; he'd discovered that people were not as pleasant close up as he had believed and wanted them to be. A couple of times he'd thought of tossing it in and doing what his father wanted him to do, join him in the small family shoe shop near his home. It had been especially tough on Pat adjusting to his shift hours and coping with the constant worry about the physical dangers involved in Ed working in such tough areas. There had been other times when he'd been offered bribes. Small amounts from motorists he'd picked up for speeding and much larger amounts from shopkeepers, restaurant owners or proprietors of clubs where illegal gambling and betting went on. Briefly he'd been tempted, but always he'd refused. He didn't think of himself as a hero or even pride himself on being an upright, moral man. It was just that he couldn't help himself. He was basically honest and dishonesty didn't come naturally to him. He realized he'd probably have got his first stripe by now if he'd gone along with offers of graft from fellow officers. But that didn't matter. All he cared about was that his wife and kids were happy and that he did his job to the best of his ability.

He stepped over now and took his cap off the peg on the wall. Turning to Ron Evans he said, 'That case does not get dropped.' He put his cap on his head, straightened it and said, 'I'm not going to let a bastard like that get away with it.'

In his thirteen years as a sergeant only one other junior officer had ever stood up to Ron Evans, and then it had turned out that he was the Assistant Commissioner's son. Confident that fate wouldn't pull the same trick twice, he didn't hesitate before saying to Ed, 'If you interfere, I'll make a report to headquarters about your total unsuitability for the positionas lockup keeper here. That will very smartly put an end to Pat's and your plans for a cushy posting for quite a while I'd say, and you'll be back on the beat. Which wouldn't be too good, would it? Added to which it would mean uprooting your boys again, and if I remember correctly that little one of yours took a long time to adjust to the change, didn't he?'

Ed took his cap off, but kept it in his hand.

'You're almost halfway through your time up here. I should think it would be a pity to throw those advantages away for a little whim, wouldn't it?' Ron Evans was quiet for almost a minute before continuing. 'I think I have made myself clear and that we understand each other perfectly.'

Ed Vickers put his cap on the table and asked, 'Why? Why is it so important to you to hush it up?' and then Ron Evans knew he'd won the game, set and match.

'Because Fred's not such a bad bloke.' Ed snorted, but not very strongly. 'And if it wasn't Fred it would be some other bloke smart enough to get in there quick. The worst thing the whitefellow ever did for the darkies was to allow them grog. If we'd kept the laws against them drinking, we'd have almost none of the trouble we have now. Sure they got liquor on the side before that, but never as much. Still it's no good crying over history. Fact is, they can't live without their drink, and all Fred's doing is supplying their demand. They're hooked on the stuff and can't do without it, even for a day, so Fred goes over on Sundays and sells it to them. If he didn't they'd almost certainly come into town and break into the hotels to get at it. Then someone would be bound to get hurt. So which is better?'

'But he sells it to them on weekdays too, before hours. Jesus, he's over there at 6 a.m. I've seen him there myself, even in the winter when he lights a fire and waits for them to come out, and in my innocence I believed what I was told, that he goes over to the West four times a day to sell them groceries and vegetables.'

'Well, that's right too, so he does. The lazy bastards are too bloody idle to walk the half-mile to the shops over here, and they can't wait for the hotels to open before they have a drink. The only way to stop it is to cut out their pension cheques and make them bloody well work for a living. Or open a pub over there twenty-four hours a day, so that they could drink themselves to death.'

Ed tried not to hear the last remark. Instead he said, 'What about the metho then? Surely you don't agree with that?'

'Look Ed, let's be realistic.' Ron Evans adopted a patronizing tone. 'There are always going to be a few who go bad. If it wasn't metho it would be something else.'

Ed picked up his cap again and ran it round and round in his hand by its rim. Jesus, Ron,' he said, 'd'you know what methylated spirits does? When Hitchcock did the p.m. on Gary Andrews he said that his liver had swollen to the size of a small pig to cope with the grog and then the metho had slowly de-stroyed it, so that it was like a huge festering mess sitting in his guts. Not only did it wipe out his liver, but it also destroyed large parts of his brain. Jesus bloody Christ man, that's what's in store for Bill Flinders if he keeps going on the stuff and you can't sit there as a man who calls himself a Christian, a bloody Catholic, and tell me that all that is OK on the basis that it satis-fies the laws of supply and demand.'

Something he had just said made Ed Vickers stop and retrace his thoughts. Then he suddenly real-ized what it was and in the same instant wondered why it was he'd taken so long. 'By Christ,' he almost shouted, 'now I see. It's because Fred Pepper's a bloody Catholic, a flaming Mick.'

'That's enough now,' Sergeant Evans was abrupt. 'Quite enough.'

'Oh, no, it bloody isn't. This is where it just be-gins.' Ed stopped running his hat round, and instead held it by its peak and flipped it up and down on the edge of the counter in rhythm with his words, while his voice took on an edge.

'And what does Father Clancy think of all this, eh? Because surely selling sly grog and metho to the boongs finds a place in his litany of sins. Fred Pepper, as a good Catholic, must feel obliged to confess to it, and what about you, what do you have to confess to, knowledge before and after the event? Do you then also take Gary Andrews' death upon yourself and confess to that too? Come to think of it, Fred Pepper is always giving you choice yellow-belly, which he catches in the weir. Do you think that counts as graft?'

Sergeant Evans began to splutter.

'Or does something even more useable exchange hands? What punishment does Father Clancy dream up for that? Fifty Hail Marys a day? Unfortunately that doesn't help poor Gary Andrews' widow and kids. But then yours is a white man's god, isn't he? So perhaps he doesn't care about what happens to the blackfellows. Clancy kills Jerry Brown, you kill Gary Andrews, and Fred Pepper finds a new victim in Bill Flinders. All the Micks together. God save me from religion!'

'I'll file a report of insubordination against you,' Sergeant Evans managed to get out.

'And I'll charge you with graft and corruption,' Ed replied calmly. The two men glared at one another, and then Ed walked to the door, put his hat carefully on his head and said, 'that is unless you personally pick up Fred Pepper and continue with the charges against him. I've not got a god to forgive me. I have to live with myself as I am, no confessions, no absolutions, and if it means going back down to Sydney and even back to Parramatta, it will be worth it, because there's no way I could continue to work with you if the matter is dropped.'

He made to leave, and then added, 'I would also like to invite you to donate generously to a relief fund which has been set up for Gary Andrews' widow and children.'

Then he went down the steps in one leap and out into the paddy wagon. Sergeant Evans closed his eyes for a brief moment and wondered if an Assistant Commissioner's son wasn't easier after all.


To be heard above the bleating of the lambs, Jim Dargan had to shout. 'Right boy, let's have it.'

Allan Foster let go of the young lamb he'd thrown to the floor and had been holding by the legs. Reprieved, the lamb scrambled back on to its feet and tried to lose itself among the other twenty animals in the pen. Allan straightened up,

'The name's Allan,' he said.

'Jesus,' Jim Dargan muttered.

'No. Not Jesus. Allan.'

The rest of the men working in the pens and at the cradle could hardly conceal their pleasure at someone standing up to the son of the property. Jim Dargan had been in two minds whether or not to take Allan on when he had arrived that afternoon with a new bunch of fellows, sent out by the employment of-fice to replace the last crew which Jim Dargan had dismissed as 'worse than bloody useless'. Allan had worked on the Dargans' property three years before and Jim knew that he was a good strong worker, but more than that, he also commanded the respect of the other Aborigines, so that under him they became a cohesive working team. This invariably meant that the shearing was done in less than half the usual time, and done well. This time the Dargans were marking and mulesing, but Jim Dargan was sure that Allan would do the job just as well as he had the last one.

At the same time, Jim also remembered, uneasily, how he had called Doug Foster a lazy bloody boong, not knowing he was Allan's brother, and how Allan had challenged him in front of the other men to a fight. The two young men from such separate worlds, the grazier and the hired hand, who unknowingly shared a common great grandfather, were of the same temperament and build, so that the fight lasted ten minutes. Jim Dargan still had nightmares about it, in which a huge fist came slowly, oh so slowly, towards him, and try as he might he could do nothing to avoid it. When it finally connected with his jaw he fell in slow, slow motion, into star-splattered darkness.

He didn't know that a blow he had landed on Allan's head was responsible for the irreversible, progressive blindness in the man's right eye. And if he had known, it would have been no compensation to him for being knocked unconscious before a crowd of Aboriginal hands.

But whatever his prejudices, no one could accuse Jim Dargan of being indecisive, so that now the moment of tension between the two men passed quickly as Jim decided that the important thing was to get the job done. 'OK. Allan, let's have it,' he said. 'And you fellows get a move on, we've got to get through this lot before dark.'

The other men, who had stopped work and were hoping for a confrontation, which would prove an excuse not to start work again, grudgingly began the awful job.

Allan grabbed another twenty-five pound lamb, knocking it, kicking, over on to its side, seized it by the legs and flung it squealing, hard down into the metal cradle. Jim Dargan deftly cut off the tail, threw it to one side, and in one quick movement of his razor-sharp knife, slashed the skin up the inside of one hind leg, across the rump, down the other leg, then ripped the fleece off, exposing the raw bleeding flesh. The animal urinated with pain. Then he stuck the knife into the scrotum and, leaning forward, squeezed the animal's two testicles into his mouth, bit them free and spat them sideways on to the floor, where they were devoured in one gulp by his favourite dog. Allan released the lamb, which had been screaming rather than bleating throughout the operation, and shoved the little beast out through the opposite side of the pen, where it staggered into a group of anxiously waiting ewes.

The heat from the mid-afternoon sun was as intense as it had been over Gary Andrews's grave the day before, but the men worked on in pairs, having a five-minute smoko at the turnabout every hour. Then the men who had been heaving lambs into the cradles changed with the men wielding the knives. By seven o'clock, when the sun had begun to lose its power, the men had finished the job and were squatting against the race, having a final mug of tea and a cigarette. All of them were smeared with blood and stank of animal fear and urine.

Jim Dargan sat on the tailboard of his ute beside the men and took great gulps of refreshing tea. He was pleased that the job was finished for another year. He hated the work, but he knew that it had to be done to prevent the sheep becoming fly-blown, for in a surprisingly few hours' time, the bare flesh around the lamb's anus would have contracted and drawn itself up, and with the tail gone, there was less possibility of dags clinging to the fleece as breeding grounds for the ubiquitous blowfly. It was a stinking and bloody job, but it was preferable to maggoty, flyblown sheep, rotting in the pastures with flesh so putrid you could poke your finger into it.

Glad that it was done, and accepting that this was due to Allan's leadership, he felt magnanimous enough toward the man to inquire, 'Your brother's back then?'

'Yeh.'

'Should have brought him out with you today. It would have been just like old times.'

Despite himself, Allan gave a small wry smile. 'He's too busy trying to get his kids back.'

'Have a hard job there. They were in a pretty bad way.'

Immediately Allan regretted opening himself up to this white man. He scowled. Jim Dargan noticed, but didn't care.

'How's Flo then?' one of the men asked.

'She'll be right,' Allan told him, 'right as she'll ever be anyway.

'Did it bring on the kid, like they said?'

Allan didn't know who 'they' were, though he realized it could be anyone, because the whole population must have heard about Dougo's attack by now. 'Stirred it up a bit. But it was almost time anyway, so if it comes a bit early, don't suppose it'll matter much.' Then, seeing Col Richards get up to pour himself another mug of tea, he said: 'Hear your wife's up the duff again too.'

'Mine?' Col asked, and shook his head. 'Not that I know of mate, but then you know what this town's like. Every other bastard would know you were dead before you bloody well knew yourself.'

The men laughed, and Allan felt he had been scored off. 'Well I don't rightly know mate,' he said, 'I only know what Dougo told me, and that was that Sylvia had told Flo she was pregnant.'

Col looked quickly back at Allan and went on pouring tea from the huge kettle so that it overflowed the side of his mug. 'Shit,' he exclaimed as the boiling liquid scalded his hand.

Realizing that he'd said the wrong thing, Allan tried to cover up. 'Well, I might have got it all wrong,' he said, which made matters worse.

He was relieved when one of the other men asked, 'What happened to Fred Pepper, is it right the lockup keeper picked him up?'

'Yeh,' Allan told him. 'Dougo and I were there when it happened. Funny as hell really. Vickers was just dropping Betty Flinders and found Bill like a sitting duck on the porch with the metho he'd just bought from Pepper. You could smell the bloody stuff from our place. I suppose it had spilt all over the bag. Vickers asked him where he got it from. You know old Bill, he hasn't got it in him to lie, so he told him straight. You should have seen Vickers roar off in his car after Pepper's van. Better than the Bathurst 500 it was. Caught up with him out on the road and made him get every tin and jar out of his van right there and then. Fucking hilarious it was. We all went across to have a better look and that made him even madder.'

'Jesus, I wish I'd been there,' the fellow laughed and the rest of the men joined in.

Someone else asked, 'Why did Vickers make him do that? Didn't he know?'

'Know what?' Jim Dargan asked. In their pleasure over Fred Pepper's arrest, the black men had forgotten he was there, and there was a moment's embarrassment before Allan said, 'That he's the sly grog merchant.'

'Fred Pepper?' Dargan was genuinely shocked. 'But I've known him since I was a boy.'

'That doesn't mean to say you know the man,' Allan replied.

'Why hasn't he been picked up before then?'

'Cos the cops know about him, what d'you think?' someone said, and then another voice added,

'He sells metho too.'

'Yes, it was him what knocked off Gary,' his friend chipped in.

'I don't believe it.' Jim Dargan got off the tail-board.

'You don't have to believe him mate,' someone said. 'You can go and see him for yourself in the-lockup.'

'No, he can't,' Allan interrupted. 'Evans let him out again.'

'The fucking bastard.'

'Well there you are, you see,' Jim Dargan said. 'I knew you must have got it wrong.'

'That's right mate, you can't trust a bloody boong to get things right,' Allan said, and tipped the dregs of his tea on to the ground. He wiped the blood off his stiletto knife on the thigh of his jeans, and stuck it into his belt. 'Well, dig,' he looked up at Jim Dargan, 'you going to run us back into town then?

Without waiting for his reply, the other men all got to their feet and piled into the back of Dargan's ute, roasting Col Richards for being the last on board.

Allan tried to avoid looking at the man, as he slid home the catches on the tailboard.

'Don't any of you bastards forget the fund-raising dance at the Hall on Saturday night either,' he said. 'I want to see every one of you there. Gary's wife needs every penny we can raise. The tickets are only fifty cents and you'll be paid tomorrow. Won't they?' He looked towards Dargan, who was about to get in behind the wheel. 'So there's no excuses.'

He yanked hard at the tailboard to make sure it was secure, and then walked round and, uninvited, slid in beside Jim Dargan. Looking straight ahead, he said, 'You're not invited. No whitefellows allowed.'

# CHAPTER SEVEN

## FRIDAY

It was the uniform that did it. On his way in to the police station he'd rehearsed what he was going to say over and over again, until he was word perfect. But, the moment he walked up the steps into the station and saw that uniform, his mind went blank. Now he stood there awkward and mute.

'G'day Dougo,' Sergeant Evans said with artificial friendliness. 'Good to see you back. What are you up to?'

Doug half-opened his mouth, but the words careering around in his brain refused to come out. 'Ummmm.. it's about, aah . . .'

Sergeant Evans stared straight at him, ran his tongue round his teeth and made no effort to help.

'My kids,' Doug managed to get out.

'Yes,' Ron Evans said slowly, 'your kids.'

A heavy truck rumbled along the main street loaded with three tiers of sheep on their way to the abattoirs in Bourke. The 400 blank-faced animals stood silently, pressed close to each other, staring out with their monochrome vision at children on their way to school and shopkeepers opening up their storefronts.

'Your kids,' the sergeant repeated.

'I want to get them back,' Dougo told him.

'Yes, well Dougo, it's not as simple as that. Fact is they've been made wards of the State. It's Flo who'd have to appeal and if she did that, then the court would have to consider whether or not she was now a fit person to care for the children. I doubt if there's much hope of that, not after the way they were when we took them in.'

'But now that I'm back why can't I have the children? I can look after them. I want them. They're mine.'

'They might be.' Doug didn't like the way Sergeant Evans said that, but before he could think of how to tell him so, Evans continued, 'But you and Flo aren't married. She couldn't even produce birth certificates for them. As far as the court's concerned Flo's their mother, she's responsible for them. She was the one who neglected them, and so they were taken away from her. What you are, father or not, or who you are, doesn't come into it.'

Doug felt instinctively that this couldn't be true. He didn't actually know anything about the law, that was the whitefellow's business, or even how to begin to find his way round the system, but he sensed that what the policeman was telling him was not the complete truth, and he wondered why he was lying.

Sergeant Evans pulled open a cabinet and took out a file of papers. For a moment Doug thought that he was going to receive an explanation, then as the policeman started to examine the folder, Doug realized that he had been dismissed. He felt the old anger return and despite the uniform, he heard himself shout, 'I want my kids.'

Ron Evans looked up in mock surprise at seeing Doug still there.

'Can't help you I'm afraid Dougo. That's the law. I don't make it. I only carry it out. Better go and see your people across the road.'

Doug knew that the Aboriginal Legal Service office on the other side of the street never opened until eleven o'clock at the earliest, and he knew that Sergeant Evans knew that too. He also sensed that the policeman had heard that Allan had tried to get the Service to take up his case and that they had refused. Allan hadn't explained why, just mumbled something about politics, but Doug felt that not only did Sergeant Evans know the Legal Service had refused to help, but also knew why. His stomach tightened and he yelled, 'I want my kids back.'

Even as his words still hung in the air, he heard a noise behind him. He put up his fists and turned quickly, in anticipation of being grabbed and handcuffed as he had been in prison when he had shouted at another white man in uniform.

Startled by the menacing face, fists and stance, Ed Vickers took a step backwards. 'Easy on mate,' he said.

Doug relaxed a little, and examined this new policeman, whom he'd only seen once before during the episode with Fred Pepper on the previous afternoon. The constable patted him on the shoulder and reached behind him to pick up the pile of charge sheets. Funny bastard, this one, Doug thought. Arrests Fred Pepper and now slaps me on the shoulder like I'm a friend. He didn't have time to pursue the thought because Sergeant, Evans moved quickly from the other end of the counter and banged his palm down on the charge sheets.

'No you don't, laddie.' Evans spoke across Doug as though he were invisible, to Constable Vickers.

'What d'you mean?'

'I mean you're suspended from duties until further notice.'

'You can't do that, you don't have that sort of authority.'

'No, you're quite right, I don't, but, ...'Ron Evans smiled unpleasantly, 'that order comes from headquarters. I phoned them when you went off duty yesterday, and their orders are that you should be suspended from duties pending an inquiry.' He picked up the charge sheets and put them into a manila folder, which he tucked under his arm. 'You're quite at liberty to check with Sydney if you don't want to take my word. There's the phone.'

Ed Vickers didn't move. Doug looked from one policeman to another.

'It'll mean extra work for the rest of the boys for a while,' Ron Evans said, 'but I'm sure they won't complain about the extra pay.'

'You won't get away with this,' Ed said quietly but forcefully.

'I wouldn't be too sure, laddie.' Ron Evans smiled again. 'There's more to all this than you know about. Now if you don't mind I'd like you out of this station. You're welcome to stay in your house of course, as long as you don't go across into the lockup area, and you won't lose any pay or benefits accruing to you. My suggestion is that you take a week of the holiday you've earned, By the time you get back, I'm sure there'll be someone up here from Sydney looking at the situation and sorting things out.'

The young constable wheeled about and left the station. The draught his hasty exit created lifted the bottom corners of a 'Wanted' poster, and on it the Aboriginal faces, with their institutional stares, rippled slightly.

Ron Evans smiled to himself, recalling the conversation he'd had with a superintendent in Sydney who'd told him that headquarters wanted no trouble at all with the Aborigines, and that they would take his advice and transfer Vickers back to Sydney where they could keep an eye on him. His smile broadened to a grin and then he became aware that Doug was still standing by the counter. Buoyant with success and self confidence, Sergeant Evans said, 'OK boy, you've had your entertainment for the day. What about doing something useful like going and drinking another nail into your coffin?'

Ron Evans was saved from having his face smashed in by an urgent voice at the door. 'Dougo, Dougo. The baby's started.'

Doug's rage was transposed into panic as he turned and stared into Sylvia Richards's face.

'The baby?' he asked, and then, 'Christ, the baby!'


Colin Richards was lying on the bed smoking when Sylvia came home.

'Oh Christ!' she exclaimed as she walked into the room.

'Give you a shock, did I Syl?' he sneered.

'Well, yeh, I wasn't expecting you.'

'Expecting someone else, were you?'

'Don't be bloody stupid.' She put down a cheap plastic holdall as casually as she could, trying to lose it among the litter of bedclothes and dirty garments, which spread across the floor, pushing it under the bed with her foot. 'I just wasn't expecting you back for a few more days. You said the job wouldn't be finished till after the weekend.'

'Yeh, well, it got finished early because bloody Allan Foster came out and got all the boys working like niggers. They'd lick his arse, some of those stupid bastards.'

She glanced quickly at him. He didn't normally use such violent language, and then she saw the almost empty whiskey bottle on the floor beside him. He saw her looking at the bottle.

'Want a drink, do you Syl? Come here and I'll give you one.'

She approached the bed a little warily, but even so was taken completely by surprise when he suddenly sat up and grabbed her by the arm, pulling her down on to the bed. He yanked her head back by the hair and her cries were half choked by the raw whiskey, which he poured over her face. He pulled even harder on her hair and thrust his face down into hers.

'There's your drink Syl. And now you tell me where you were when I got home last night, eh?'

His knee was pressed hard into her kidneys and he held her head so far back that she had difficulty swallowing, and felt that her neck would snap. His face was distorted with anger and his eyes bulged, the whites yellowed and bloodshot.

'Well, you bitch,' he yanked and she grimaced in pain, 'where were you?'

'I'll tell you, Col,' she gasped. 'Only let go of me.'

He grasped her left arm and let go of her hair, but as she sat up he held her arm twisted up behind her back just hard enough for her to have to lean forward in order to ease the tearing pain in her shoulder. 'Well?' he demanded.

'I . . . I was at Di's place.'

He pulled her arm up and she cried out with pain.

'You stupid bloody bitch, don't you lie to me.'

'It's not a lie,' she gasped in desperation. 'I stayed with Di and Les.'

She screamed as he pushed her forward on to the floor and then fell heavily on top of her, wrenching her arm almost out of its socket.

The relief when he let go of the limb was so intense that she began to cry. He sat full on her buttocks, his weight crushing her pelvis against the bare board floor. She felt some of the weight ease off her right side as he stretched across under the bed and dragged out her plastic holdall. He dumped it on the small of her back and then he pulled her head up off the floor by her hair.

'Since when d'you take this with you when you stay over at Di's? Eh?'

He let go of her head, ripped open the holdall, turned it upside down and shook the contents over her. She was showered with an assortment of bedraggled underclothes and toiletries.

'What's this, eh?'

Her face was pressed hard into the boards so she couldn't see what he held in his hand, but in the

next instant he had shaken dozens of pills and capsules on to the floor beside her.

In one violent movement he rolled her over on
to her back and sat astride her chest. Her breasts were
trapped beneath the powerful grip of his thighs and
painfully pinched by his knees, her ribs crushed by his
weight.

'Got these from Di, did you? You bitch.' He
grabbed a handful of the yellow pills and red and blue
capsules from the floor and smashed them against her
mouth. Instinctively she opened it to cry and then
spluttered and spat the tablets out.

'You'll kill me with all those pills,' she gasped.

'I'll do worse than bloody kill you, you bitch.'
He belched, and swallowed the thin alcohol vomit.
'Uggh, Christ,' he grunted.

She took advantage of his distraction to scram-
ble out from under him and made it to the door.He
caught her in the hall and brought her down heavily.
She hit her head on a door handle as she fell, feeling
the blood beginning to ooze.

'No you don't, you bitch. You don't go anywhere until you tell me why you were up at the hospital. Yeh, see, I bloody well know where you were, and
I bloody well know why you were there too, you
whore, but I want to hear it from your own mouth.'
He grabbed her by the hair and ears and pinned her
down, keeping his face close to hers. 'Tell me.' He
banged her head on the floor and she saw stars.

'They said I'd die,' she sobbed. 'I was bleeding
inside, they said I'd go rotten. They had to clean it all
out.'

'Clean what all out, the baby?' he screamed. She nodded as best she could with him still clutching her hair.

He let her go and got off her, but when she attempted to get up, he hit her across the face, so she lay still beside him as he leaned against the wall with his eyes shut. His face was shiny with sweat and his voice low as he said,

'Tell me. Tell me what you told Flo Foster.'

So that was how he knew. She cursed herself for talking to Flo. But she was glad that at least he hadn't heard it from the children, because she still hoped that they didn't know. She wondered where they all were. He looked less angry now, but she knew better than to be deceived. She knew him well enough to be more frightened of him now, than when he was shouting or hitting her. His cold detached fury was far more terrifying. She wondered how much Flo had told, and also how much she had told Flo, for she had been so distraught that she couldn't recall the details of their conversation.

Almost as though he sensed what she was thinking, he said, 'Tell me it all. I want it all.,

She tried to sit up, but lay down again quickly before his outstretched palm hit her face. She told him all in one quick jumble. 'I got pregnant and I tried to get rid of it and then it wouldn't stop bleeding so I went to Hitchcock and he told me I'd die if I didn't go up the hospital and they operated on me, and now they say I'll be right.'

'Whose was it?'

She didn't answer, and he opened his eyes and stared at her. 'Tell me.'

'They don't know it wasn't yours, Col. Honest. I didn't tell nobody that it couldn't have been yours, and I won't ever, I promise. I must have talked to Flo when I was half dopey from the operation, but I know I didn't tell her that,' she lied. 'She's in a bad way too, you know. It's on the way, but real slow and she don't even know whose kid it is. She told me that herself. It wasn't my fault Col, honest, it was while you were away last month, it must have been.'

'Who was it? Tell me.'

Sylvia heard a radio blaring from the house next door, and a child crying. Her throat was dry and the pit of her stomach was cold and heavy with fear.

'Tell me,' he yelled.

'It was,' she started, 'it was these fellows. .

'Fellows? he echoed, emphasizing the plural.

'. . . from Brisbane,' she got out.

He leaned forward from the wall. 'From Brisbane. Whitefellows, eh?'

She nodded miserably.

'You fucking bitch,' he said slowly, and then again, louder and again louder still, filling the narrow mean hallway with his shouts, 'I'll teach you to be a white man's cunt,' he yelled.

She heard the snap as he grabbed the broom and broke off the head. She screamed as he ripped off her dress, and she tried to struggle back up the hall away from him, but he was like a wild beast. The pain as he forced the broom handle up into her body was so excruciating that she fell, still screaming, into merciful oblivion.

Her body burst open the kitchen door to reveal her two youngest children playing with some empty beer bottles on the dirty floor.

A goanna slithered away from them through the coarse, brown grass and they stopped to watch the startled reptile climb flat-footed up into a spotted gum. It eased itself out as far as it dared along a high branch, and Lesley laughed.

'It's just like a child, it thinks if it stays still for long enough it will become invisible.'

The brown and green mottled skin of the goanna blended in so well with the foliage that unless someone knew it was there, they wouldn't notice it. Perfectly motionless it lay, watching them with its round unblinking eyes.

'It's a big one isn't it?' she commented. 'It must be a good three feet.'

'Have you ever eaten goanna?' Allan asked.

'No, of course not,' she laughed, 'and nor have you, so don't tell me you have because I shan't believe you.' She gave his arm a playful small punch. 'And don't put on your "I am an Aborigine" face.'

He remained serious. 'Yes I have, many times. When I was a child. Mum would take us off fencing or mustering with Dad. Camp followers, I suppose we were. We'd follow the men wherever their job took them, and we'd live out in the bush for weeks on end. The men would catch roo and pig and sometimes we'd eat goannas or even emu eggs when they were in season.Good tucker, goanna. A bit strong tasting, but I liked it.'

Lesley thought of her own very urban upbringing when the only contact she'd had with animals was with the family dog and her own white rabbit. She'd called the rabbit George Sandp because it had a masculine intelligence in a female body. How much more dissimilar could you get than George Sand and goanna cooked over an open fire, she thought.

'What happened to your Dad?'

Allan picked up some small loose clods of earth and aimed them gently at the goanna. They landed softly on his back, but he didn't even blink an eyelid.

'Went walkabout. Suppose he forgot about us.'

'How old were you?'

'Nine, I think, 'bout that. Mum had just had Irene, I remember that.'

'Haven't you any idea what happened to him or where he is?'

'No. Never heard a word. Guess he's got another wife and a few more kids. Maybe he's left that one too. He wasn't a bad bloke. Worked damn hard and didn't drink that much, only when we finished a job and came into town for a spell.'

'Does your mother ever talk about him?'

'No. It's not such a big deal as it is with your people. Most of us have a couple of wives in different places. I suppose it's the black in us. Tribal Aboriginal men were never expected to be monogamous. That idea came with the missionaries. Same thing with going walkabout. Ask any blackfellow, part-blackfellow I mean, and he'll tell you that every now and again he gets this urge to move on. He can't tell you what it is, it's just in his blood.'

The goanna blinked.

'And what does your white blood do for you?'

Allan dropped the rest of the clods on to the soil.

'Makes me the nasty aggressive bastard that I am. And the two together louse up my brain.'

He began walking again, and Lesley fell in with him. They were beside the muddy river which flowed fast and deep between its steep banks, though even in the last few days it had dropped noticeably because the heavy rain further north had cleared. In a week or so it would be flowing much more slowly, and unless there- were further rains upstream, in two months it would be reduced to a trickle. Looking at it now it was hard to imagine that it could ever be depleted.

'Fucked in the head, that's what I am.' Allan pushed his hands further down into the pockets of his shorts. 'I look at Dougo, you know, and I envy him, yeh, really. He's a simple bloke. Not stupid, simple. The things he wants are very basic. They're what all normal average men want. A wife who loves him, kids, a home of his own, a job when he needs it and to be left alone the rest of the time. He's not interested in politics, the future of his people. I don't think he con- sciously even thinks of them as his people. He never looks at himself from the outside. Never examines his thoughts and reactions. Ignorance really is bliss as far as Dougo is concerned. I envy him his bliss.'

Lesley put her arm through his.

'Look at me,' he said. 'I am so screwed up I want to stop.'

He stopped walking and she stood silent beside him. A flock of white cockatoos flew into a tree over- head, the flash of yellow on their heads vivid in the morning sun.

'I want to stop being me, and be someone else, someone who doesn't care. Doesn't care because he doesn't see. I want to stop being aggressively what I am. Aggressively black. I don't want to be white par- ticularly, only that whites don't have to be conscious the whole time of being white. I swing violently between being proud and being ashamed, and all I really want is just to be me.

'I'd be better off if I was up in the Territory working on a property. The full bloods out there speak their own language and keep to tribal ways. They work through the dry and go bush in the wet. The whitefellows they work for can't afford to be paternalistic to them, because they are so dependent on them. D'you know there's whitefellows up there that speak Aboriginal languages? Fair dinkum.'

He was quiet for a while, scuffing the earth, and then: 'I should either go up there or down to Sydney and work in the Movement. At least there I'd be with other people who are equally messed up. Down there it's not only blacks who are fucked in the head, they almost all are, otherwise they wouldn't be there in the first place. But at least they have to be more tolerant, because there are so many oddballs there that even a bloody boong is accepted as part of the scenery.'

He sighed, and hunched his shoulders. 'But I won't go anywhere. I know I won't. That's what's so bloody awful. I'll stay here getting more and more messed up and end up like the rest, drinking myself to a slow death. I'll stay because this is my country.'

He bent down, picked up a handful of dirt and looked out across the flat plain, then back at his own hand, He opened his fingers and let the dry red soil flow through, leaving three pieces of white bone in his palm. Then he took Lesley's hand and put the pieces into it. 'My people,' he said.

She brought her hand closer to her face and examined the pieces of white bone; each was about an irregular inch square, curved, and almost half an inch thick. Between the inside and outside surfaces of the curve, which were smooth, was soft, grey, porous bone. She shivered in the bright sunlight as she recognized the bones as parts of a human skull. Then she looked down at the ground where they were standing and gasped. Allan was still scuffing at the topsoil, and as he did so, parts of human bone surfaced everywhere. She dropped the skull particles and wiped her hand hard on the side of her dress.

'What is it, Allan?' she asked in a low voice. 'Where are we? Is it an old graveyard or burial place or something?'

'No, they were never buried,' Allan said, still continuing to scuff around with his foot. 'They lay where they fell. It was a massacre. This is Hospital Creek. The whitefellows came through here and wiped out over a hundred Aborigines in one hit. They don't teach us about that in school, do they?' He said it without bitterness, but still she couldn't look at him.

'No one's sure exactly when it happened. Sometime in the 1830s is the most likely time. And the stories about why it happened vary too. Some say it was retaliation over some cattle the blacks pinched. Others say a white woman was raped and her husband got a licence from the government to shoot three hundred blacks. We'll never know the truth now, but it's for sure that it happened and when you see how many bones there are out here, it's obvious that they killed plenty.

'Come, I have something I want to show you.'
She followed him through the sword grass, wishing she had asked him, when he suggested going for a walk, where they were going. She would have covered

her legs, which were now criss-crossed with painful shallow cuts from the razor-sharp grass. They slithered down the edge of the bank and came to rest by the edge of the river on some small, smooth, round grey stones.

'Look.' He pointed back up the slope. 'You get the best view from here.'

She looked in the direction he was pointing and saw an enormous spotted gum with a huge scar on its trunk. 'What is it?' she asked. 'What made it grow like that?'

'It didn't grow like that,' he told her. 'It's what we call a coolamon. My grandfather cut it out with a stone axe when he was eleven years old. He cut the bark off in one piece and made a big canoe. He told me it was the biggest one in the area, about seven feet long. He'd go out fishing with his brothers, and they'd also go bird nesting. The scar is where the tree tried to coverup the wound.'

They clambered up and stood beside the trunk. One on either side, they ran their fingers round the curve and up as far as they could reach, both of them thinking about the boy who had hacked out the bark canoe.

'Wonderful,' Lesley smiled. 'How wonderful, and doesn't it make you realize how temporary life is. Just to think of your grandpa paddling up and down this same river catching fish and stealing birds' eggs. Now he's dead, but life goes on, just as it will when we're dead. I like that.It makes me feel part of the flow of life.'

What she said pleased him. 'And up there,' he said, pointing a little further up the riverbank, 'you can see a smaller coolamon, see?'

'Yes! Yes!' She was excited. 'What's that for? Not a baby's canoe, surely?'

'No. That's where they cut into a hollow tree to get out a possum, or perhaps a goanna, which was inside. Possum tastes good too. Next to it you can see where those other trees have been ringbarked. That was done with a metal axe, you can tell by the harsher marks. Chinamen would have done that. They were employed all through here as ringbarkers in the late eighteen hundreds and early nineteen hundreds.' He held out his hand to help her up the last bit of the steep bank.

'Something else,' he said quietly.

They walked a hundred yards to where a huge gum spread its branches above a small gully, which had been cut out, by the floods, exposing part of the root system. The gully was littered with rusty tins, shiny aluminium cans and shattered bottles. Allan knelt between the two huge roots, which stuck up out of the earth and began to gently rub aside the soil. Lesley stood beside him. The bush was silent in the intense afternoon heat.

As she watched, Allan scooped the soil into little heaps and she saw what was unmistakably a long shinbone appear. Beside it he revealed another, and as he worked up towards the trunk of the tree, he gradually uncovered the thighbone, broken in three places, the pelvis, the vertebrae, the right arm and then the skull. Lesley's mouth was dry and she felt the blood pounding in her head as though she were about to faint, but she kept watching as Allan dug beside the left side of the skeleton and uncovered a jumbled heap of much smaller bones.

'My God,' she breathed. 'It's a child!'

Allan knelt back on to his heels and looked at what he had exposed, and Lesley fell to her knees beside him and stared at the bones. 'My God,' she whispered again.

Without looking at her Allan said, 'It's my great-great-grandmother. I've never shown her to anyone else. Not even Dougo. I don't think he'd understand.'

'But how, I mean why, I mean, I don't understand. . Lesley stammered.

'My grandfather told me. This is his wife's grandmother and her child. They were killed in the massacre.'

Allan stood up and looked out across the plain. He spoke slowly. 'I don't know that I really believe him. It could just be a legend, which grew, like so many Aboriginal legends. But that's what Grandfather told me. The baby was less than a year old. In this dry climate out here they will be preserved for hundreds of years, that's how all these other bones are still intact. Anyway, even if it isn't actually my great-great-grandmother, it doesn't really matter. She was one of my people. Their graves are all along the river here where their campfires are. Some of the ashes from those fires go down forty feet. That's how long my people have lived here. They died where they had lived for thousands and thousands of years. So you can see now why I can't leave and go to Sydney, even though I want to get away.' He looked at her. 'I belong here. This is my land.These are my people.'

It didn't seem like a very appropriate moment, but she said it anyway. 'They know about us,Allan. Jeanna Taylor told Gordon Wright. He called her in and bullied her so much that she didn't know what she was saying. She didn't tell him to be mean, it just came out.'

'It doesn't matter. They would have found out sooner or later.'

He was silent for a moment and then said, 'There's no future for us together, they know that, and you know it too, don't you?'

She looked down at the grave and nodded. He went back down on his knees and began to gently re-cover the bones.


'Aahh, come on, don't be such a bloody piker, mate. It's not going to cost you anything, for Christ's sake. They're giving it to you for free, all they want's the grog.'

Greg Fletcher reached under the car seat, brought out a flagon of red wine, put it between Ian Maconachie's knees and then went back down and brought out another, which he held on to himself.

'There,' he said. 'Three gins for a couple of flag-ons. Not doing too bad for city slickers, are we?'

In the week the trio had been in Woongarra Greg had taken on many of the coarser traits of his elder publi-can brother. On the other side of Ian sat Darren Jones with a big grin on his face.

'Right on, sport,' he said. 'Wait till I tell the blokes back at the factory how easy it is to get a chick up here. They'll be coming up in bloody droves, they will.' He grabbed the flagon from between Ian's knees and made to open the car door.

'Wait on a bit,' Greg said, and turned to Ian. 'We can't just leave you here, mate. What's up with you? You go well enough down in Sydney with that little blonde hot pants you've got, why not give this lot a go? We're not going to be watching you, you know mate, we'll be too bloody busy on the job ourselves.' He laughed. 'Or don't you fancy a bit of black velvet, eh? Yeh, that's it, can't come at it, eh? Well just close your bloody eyes and pretend it's your little blonde bit. They're all the same between the thighs you know, and that's the only place it matters, right?' He laughed again.

'What if they've got a dose?'

Jesus Christ mate, you can't spend your life worrying about that, or you'd never get your rocks off. And anyway, if that's what's worrying you, I know a quack in Sydney who'd fix you up in no time flat. They got pills and junk for that sort of thing nowadays. Anyway, I'm sure there's more risk of getting it down home than there is up here, and I'm certain as hell that you stand a greater risk of being run over by a bus, outside your own house, than of getting a dose of clap from a gin.'

On the other side of the car Darren began fiddling with the door handle again.

'Aahh, come on, Greg. Don't worry about him. If he wants to miss out on a good time, let him.He can always walk back to the pub and take a pull at himself instead.'

Ian gave him a withering look. Neither young man really liked the other, they merely tolerated each other because they both admired and envied Greg. He was the catalyst, which held the threesome together. They even liked him a little.

'Shut up, you randy bastard,' Greg ordered. 'Can't wait to get one, can you?'

'Too bloody right, mate. Your brother said that once you get some grog into them they go off like a packet of crackers.' He gave what he imagined to be a sexy growl.

It was almost eleven o'clock and the pubs having been closed an hour most residents of theWest were now at home. There was obviously a party going on at the other end of the street because there was loud music and a few people in the crowd were even attempting to dance in the road amongst the refuse. But where the men were parked there was only muted noise from inside the homes, although the lights were still on. Across the street a few people were drinking on some porch steps, but they took no notice of the three young men in the utility,and because there was no street lighting they couldn't see that they were white.

'How old are these chicks anyway?' Ian asked.

'Jesus,' Darren exploded, 'he'll be wanting to see their bloody birth certificates next. What does it matter as long as they're a good fuck?'

'It matters one hell of a lot mate,' Ian retorted. 'I'm not getting stuck into any jail bait, thanks.'

'They're fifteen, almost sixteen,' Greg lied, knowing that one of them was thirteen, but also knowing that he was going to have her himself, to start off with anyway, because Harry had said, 'Make sure you have a go at her. She's so bloody keen, her legs fall apart as soon as you look at her.'

'That's what I thought,' Ian said. 'Under age. And what happens if they report us, or if some big blackfellow walks in on us and decides to do us over? I've seen a couple of real nasty bastards around town.'

187

Jesus mate, there's no bloody way they'd dob us in. They want it as much as we do. Specially when they see the grog.' Greg glossed over the idea of being discovered by an Aboriginal because he had already considered the possibility, and was so nervous about it that he'd stuckHarry's hunting knife down the waist of his trousers.

'How come your brother knows so much about these chicks anyway?'

'Oh Jesus bloody Christ, mate.' It was Darren again, becoming increasingly impatient.

'How d'you think he knows? Maybe a little birdie told him, Greg jeered. 'Christ man, he knows because he's tried them on for size himself. just because he can get it regular and legal whenever he likes, doesn't mean he doesn't want a bit on the side once in a while. Most normal blokes aren't satisfied with just one woman, and they don't let their women bloody well tie them to their apron strings just because they married them, or worse still, because they just promised to marry them.'

Ian flushed at the direct reference to his engagement, and the doubt cast on his manhood by the person whom he most wanted to emulate and be liked by. 'Aahh well,' he said. 'Suppose I should give it a whirl. After all every one you knock back is one you never get again, eh?' He gave a hollow laugh, hoping to regain their acceptance.

'About bloody time too, mate,' Darren said, opening the door.

Ian slid out after Greg. 'Thought your brother didn't like the blacks?'

'You don't have to like something to fuck it, do you?'

The three men walked through the littered yard and Greg kicked a smashed bottle off the bottom step.

'I feel a bit empty-handed, mate,' Ian said nervously. 'Should have brought three flagons, shouldn't we?'

'Nah,' Greg assured him. 'Harry says he only ever brings a bottle of port or half a flagon. That's the going rate. They'll think their luck's changed and all their Christmases have come at once, when they see this lot.'

He raised his flagon and Darren did the same. They toasted each other with mock solemnity.

'Here's mud in your eye, mate,' Greg said.

'Mud in your eye be buggered,' Darren replied, 'here's to a hot little cunt.'

Irene Foster was waiting for them. She lolled self-assuredly across the mattress, her school pants showing underneath her short skirt, her small still-forming breasts hard under her white uniform blouse. Her two friends, Bill and Betty Flinders's fifteen-year-old daughter Jilly, and Molly Brown's sixteen year-old daughter Debbie, sat awkwardly beside her, their vulnerable faces scarred with vivid red lips as a badge of sophistication. They all giggled self-consciously.

'Drink up, girls.' Greg presented Irene with his flagon. 'This is going to be one hell of a night.'

# CHAPTER EIGHT

SATURDAY

'**M**r. Foster.'

'What? What? Yes. What?' Doug shook his head and opened his eyes, but shut them again immediately to keep out the glare of the neon lights. He became aware of a stiffness in his neck, and grimaced as he twisted it to try and ease the pain. He sat forward on the hard bench and put his head in his hands, running his fingers back through his hair, still shaking his head. He felt as though he was at the bottom of a deep pit and was wearing big heavy boots, which made it impossible for him to climb out.

'Mr. Foster.'

He opened his fingers and looked up through them at Sister Phyllis Hutchins. 'Must have dropped off for a second,' he explained.

'I'm not surprised,' she said. 'Now why don't you go home and try to get some proper sleep?'

Doug was surprised by her friendly tone of voice.

'There's nothing you can do here, Flo will be all right. It just looks as though it's going to take a bit longer than we expected. We'll give you a call the moment anything happens.'

Doug shook his head. 'No, I'll be right thanks. I'll stay here. Something might happen quickly and she might need me.'

Sister Hutchins had changed her opinion of Doug and was impressed by the way he'd been to the hospital every day and stayed continuously for the past twenty-four hours. She'd marvelled at his obvious affection for his wife. Though god knows why, because she's such a hopeless slut, she thought. And she couldn't fail to notice how Flo was soothed by her husband's presence.

The baby, which had shown signs of imminent arrival the previous morning, was now lying heavy and still in the pelvic opening. Doug had spent hours yesterday rubbing the small of Flo's back. The contractions would begin again, mount to a crescendo and just when the nursing staff were sure that things were starting to really happen, they'd fade away. Dr. Hitchcock had been called out twice from his private surgery and both times he'd gone back disgruntled at being disturbed, knowing that in his absence the queue of patients would have grown even longer. By the third time, which came in the middle of the night, Doug was at screaming point. He couldn't bear to see Flo suffer so badly and he felt like putting his hand in and wrenching the baby out. He was beginning to hate this new creature which was causing such worry and agony.

Flo was still being fed from a drip bag and the bandage which still covered her right eye and ear looked like a cap set at a jaunty angle. It struck a bizarre note in these surroundings. The stitches had been taken out, leaving a long thin scar which pulled slightly at her top lip. But he worst of it was that she was tired. Very, very tired. The contractions had worn through her physical resources and all she wanted now was to get rid of this thing inside her, and sleep.

'Well at least get something to eat,' Sister Hutchins interrupted Doug's reverie. 'You didn't eat anything yesterday, and we don't want another patient on our hands, thank you, we have quite enough to cope with as we are.'

She smiled in the closest attempt she had ever made in her entire life to be friendly to anAboriginal. A gaunt, big-boned woman, she had been born on a property in the area and had lived in Woongarra all her life. Her father, who had worked harder than many men, had lost everything in the Depression, and she and her brothers had had to leave school early to begin working for other people. Her parents had never recovered from the blow, and her eldest brother, who had always anticipated inheriting the family property, was still bitter about what he considered the raw hand life had dealt him. Phyllis had gone into nursing and had married a Walgett fellow whose parents had also lost out in the dfepression, and who was now a linesman with the electricity commission. Together they had worked hard and saved up enough money for the down-payment on a block of land.Just enough for a house, which they had built themselves, with room left over to run a few cattle. The cattle market wasn't so good at the moment, but it would pick up again, it always did eventually, and anyway at least they had some dirt of their own. Their only disappointment was that they had no children. They had worked hard to help themselves and like the majority of other whites in the area, they despised the Aborigines as bludgers, no-hopers and alcoholic losers, who wouldn't do an honest day's work for a day's pay, who preferred to sponge off the government and take the tax-payers' money, in other words Phyllis and her husband's money, rather than work for a living.

These feelings had been reinforced in Phyllis Hutchins by her work as a nurse specializing in child care. She'd seen so many children suffering hideously and unnecessarily from neglect.'Let them drink themselves to death,' she had often said, 'but how dare they make those little children suffer!'

Now, as she looked down at Doug Foster, Phyllis Hutchins felt a compassion she had never experienced before for an adult Aborigine. Every day he had come twice to visit his wife. He hadn't said much, just sat by the bed. They hadn't even held hands, but Sister Hutchins could sense an unspoken communication between them. She'd heard from George Davies that Doug had also been out to see his children every day after school, and that he was trying to get them back. She knew all about Doug's past, his drinking and fighting, his imprisonment. She'd found his children maggot-ridden and suffering from exhaustion. She'd heard of Flo's past and knew that while Doug was in prison Flo had slept around with other men. Yet as she looked into Doug's eyes, somewhere in her deep subconscious, almost obliterated by years of conditioning and experience, the germ of a new feeling began to formulate. It was quite a revolutionary thought for someone like Phyllis Hutchins and it was simply that perhaps, after all, it wasn't all Doug and Flo's fault. That maybe they were caught in something bigger than themselves, something over which they had no ultimate control.

Perhaps some of these jumbled half-formed ideas communicated themselves to Doug Foster, because he felt able to ask this white uniformed woman, 'It's not right, is it? Something's wrong, isn't there? I mean she never had any of this trouble with the last two.'

'Now don't you worry, Mr. Foster.' Phyllis actually sat down beside him and put her hand on his knee. 'She's going to be all right. It's taking a little longer, that's all. When you're tired everything seems worse, so why don't you go home and get some sleep.'

Doug was tempted to tell her that no one could sleep in the West during the day, unless they first deadened themselves with alcohol to shut out the noise of blaring radio and television sets, screaming children, bickering women and arguing men. 'No, I'll be right thanks,' he insisted, 'but I will go and get some coffee and perhaps a bite to eat.' He stood up, feeling every muscle complain. 'I'll be over at the cafe if anything happens.'

'All right, I promise I'll send for you if anything does happen. But from the way she looks right now, I don't think you need eat your breakfast too quickly,' she said with a friendly smile.

'I'll just take a quick look at her before I go off,' he said.

'Don't trust me, eh?' she said pleasantly, and watched as he went off down the corridor and turned into the small ward.

Doug stood at the end of his wife's bed and sighed in sympathy as she moved uncomfortably in her drugged half sleep. The baby lay huge and dormant.

Flo opened her eyes drowsily.

'G'day,' Doug said quietly.

She said nothing, only smiled a little.

'I'm just going off to get some tucker. I'll only be gone half an hour. You be right?'

She nodded. He touched her hand quickly where it lay, unresisting, alongside her body.

Coming out into the corridor he almost collided with Jake Jones, whom he hadn't seen since he returned. Jake was flushed with excitement. His long red hair was tousled, he had a day's stubble and Doug noticed, as he always did with Jake, that he still hadn't had his teeth fixed, though he was always saying that he was going to. They grew from his gums like an irregular picket fence with several posts missing.

'G'day, Dougo. What d'you know? I'm a father!' He laughed and revealed even more distorted teeth. 'Yeh, what about that, me a dad!'

'Well, that's great. What is it?'

'Boy, of course. Told Emma straight, got to be a boy, or else!'

Jake was a Sydney boy who had travelled around New South Wales shearing. He'd arrived in Woongarra last season and started taking out Emma Marshall, Ann's younger sister. When Emma showed obvious signs of being pregnant, no one was surprised. What did surprise them was when Jake announced that he and Emma were getting married. But the biggest surprise was that Jake insisted on a church wedding, with both his and Emma's parents present. It had been Woongarra's wedding of the year. Jake in his hired dinner suit, grinning and showing off his teeth, Emma hugely pregnant and beautiful in a dress made by her mother. The wedding was a great success and Jake's parents didn't seem the least concerned by the fact that they were the only white people at the celebration.

'What are you going to call him?'

'Opal, of course. What else? Red on black. Right?' Jake laughed again, and Doug laughed with him. They were at the main door. 'I'll let you buy me a celebration drink, mate,' Jake was saying, as Dr Hitchcock came out of the reception area.

'Mr. Foster,' he said, 'can I have a word with you?'

'Wait for you outside, mate,' Jake said.

Doug's heart began beating faster. 'Yeh, what's up?'

'Nothing's up, Mr. Foster, not yet anyway. But I thought I should tell you that unless something definite happens by midday, I'm planning to operate.'

'Operate? What d'you mean operate?'

'A caesarian section, Mr. Foster. Your wife is very, very tired. If her labour continues at this slow pace there is a very real threat of the baby's life being in danger.'

'But what about Flo?' Doug had already dismissed the child. All he wanted was for his wife to be all right.

'It's a quite common operation, Mr. Foster. I've performed many, and we'll take all the precautions which are available to care for your wife.'

The two men stood side by side. The white man holding the life of the black man's wife and child in his hands, the black man unable to do anything to help either them or himself.

Dave Foster forced the hook through the neck of the decapitated animal, sliced free a flap of skin and clamped it into the teeth of the huge machine which with terrifying surety moved backwards, ripping the whole skin away and exposing the raw flesh beneath. The shooters had already gutted the kangaroos and removed the paws and heads, so that the skinless carcass, which Dave now passed on to his older brother Bob, was ready to be boned. In several quick, seemingly easy slashes of his incredibly sharp pointed knife, Bob Foster separated the soft red meat, tossing it into one huge tub, from the bones, which went into a separate tub. At frequent intervals these tubs were collected by another workman, who wheeled them away into enormous refrigerated rooms for storage prior to the bi-weekly trucking down to Sydney, where the kangaroo would be processed into pet food.

The two brothers had often worked as a boning team at Les Cullen's roo works. They'd work for several months at a stretch, and Les was always glad to see them, for they arrived on time and got through a great deal of work during the day. Then suddenly, without any warning, one day they would simply not turn up and Les would curse the lackadaisical Aboriginal mentality, but always take them back when, in a couple of months, they came round again asking for work.

This time the Foster brothers had been at the works for three months through the heat of midsummer, so they were very close to feeling that it was time for a break. Les Cullen realized this, and had offered the young men more money to stay on, because right now, after the lifting of the government's export restrictions, the kangaroo market had never been better.

'I'm offering you three times what you'd get on the pension,' he'd said, trying to tempt them into continuing work. But the young men were not tempted. They knew when they'd had enough of hacking up dead beasts and finishing each day spattered with blood. No amount of money could persuade them to continue. Even though he was married to an Aboriginal, Les Cullen still didn't understand how a man could give up a job and take a far smaller amount on an unemployment cheque. He sometimes wondered if he would ever understand Aborigines,and after yesterday's events he was wondering whether that also meant he would never understand his wife.

He'd gone home early yesterday afternoon wanting to surprise her, and treat the kids to a swim. He'd found her sobbing on the bed. She didn't appear in the least pleased to see him.

'What's up, love?' he asked.

'Nothing. Nothing. Just leave me alone.'

Perhaps it's time for her period, he thought, and tried to work out what date the last one had been, but then that wasn't much point because, since she'd come off the pill, on Hitchcock's instructions that she should give it a rest for a while, her menstrual cycle had been all over the place and the accompanying depressions had been worse than ever. He sat beside her on the bed and stroked her hair.

'Come on, love, you'll feel better if you have a swim, there's a girl.'

'I don't want a swim!' she shouted. Her sobs increased till she was wailing, and then stopped abruptly. 'What the hell does it bloody matter anyway?' she said violently. 'It's her own fault.'

'Whose fault, love?

'Sylvia! Sylvia. Who do you think? Haven't you heard?'

'Haven't I heard what?'

Between her wails he managed to work out that Sylvia was in hospital. 'Now stop crying. Pull yourself together and tell me what's happened.'

'It was Col. It must have been him. They can't find him. So it must have been him who did it.'

'Did what?'

'Rammed a broom up her cunt,' she yelled.

Les stopped stroking her neck and sat up stiff with shock. He'd never heard Dianne use such a word. She hardly ever swore, and then only on extreme occasions came out with a 'bloody'. She turned over on her back and he saw how puffy and swollen her face was. Then she threw herself on to him and clung to him, sobbing.

'It's my fault! It's all my fault. If she dies I will have killed her.'

'Now, now.' He rocked her to and fro in his arms. 'Don't be silly, how can it be your fault?'

'Because she came here on Wednesday and asked me for money and I said I didn't have any so she went and got rid of the baby herself and ended up in hospital, and Col must have found out and that's why he did it.'

The pieces of the jigsaw were beginning to fit. 'You mean Sylvia was pregnant and wanted to have an abortion, but didn't have the money, so she did it to herself and Col found out and...' Les paused, 'and did that to her?'

Dianne nodded into his chest.

'Why didn't she have the baby? One more wouldn't make much difference.'

'Because it wasn't Col's. It was a white one,' she told him, and began a renewed spate of sobs.

Les closed his eyes. 'Oh my God.' Then he opened them and asked, 'Well, if she told you all this and asked you for some money, why didn't you give her some?'

Her sobs stopped, she flung herself off the bed and then turned back to face him. 'Because I don't have any, you stupid bastard.'

Les flinched. She had never before sworn directly at him, nor had he ever seen her face so distorted with anger and even hatred. Anger for him? Les shivered involuntarily. 'But why didn't you ask me for some?' he said simply.

'Why?' she screamed. 'Because I never have and I never will. I'll take what you give, but I'll never ask, what d'you think I am, your black whore?'

'Dianne...'

'Dianne, Dianne. Don't you Dianne me. It's true, that's all I am. I might just as well be handing out my favours round the West as living in this place. At least I'd be with my own people.'

She'd never talked about the Aborigines as her own people before. He sat very still with his head down, looking at the pattern on the imported German rug, but not registering it.

'I thought I could become like a white woman just by living like one. Shit!' She swept her hand over a low dressing table, knocking perfumes and cosmetics on to the floor. Some of them collided and smashed and Les watched as the contents seeped into the pile of the rug.

'And what am I left with? Nothing. No family. No friends Oh, yes, your white friends appear friendly enough, they'll still drink with you in the hotel, but do they ever ask us to their homes? No. Nor do any of my friends or even my family. I haven't seen Mum for over a bloody year, and she only lives down at the West. I haven't been to the West for all that time The only member of my family I've seen has been Sylvia and she only comes to me when she needs money. They despise me, do you know that? Yes, they do. I used to despise them for not getting off their arses and doing something for themselves. I thought I was the smart one, the clever one who got herself a white-fellow. But now they despise me and they're right too. All I am is a whitefellow's wife. What does that make me? Worse than dirt. A kept woman who can't even ask for money to help her sister. Shit! Shit! Shit!'

Dianne dropped amongst the broken bottles and jars and began to sob again. Much of what she'd said hadn't been her true feelings, but more self-abuse. She hadn't really married Les simply in an attempt to become a white woman, she had married him also because she loved him. But she wanted, needed, to punish herself, and a single thought kept repeating itself in her mind: Why didn't I get the money for her?

Les didn't understand the ramifications of his wife's guilt. All he felt was that his world had crumbled. He loved Dianne and their children. He thought of her simply as a woman, not a black woman. He never analysed why he loved her or had married her. What she had said was an attack on everything he had always happily taken for granted. His reaction was to need to get away, and he ran from the room, leaving her sobbing on the floor.

He'd spent the night in his car somewhere on the road between Woongarra and Goodooga. He hadn't slept much, just pushed the reclining car seats back and looked out into the vastness of the night sky, dense with bright stars. He must have dropped off about four o'clock, f when he woke with a start it was already daylight. He drove slowly back down to the meat works, glad that at least, as it was Saturday, he'd only have to work half a day.

The men were waiting for him, smoking on the loading bays, and he realized that they must all know about the attack on his wife's sister. In strained silence he opened up and gave them their orders for the morning before retiring to his office, where he now sat trying to concentrate on a backlog of paperwork. He systematically pushed every thought of Dianne, his children, Sylvia and Col from his mind.

At nine-thirty his door opened and he looked up expecting to see his secretary, who was invariably late and always profusely apologetic. Instead it was his wife. Dianne Cullen stood hesitantly in the doorway. Les got up. She was the first to speak. 'I'm sorry, Les.'

He walked quickly across to her and wrapped his arms around her. 'It's all right, Di,' he said. And then, 'We'll work things out.'

Over her shoulder through the open door he saw Bob Foster glance at him before he sliced up another carcass.


Almost every Saturday evening for the past twenty-one years George Davies had led a street service in the main street of the town between the Imperial and the Woongarra hotels. The only times he missed were when he was ill, which was practically never, or when he was in Sydney or Canberra talking to government people, lawyers or social workers about his extended family. Those were the only matters which he would allow to prevent his being there in the street on Saturday evening. In twenty-one years he had probably missed only a dozen services.

Tonight there were eleven members of the gospel church at the service. Ten really, because George didn't count Bruce Stannard. For a start he was white and also George knew that Bruce wasn't totally committed to the faith; that he found difficulty in accepting even such basic tenets as the creation of the universe in seven days or the picture of hell fire and damnation which George painted and promised to all those who did not accept the faith in its totality.

Still, George thought, I suppose I should be grateful for every small mercy, and it's a fact that since Bruce started coming along with his guitar a few of the young ones have been more regular in their attendance. He looked round at the members. They were all familiar faces, the only unusual one was Richard Brown, who hung back self-consciously at the edge of the group. George felt sorry for the boy: his own past so nearly echoed Richard's experiences.George's father had died too when he was only fourteen, not in prison like Richard's, but by a gunshot in the head. The white farmer who fired the shot said in his defence that he had thought George's father was an illegal roo-shooter. He said no one had been more surprised or sorry than he, when he found out that what he had taken to be a gun in the man's hand was merely a stick, and that he had shot one of his finest stockmen. The court had accepted his explanation and public apology to George Davies's mother, but that didn't help her much with bringing up thirteen children.

Before she had time to recover from her sudden bereavement, George had already taken himself out of school and started to drink, which at that time was still illegal for Aborigines.It took the police three months to discover who was breaking into the storeroom at the Imperial and stealing large quantities of cheap port, and when they realized they had been tricked by a fourteen-year-old boy, they were so incensed that they committed him to state care, even though it was only his first offence.

It was his experiences in orphanages in Sydney, experiences which he had buried deep in his mind and refused to recall, which later in life made George decide to run a home of his own for state wards. But before that eventuated, he spent nine hideous years in and out of courts, orphanages and prison. It was in prison that he met an evangelist, a woman, who came once a week to talk to any of the prisoners who would listen. Most of the prisoners only went along for a laugh and to break the boredom of prison routine, but right from the start George could see some glimmering of salvation in her teaching. By the time he finished his two-year sentence, he was quite certain what he wanted to do: that he had been called by the Lord to give up drinking, smoking, gambling and swearing, and to return to Woongarra to help his people.

George knew the words of all the songs so well that he could sing them automatically, leaving his mind free to consider other matters. He looked again around the group and wondered how many people would consider it a worthwhile lifetime project. I'm forty-seven, he thought, and so far I've brought up thirty-seven children plus my own four. If the Lord allows me another twenty years I may manage another fifteen. George knew he'd have to accept at least a ten per cent failure rate, so that left about forty at best who might make something of their lives. Forty, he sighed. Forty out of all those thousands.

A group of about ten young Aboriginal men came out of the Garra, singing noisily and colliding intentionally with one another. George had his back to them but he saw Richard Brown stiffen and look about for a place to hide. George kept staring at the boy and when, in his panic, Richard caught his look, George's eyes compelled him to stay still.

Jesus, man, look who's here!' George recognized the voice of Bob Foster. 'It's bloody Richard.What you doing with this mob of bloody idiots, eh?'

The young men had circled the group of worshippers and Bob Foster lurched into Richard.'Come on, mate, come and have a bloody drink. No good hanging round with this lot.'

George kept looking at Richard. The small band continued singing and only Bruce Stannard showed any sign of embarrassment. He muffed a couple of chords. Richard Brown wavered and, still with his eyes on George, opened his mouth to say something to Bob Foster. Suddenly George burst into a loud, solo, melodic accompaniment to the hymn, sending his voice deeper than the other singers and then higher. Richard shut his mouth and Dave Foster grabbed his brother by the arm.

'Come on, Bob,' he said, 'let the stupid bastards alone. If they want to waste their bloody time, let them.'

Bob staggered slightly, then righted himself and the two brothers, celebrating their self-dismissal from the kangaroo meat works, lurched off up the street to catch up with their friends.

Richard Brown lowered his eyes and George felt he had gained a small victory for the boy. If only he could have him out at his place for a while, George was sure that he could put the boy right again. He'd even approached his mother, Molly, with the suggestion, but at the time she had still been so distressed over her husband's death that he couldn't persuade her to make a decision.

For once, George thought, I would like to have a chance at prevention, rather than cure. George was sure that the boy would go bad. He knew Richard was already an alcoholic. He'll end up in the criminal court, George said to himself. Get sent down to a home in Sydney, because they never give me the older ones. Whenever I've tried it Pete Mathews has always worked against me. Just can't take it that I go my own way without grants or government aid.

George noticed that Richard had started to join in the singing. He thought again about Pete Mathews. A real little wheeler-dealer, always playing one group off against the other, too much of the whitefellow in him. Now he's sold out Doug Foster's kids just to get a grant. And it's only a promise, a whitefellow's promise. Worthless. George sighed. They use little power-hungry people like Pete Mathews to divide us. Divide and rule. And we're such fools, we let them.

George recalled the confrontation he'd had with Pete over renovations at the old mission.There had been nine-inch gaps between the wooden walls and sagging floorboards and George had asked the bank manager for a loan of two hundred dollars to buy the materials to do the job himself. The manager had refused on the grounds that George had no collateral and had suggested instead that he should stuff rags in to fill up the holes. George had been very, very angry but wouldn't give the white man the satisfaction of seeing it, so he said nothing.Obviously the bank manager was rather pleased with his behaviour because within three hours Pete Mathews came out to the old mission and told him the news was all over town that the bank manager had rejected his plea for help. 'You shouldn't go crawling to a white bastard like that for help,' he said 'it makes us look like idiots. You should apply for a building grant from the Department of Aboriginal Affairs.'

'No thanks, mate,' George said.

'Why not?'

'I'm old fashioned I suppose, but I don't like to be beholden to anyone, specially not a government department.'

'But it's our department.'

'Well you might think that, Pete,' George said, 'but to me it's still a whitefellow's outfit with a few token blacks to make it look respectable. I don't like politicians or politics. I like to do things for myself and then if they don't work out, I can only blame myself. But at least I don't have anyone else on my back telling me what to do or how to do it.'

'You're a fool,' Pete Mathews said bluntly.

George didn't get angry, he just said, 'Yep. An old fool, and you can't teach new tricks to an old fool,' and paused before finishing, 'only to young fools.'

Pete Mathews had left without saying another word. George had patched up the walls with bits of tin and wood he'd cadged off various people, and the two men had spoken to one another only when it was strictly necessary, at court cases usually, and then as little as possible.

Richard Brown was obviously enjoying himself now and singing quite unrestrainedly. George gave him a congratulatory smile. Another crowd came out of the Garra and up towards them, arguing noisily all the way. George turned to watch one of them who, with arms outstretched like a tightrope walker, was balancing precariously on the edge of the pavement. When he fell off into the gutter his friends screamed with laughter, and it was at this moment that Lesley Armstrong came out of the main door of the pub from behind them. George wondered what she had been doing in there, because he knew that she very rarely went to either pub. The young Aborigines whistled and hooted as she walked quickly past them, and she gave them a half-smile.

No doubt, George thought, they all know, like everyone else in this town full of busybodies, that she's sleeping with Allan Foster. You can't scratch yourself here without everyone talking about it. George couldn't help admiring Lesley, and even liking her a little, even though he disapproved very strongly of her morals. George wondered about the reasons why Lesley was having this affair with Allan Foster. If she thinks she's doing the black cause a good turn, she's barking up the wrong tree, he thought. Sleeping with a blackfellow isn't going to do any good. In fact it'll just make things worse. It'll only make the two of you unhappy.

Bruce Stannard had also noticed Lesley, and now looked down at his guitar and blushed. Lesley stepped down into the road to pass them. She was walking quickly, but she gave a small nod to George, who nodded back and continued to sing. When Bruce looked up, George caught his eye and saw the physical ache. Well young fellow, he thought, you can't blame Allan for getting it.You should have been a bit quicker off the mark, though I doubt if you're her type. Surprised and embarrassed by such a carnal thought, George Davies indicated to the worshippers that this was the last hymn, and prepared to begin his sermon on the evils of fornication and adultery.

Lesley hated going into the whitefellow's bars in the hotels, but she had to find Jeanna, and that was where she had been told Jeanna would be. She wanted to tell her that she wasn't angry with her for telling Gordon Wright about her relationship with Allan. Stupid bitch, she thought, annoyed at having to go into the bar, something she so intensely disliked. As if I'dblame her.

She'd looked into the white bar at the Garra, hoping to find Jeanna there, because she was even less happy about visiting the Imperial. But Jeanna hadn't been in the Garra, and if she didn't find her soon, Jeanna would miss out on the parade and judging at the RSL Ball.

Every year the RSL held a ball for the under-eighteens. It was a great social event for the bored white teenagers in Woongarra. Especially the girls, who spent weeks designing and making dresses. Some of them made special trips to Dubbo or even to Sydney to buy a dress for the occasion. Lesley knew that Jeanna had been looking forward to the ball and there had been much bitchy speculation amongst her friends about what she would wear. In a conspiratorial moment Jeanna had confided to Lesley that it was 'a knockout, bloody near topless'.

The boys pretended that they weren't very keen on the affair, mostly because there was no liquor sold, but they too put on their new or at least very best clothes. Every year the RSL hired a band; this time they'd got The Rockaires, a group well known in the northern part of the State, where they travelled up to five hundred miles to play for an evening. And every year the boys smuggled alcohol into the club and several got drunk and threw up. It was all part of the occasion and the evening wouldn't have been considered a success without it, any more than it would have been without the crepe paper decorations and the limp balloons.

This year there was an additional attraction. There was a Belle of the Ball competition, judged by the wives of RSL committee members. The winner would have a weekend in SurfersParadise for two, and the prize was to be awarded by a young man described on the programme as 'star of country television, Dubbo's own Garth Hudson'.

Every teacher from the high school was expected to attend, partly to chaperone their pupils, but also because the young people wanted to show how grown-up they could look to the people who only ever saw them as children. A few weeks ago when Lesley had been asked she had agreed to come, but not before she had told her whole class that this was the only occasion she would visit the club, because she didn't approve of its policy of not admitting Aborigines. Almost none of the twenty-six black children in her class of thirty-three could have cared less whether their teacher went to the white kids' ball or not. But there were two or three of them whom she felt she was beginning to relate to, and who were glad that she had said this in front of the white kids, all of whom ignored her explanations, except for Jeanna who had actually cheered her remarks. As she did, one of the white boys, a young Dargan, had turned round to Jeanna and said, 'If you're so bloody keen on the boongs why d'you want to come to the dance yourself then?'

'Because what else is there to do in Woongarra?' Lesley had answered for her, and Jeanna had stayed thankfully silent.

And then, when Lesley had heard that there was to be a fund-raising dance for Gary Andrew's widow, held on the same night in the Memorial Hall, she had been very tempted to give that as an excuse not to attend the ball. But in the end she had decided that she must at least put in an appearance. Because of all this, Lesley was even more disappointed when she heard that Jeanna had decided that she couldn't face her at the ball. She hadn't come to school on either Thursday or Friday after Lesley had been confronted by Gordon Wright, and Lesley had felt it best to leave Jeanna to make her own decision about when she would come, and explain to her how Gordon was told about her affair with Allan Foster. She was disappointed that the girl was now behaving in such a childish manner.

Lesley had overheard a conversation she was obviously intended to overhear between a couple of girls in the class. They could hardly conceal their delight over the news that Jeanna had decided not to come, because they knew she was certain to outshine every other girl there.'She says she's going to get pissed instead, miss,' one girl said. Taking great pleasure in using such language, she added, 'that's Jeanna's word, not mine.' Her friend giggled, and Lesley marvelled, as she often did, at the absolute inanity of most teenage girls.

'I see, and did she say where she was going to get pissed?' Lesley underlined the word to make the girl realize that she was neither amused nor impressed.

'Yes miss, up at the hotel.'

'Which one?'

'Oh, I don't know that miss,' and the other one spoke up, 'But she'll be in the whitefellow's bar, that's for sure.'

Lesley hadn't even bothered to make a reply.

So here she was pushing open the door to the Imperial's little saloon bar and seeing a crowd of white, male faces turn towards her.

'Well now, if it isn't the blackfellow's delight,' someone said, and someone else opened the door wide and grabbed her around the waist, forcing her in, closing the door behind, and propelling her towards the bar. 'What'll you have to drink? Bottle of plonk, eh? Or would you like some port?'

Lesley looked quickly round the room at the sea of faces. She knew almost all of them by sight, but only a few by name. Jim Dargan sat on a stool beside his father, among a group of other people from properties around the area. Fred Pepper was lounging by the fireplace which was empty on this hot summer evening, and beside him was John Smith, the Clerk of Petty Sessions, and Sergeant Ron Evans, who was still in uniform, and had been on duty for eight hours straight because the station was now under-manned as a result of Ed Vickers's suspension. Father Clancy had propped his large stomach against one end of the bar alongside Johnny Phillips, and next to them were three strangers, whom she guessed correctly were Greg Fletcher and his friends. Harry Fletcher stood smirking at her from behind the bar.When his brother had told him what Jeanna had said about Allan Foster's visits to Lesley's rooms, he'd been delighted to help spread the news among his customers. Unconsciously he felt that this gossip helped take the heat off the possibility of too many people finding out about his own exploits in the West.

Lesley was surprised to see Gordon Wright, who had always intimated that the hotels were hardly the sort of place at which he would choose to drink. But then she realized that he had been ousted from drinking at his favourite place, the RSL, by the ball, which reminded her of why she was here, and seeing that Jeanna was not around, she tried to pull away from the man who held her by the waist. She didn't know him by name, only that he had a property out on the Bourke road, and didn't come into town very often. He looked about fifty, and was obviously rather drunk.

'Please let go of me,' she demanded, and when he didn't she tried to unloose his grip. He held her tight, pulling her up close to his face so that she smelt the alcohol on his breath.

'Wha's matter,' he slurred his words, 'don't you like whi'fellows?'

She brought her other hand round to push at his chest, but he caught her wrist and bent it back. She gasped a little at the sharp pain. The bar was very silent. No one spoke. Lesley looked quickly at the other men, and registering the antipathy towards her in their faces, shewent cold with fear.

'Mind you don't get too close to her,' someone in Jim Dargan's group said, 'never know what you might catch from a blackfeller's tart.'

'Yeh, blackfeller's clap is a pretty rough dose,' his friend Said, 'rots your brains and you end up like them; only good for the knacker's yard.'

Jim Dargan laughed and asked, 'Does he really have a twelve-inch prick or is that just another Dreamtime legend?'

Lesley could tolerate prejudice and racial bigotry from people she didn't know, because she could tell herself that perhaps they didn't know any better, but she knew Jim Dargan had been educated at King's School in Sydney, and had had all the advantages of being the son of an affluent white grazier. He had asked her out to his place a couple of times when she first arrived in Woongarra. On the second occasion he had taken her out into the bush on his motorbike and then threatened to leave her there unless she had intercourse with him. She'd refused, and he'd ridden off. She'd told herself that it was just to scare her, but even so she was very relieved an hour later to hear the bike coming back. He hadn't said anything, just picked her up and ridden back to the property from where she had driven herself back to town. She hadn't seen him since, and now he taunted her: 'Well, come on now. You're not afraid to admit you've been sleeping with the blackfellows, are you?'

The fear left her and in its place she felt an icy anger. 'No,' she said. 'I don't have anything to be ashamed of. He didn't have to force me. I did it voluntarily. He didn't have to threaten me like you did.'

A couple of the men chuckled, and Jim Dargan took a swig of beer to cover his embarrassment.

'I'm not ashamed of sleeping with Allan Foster, he's a good man, an honest man.'

'Yes, but is he a good fuck?' someone yelled.

So, she thought, they want a confrontation. Well, then they shall have one. And she gathered herself together before replying, 'Yes, he's a good fuck too, if that's what you want to know.'

'He's a fucking bludger, that's what I know,' Harry Fletcher said. 'Just like all the rest of them, they'd all be better off with a bullet between the eyes.'

'Nah, that'd be too bloody quick,' someone said, 'more fun to pour sheep dip in the water tank across at the wild West and poison 'em.'

'Bit cruel aren't you, mate?' someone else said. 'Do just as well filling the tank with plonk and let them drink themselves to death.'

'They're doing that already,' Harry said.

'Well, you're making a bloody good living out of selling it to them, aren't you?' Lesley shouted. 'You came up here two years ago with nothing and now you've paid the place off and you're sticking money in the bank as fast as you can. Saving up for that place in Surfers.Well there won't be any black girls up there for you to screw when your wife won't come across.

Up there in Surfers you'll have to pay more than half a flagon of wine like you do now, over in the West.'

Harry Fletcher leant across the counter, his face contorted with rage. 'You watch what you're saying, you fucking little whore,' he said. 'I'll break every bone in your body as soon as look at you, if you go round spreading rumours like that about me.

In the crackling silence, she flung herself into the middle of the room and turned a full circle, so as to include every one of them. 'What's the matter with you all? You have everything you want. You're the lucky ones, the lucky white bastards. Why can't you find it in your hearts to have a little love and humanity for those who aren't so bloody lucky?'

'We'll leave the loving to you,' Father Clancy said, easing his beer gut off the counter, 'but as for the humanity, we've all tried that, and where does that get us? Nowhere. They don't want anyone to help them. They're happy as they are.'

'Happy!' She spat out the word. 'Do you think Jerry Brown was happy when his wife had to have her breast removed and he was left on his own to look after eleven children? D'you think it was happiness which drove him to steal groceries from your house? Have you ever stopped to consider how desperate a man must be before he's reduced to stealing basics like bread and butter, sugar and milk? Have you ever imagined what you would do if you were that desperate? Or are you so insulated by your colour television and your bar full of cocktails that you are unable to imagine what it's like to be so desperate? Happy! By Christ, d'you think Jerry was happy when you hounded him to prison and he was left there to worry about how his wife was coping, and to pine to death?

To die in a stinking hole like that. Just like a trapped rat; and to be buried in an unmarked official grave. Happy? Is that how he died? Happy! You and Your lousy, stinking religion which exonerates you from having a personal conscience. I hope for your sake that your god is happy enough about your loveless-ness to forgive you.'

A few of the men shifted uneasily, and from the back bar the strains of 'Black Superman' wafted through the tense air of the saloon bar.

It was Sergeant Evans who spoke. 'If they're not happy, it's their own fault. We give them every-thing they ask for. It's us that's the underprivileged ones and the endangered species. If this government goes on spending money on them the way they are at the moment, the bloody country will go bankrupt and where will the bloody boongs be then? Tell me that. If it wasn't for us they'd still be living in the bloody stone age.'

'Perhaps that's so,' Lesley answered. 'But does it ever occur to you that they might have been better off? What have we given them that's so bloody great? They had a good thing going. A social structure which would be envied by most people today, enough to eat and a whole country to live in. What have we given them? Roads and bridges of course, and rules and regulations, and a system which is so complicated to find a way round that they are likely to meet them-selves coming backwards and give up before they start. Then of course there's the ten-dollar fines to pe-nalize them for a habit which we gave them, and the forty-eight hours in prison to protect them from themselves, so you say, and a compulsory shower and hair wash with Lysol to get rid of the fleas and lice.

We've taken away the authority of their elders and re-placed it with whiteman's rules, corrupt whiteman's rules.' She looked straight at Ron Evans. 'And if they don't or can't fit into your image of a law-abiding citizen, you can put them inside our jails, where they are put upon by every perverted warden and prisoner who isn't game enough to try it on with white prisoners.' She paused. 'All they want is a fair go.' The Australian phrase came easily to her English tongue for the first time.

'A fair go be buggered,' Fred Pepper said. It was the first time she'd ever heard him speak.Usually he preferred to remain silently in the background. 'Their idea of a fair go is the whole of the Northern Territory and that was what they were asking for last month. Christ knows what they want now. They should be satisfied with what they've got. They get a damn sight more than the whitefellows and we have just as much right to live in Australia now as they have. At least we work for a living. The bloody government pays them so much for bludging that they're better off not working. The government pays them to have kids. To feed and educate them. It gives them houses to live in and free medical care. Christ, what else do they want?'

There was a murmur of approval around the small room.

'Dignity and self-respect,' said Lesley.

'A man has to earn that,' Fred Pepper replied. 'That's one thing that doesn't come bloody free.'

'No more than the sly grog and methylated spirits you sell four times a day over at the West.'

A few of the men looked in surprise at Fred Pepper. Noticing this, Lesley said, 'That's right, gentlemen, that's what this man is. A sly-grog and metho merchant. With the approval of the Sergeant of Police here, whom he keeps supplied with fish. He sells it to the bloody boongs, taking advantage of their inability to cope with alcohol. Here's the man who murdered Gary Andrews, whose widow now has five kids to support.'

She turned back to Father Clancy, 'But then you'd know all about that, wouldn't you Father? The Sergeant and Mr Pepper, being the good Catholics they are, must have confessed these crimes to you.' Father Clancy scowled at her. She turned to Fred Pepper again. 'But you're not satisfied with just one murder, are you? Now you've got Bill Flinders on the stuff too. Do you know what methylated spirits does to a body, Mr Pepper? Black or white. It rots the brain cells; it causes paralysis by destroying the motor nerves. It eats a man alive. If it's as good as you tell us to be a bloody boong, Mr Pepper, why do you prefer to be a white man? Perhaps it's because you make such a good living out of slowly torturing them to death.'

'That's all they're bloody good for,' he snarled. 'That and white sluts like you.'

'And what about you, Gordon?' She took a step towards the headmaster. 'You're very quiet.Don't you have some insult you'd like to hurl at me? Don't you want to tell me how the blacks are all ineducable? Don't you want to come out with one of your excruciatingly unfunny puns and witticisms at their expense which illustrate your superior intelligence, and tell us how they are all of below normal intellectual capabilities, with the IQs of four-year-olds, and that a white man's education is wasted on them?'

Gordon Wright said nothing, just sipped his brandy and dry.

'Do none of you feel guilty?' She wheeled around the room. 'Is there not one of you who can find it in his heart to show a little compassion? By Christ, you've taken their country, destroyed their culture, killed thousands of them. They're a dying race. It's obvious that they'll go the way of all minorities and be swallowed up by the strongest ones, the aggressive white Aryans like you and me.' She was crying and shouting through her tears.

'Can't you find it in your hearts to ease their going? Must you kick them when they're down? Why are you so afraid of them? Is it that you feel guilty? Do you feel anything?'

The men were silent as she rushed at the door and flung it open. They heard her as she fled upstairs and into the ladies' toilet. She threw herself against the tiled wall and sobbed for several minutes, gradually becoming calm. Then she splashed cold water on her face, and looking ruefully at her blotchy skin and swollen eyes, she decided that she must go home and change and go to the ball. She'd done her best to find Jeanna. She couldn't let her other pupils down.

Coming out of the swing door into the corridor, she heard someone call, 'Is that you Harry?' and stopped. The voice came from one of the hotel's bedrooms further up the corridor. She went back and stood outside. The voice called again.

'Come on, Harry Fletcher, I'm waiting for you.'
Lesley opened the door slowly. Reclining on the bed, naked, smoking, and with a beer can in one hand, was Jeanna Taylor.

'Jesus, Harry, I thought you weren't ever coming back.' she said, and then, seeing Lesley, she clutched at a sheet and dragged it up over her, spilling the beer and burning a hole in the cover at the same time.

# CHAPTER NINE

## SATURDAY

The doctor slumped on to a hard chair. Across the chest of his green operating coat tiny drops of blood had spattered and dried, but on his rubber gloves it was still sticky. He pulled them off and dropped them uncaringly on the theatre floor, and scrubbed at his eyes with his clenched fists. It had been a long and difficult operation, the result of which had overwhelmed him.

Sister Hutchins stood wearily beside him. Her arms hanging limp, she waited and watched while the nurse made the final adjustments to the humidicrib.

'Will you tell him or shall I?' Phyllis Hutchins asked, pulling the gauze mask down off her face. Doctor Hitchcock made no move. 'I shall then,' she said, and as he still said nothing, she took that as assent.

She didn't know why she had taken this awful job on herself, when really the doctor should do it. Perhaps it was just that she felt she could break the news more gently, but it was also that she had become personally involved with Doug Foster: something which she knew a nurse should never do. She hoped that her professionalism hadn't slipped too far and that she could rely on it to help her through what she knew was going to be a very difficult time,

The nurse had finished, and glanced towards Sister Hutchins.

'Right then?' Phyllis asked. The nurse nodded. 'OK then, let's go.'

Dr Hitchcock didn't even look up as the two women wheeled the crib past him and out through the heavy swing doors. In the small protective sterile corridor the two nurses looked quickly at each other over the top of the crib and readied themselves for what was bound to come.

On the other side of the doors, Doug Foster paced up and down. He was drawn, haggard and pallid under his dark skin. He'd been at the hospital now for thirty-seven hours, but it seemed like much longer than that. So long that the bare, white, tiled walls, glaring neon lights, heavy smell of disinfectant and the sound of hushed voices had become reality and the idea of another sort of life going on anywhere else seemed unreal. He had the curious sensation of being suspended in time, of being one stage removed from events and of viewing them through a clouded screen. Sometimes he wondered if all this wasn't a dream from which he would wake and find himself down by the river, dozing over a fishing line, or perhaps he would come to on his prison bunk. Or was prison another dream? Then he would shake his head and go to the front door to take great gulps of fresh air.

He'd had nothing to eat since morning, when he'd gone across to the cafe for half an hour and hurriedly eaten some steak and eggs and a large cup of coffee. But he was past hunger. He'd tried to snooze on the hard waiting bench, but his mind kept playing tricks with him, throwing up jumbled, half-forgotten memories and mixing them with his plans for the future. He was past sleep.

How much bloody longer can they be? he thought. They've had her in there for bloody hours.He wasn't sure exactly how long it had been because he'd lost track of time, but he knew there had still been bright mid-afternoon sunlight pouring through the windows when Dr Hitchcock had come into the ward, where he was sitting beside Flo's bed. 'Excuse me, Mr. Foster,' he'd said, 'I'd like to examine your wife. Would you please wait in the corridor?'

Over the past two days all the hospital staff, including Dr Hitchcock, had become increasingly polite and friendly towards Doug. He heard Flo sigh with pain before the doctor joined him. He was grim-faced. 'I'm sorry, Mr Foster, but I'm going to have to operate.'

Doug went back into Flo's room to have a last word with her, but she was already only semi-conscious from the injection she'd been given. He stroked her hand until the orderlies came and moved her over on to a trolley. Then he sat and watched as they rolled her away. The last view he'd had of his wife was the huge stomach disappearing towards the operating theatre.

Now the heavy swing doors burst open again and he stopped pacing for a second before running towards Sister Hutchins. 'What is it? What's happened? How is she?'

Sister Hutchins put her hand up. 'She's fine, it's a boy and everything is going to be all right.'

The nurses kept walking quickly. Doug fell in beside them and stared down into the humidicrib at the tiny silent thing. There was a tube pushed up one nostril and another one down its throat. It was naked except for a patch of bloody gauze over the severed umbilical cord. He immediately registered that there was something strange about the baby, but it took him several seconds to realize what, and all the time he had to almost run to keep up with the pace of the two women.

As they turned to go into the nursery the quality of the oddity formed into words and Doug shouted, 'Why's its head so big?'

Sister Hutchins put up her hand to silence him. 'I'll be with you in a minute,' she said, and shut the glass door in his face.

Doug walked back a few steps, clinging to the glass wall of the nursery, peering in as the women worked smoothly and efficiently, reconnecting the humidicrib, adjusting the thermometer and linking up the complicated equipment. Doug kept staring at the creature over which they were taking such infinite care. It was long and thin. Its soft brown limbs lay limply on the sheet and its genitals were swollen. None of this did Doug look at because he couldn't take his eyes off the grossly distorted head, so huge it made the rest of the body appear wasted. It looked like a parody of a baby, the sort of thing a child might draw, or a pregnant woman see in nightmares. There were two small red marks, one on each temple. Its eyes were closed and it lay very still.

It's dead, Doug suddenly thought. Thank God it's dead. The thought came to him from nowhere, but he hugged it to himself. It's dead. They didn't like to tell me. But once they see that I don't mind, they'll come and say so. A wave of relief swept over him, making him feel weak in the knees.

Then he saw that the young nurse was holding the baby's arm while Sister Hutchins inserted a large needle into the vein. Just as suddenly he realized that they were trying to save its life.He hammered on the glass, yelling, 'No. No.'

Sister Hutchins looked up and frowned at him, but he continued to hammer. She finished inserting the needle, spoke briefly to the nurse, who nodded her reply, and then came briskly out into the corridor.

'Mr. Foster, stop that at once,' she commanded.

'But it's dead,' he shouted. 'Leave it dead.'

'It's nothing of the sort, Mr. Foster. Your baby is very much alive and we'll do all we can to make sure it stays that way.'

'But why?' He stared at her in amazement. 'Look at its head. Can't you see? It's got something wrong with it. Look at it.' He flung himself at the glass again and watched as the nurse closed down the crib. 'Jesus Christ, what's wrong with it?' he yelled.

Sister Phyllis Hutchins sighed and put her hand on his shoulder.

'Mr. Foster, I'm sorry. Truly I am very sorry. You can see for yourself that your son is not quite right.'

'Not quite right!' he yelled. 'It's a monster. It's not my son. It's a monster!'

'Mr. Foster! 'Her voice was sharp now. 'Pull yourself together. There are far worse things which could have happened. At least your wife is going to be all right. Now, be a man about it.You have a deformed child with probably quite an amount of brain damage. It may be superficial, it may not. We'll have to wait to find that out. But it's a fact, and now you must stop this nonsense.'

He continued to press his big hands and his face against the glass, flattening his nose, to stare through at the grossly deformed child. Then suddenly great sobs of anguish burst from him and he slithered down the glass and lay in a crumpled heap on the corridor floor.

Sister Hutchins knelt beside him and took his large hand in hers. 'I'm so sorry,' she kept repeating. Eventually he turned his tear-swollen face towards her, wiping his nose with his other hand.'Let it die,' he breathed - 'Please let it die.'

She shook her head slowly. 'I can't. I can't.'

And though Sister Phyllis Hutchins did nothing positive to help the child live, she couldn't bring herself to do anything negative. So with the miraculous aid of twentieth century medicine, the mongoloid boy was destined to live for twelve years.

After a while Sister Hutchins and Doug got up off the highly polished institutional linoleum, and she took him into the intensive care ward to see his wife. Flo was snoring heavily. Her mouth open. Despite the fresh, raffish bandage which still covered her right eye and ear, she looked relaxed and smooth-skinned. The covers lay flat across her stomach. She looked as he had always pictured her when he conjured up visions of her as he lay on his prison bed. She's beautiful, Doug thought, and wishing that he could capture the moment forever, he bent down and kissed his wife on the mouth for the last time.

In the next ward, Dr Hitchcock leant across and closed Sylvia Richards' staring eyes, before pulling the sheet up over her face.

The Rockaires were in full swing by the time Lesley arrived at the RSL Club. The singer had wrapped himself around the microphone in a poor imitation of someone he'd obviously seen on television. Below the stage, on the floor, no one took any notice at all of their posturing, they were too busy dancing, and those who weren't dancing were eyeing up possible partners.

Lesley squeezed between the poker machines and the tables which were crowded with young men drinking large glasses of what had started out as lemonade, but was now, after the addition of large quantities of beer poured surreptitiously from cans wrapped in brown paper bags, very strong shandy. Someone pinched her bottom as she eased her way through,and this was followed by a burst of barely stifled laughter. She didn't bother to turn round,but just struggled on until she reached the edge of the floor where she stood and watched the dancers. It was odd to see children with whom she had spent hours, trying to whip up an enthusiasm, or simply an interest in social issues, dressed in their very best clothes and trying desperately to appear adult. Some of the girls were as unrecognizable as a frog would be to a tadpole. When the number finished and the band announced that it was taking a ten-minute break, there was a small amount of scattered applause and the couples immediately separated, as if relieved to be free of each other's grasp.

The boys all rushed the bar, bought glasses of lemonade and then rejoined their friends at the tables. The girls went to the tables around the walls of the big hall, where they sipped their soft drinks and began to compare notes about their experiences on the dance floor. Several of the girls walked self-consciously up through the hall towards the ladies' room, smiling artificially at one another and adjusting their unaccustomed long dresses. As they got closer to where the boys sat, they shot quick, hopefully suggestive looks in that direction.

Several of the twisted crepe paper streamers had come unpinned and floated negligently from the centre of the ceiling. A small dark-haired girl suddenly leapt on to her table and reaching up with her cigarette, popped two or three balloons in the cluster above her head. As she sat down again her friends all burst into uncontrolled laughter and looked around to see who they had impressed.

One of them saw Lesley and called, 'Miss Armstrong! Miss Armstrong!' signalling for her to join them. It was a moment before she recognized Jeanna's classmate under the lashings of makeup and the long flowery gown, and as she walked towards her, she cursed herself for not having had the foresight to have a drink before coming to the dance. She hardly ever drank,but she felt that she could have done with one tonight.

'Hello Miss Armstrong,' the girl smirked. 'We were worried you wouldn't ever get here. Did you find Jeanna?

'No, I'm afraid I didn't,' she lied.

'Oh, what a pity,' the girl said with such insincerity that even she had the grace to blush before adding significantly, 'Well she must have gone off somewhere, mustn't she? Pity she missed the parade and the judging.'

'Yes.' Lesley sensed that more was expected of her and she asked, 'Who won?'

With false modesty the girl looked down and then up, 'Well I did, miss.'

'That's lovely, congratulations, and now if you'll...'but she didn't have to excuse herself because The Rockaires returned and with no introduction launched into a loud number, the lead guitarist immediately beginning to gyrate as if he were a mechanical doll which someone had wound up and let go.

The girls pretended to continue talking to one another, while all the time they were watching out of the comers of their eyes and waiting hopefully for the young men to put their shandies down and casually saunter towards them like birds seeking their prey. The first couples who started to dance were whistled and hooted at as they clung to the edge of the floor. Then a few more joined them and gradually the dance area filled with empty smiling faces.

Lesley felt a tap on her shoulder and turned to face the young Dargan from her class, Jim's younger brother Dick.

'Dance?' he demanded rather than asked.
She almost refused, but then realizing that his friends were watching, and that he had probably been dared by them to ask her, she decided that it would be churlish to embarrass him, so she smiled and inclined her head.

She was surprised at how well he danced, but then she remembered that he had followed his brother to King's School in Sydney for two years before dropping out through a mixture of boredom and distaste to return home. No doubt he's had plenty of practice in various Kings Cross nightspots, she thought. Smiling a little the whole while, Dick Dargan shook and stepped and swivelled and swayed in easy time with the slightly unsyncopated music. Entering into the spirit of the occasion, Lesley danced a few feet away from him, and actually began to enjoy herself. It was so long since she'd danced, and it was one of the things she enjoyed enormously. A couple of numbers later she had begun to let herself go and her uninhibited dancing was raising a few eyebrows among some of the parents who had escorted their children and were sitting in a far corner of the hall. She knew it, but didn't care. It was a great release.

She could understand why Jeanna felt trapped in Woongarra and why she went easily from man to man. The pressure-cooker atmosphere of a small town made everyone, black and white, behave in an exaggerated way. Something which would pass as merely an unimportant detail in a bigger town, here assumed enormous proportions. Living in a tiny township like Woongarra, isolated mentally and physically from other ways of life, created an artificial situation in which rumours and gossip sprouted like fungus, causing emotions to mount until they had to be vented in drink, sex or violence.

Tonight, she thought, I'll dance it off. I'll dance till it doesn't matter that everyone in this hall knows about Allan and me. I'll dance till I don't care about Gordon Wright, or Father Clancy or Sergeant Evans or Fred Pepper or Harry Fletcher and Jeanna or Jim Dargan. Thinking of Jim reminded her that she was dancing with his brother. She smiled at him and he grinned back. She wondered briefly if he also danced to purge himself, but her thoughts were interrupted by the singer who huffed into the microphone in what he hoped was a sensuous manner: 'And now ... for all those out there who are in love... or for all those who can remember ... we'll play a slow one so that you can hold her in your arms.' He gave a throaty chuckle and there was an air of eager anticipation in the hall.

Lesley moved to leave the floor, but Dick Dargan caught her in his arms and, surprised by the young man's strength, she let him hold her close and propel her slowly round the room.They shuffled past the other couples and she smelt beer and his after-shave as he put his face against hers. Cheeky little bastard, she thought, and grinned, and was still grinning when she saw, over Dick's shoulder, Gordon Wright come in through the door followed by Father Clancy and Johnny Phillips. They all made for the bar and Lesley realized that it must be eleven o'clock, closing time. She wondered if Harry Fletcher would come over, or if he would be otherwise occupied. Her grin grew wider as she imagined how he would feel when Jeanna told him what Lesley had seen. She felt so generally pleased with herself and life that she leant back a little way in Dick Dargan's arms to smile and say, 'A good night, eh?'

It was then that a scuffle broke out at the door, but Lesley didn't see it begin, because Dick Dargan chose that moment to spin her round and laugh in agreement.

'What you doing here, black boy?'

Jim Dargan tried to shoulder Allan Foster aside. The frosted glass front door of the RSL slammed shut and Allan, who had been holding it open and peering inside to see if he could spot Lesley, had to hang on to the handle to prevent himself from toppling down the stairs.

He righted himself and glared at Jim Dargan, narrowing his eyes and flexing his shoulders.On the steps below Dargan stood two of the other young men who'd also been drinking in theImperial with Dargan.

'Well, if it isn't the walking prick,' one of them said.

'Yeh, it's Woongarra's big black stud,' said the other.

Allan cursed himself for coming to the RSL but when his brother had told him about the baby,without knowing why, he felt he had to tell Lesley. Allan ignored the other two and giving onewithering look at Jim Dargan he made to walk past him and down the steps.

As Allan stepped down, Dargan shoved him with all his weight, but as he fell, Allan grabbed at Dargan's leg and brought him over on top of him. They landed on some freshly watered balsam, which was smashed to a pulp by the men's weight and spread greenish waxy slime over their shirts.

As Allan struggled to get up, Dargan threw himself on top of him and the two men rolled over and over, grappling with one another, trying to land punches. Allan fought free and managed to get up and sit astride Jim Dargan, pinning his arms to the earth. Both men were breathing heavily.

'Get this black bastard off me, will you?' Dargan yelled, and Allan just had time to land a fearful blow on Dargan's cheek before he was hauled off from behind by the other two men. Dargan scrambled up, the bruise already beginning to swell on his face- The men twisted both Allan's arms back behind him, that he doubled forward and one of them grabbed him by the hair, Pulling his head back so that his jaw jutted out ready to take Jim Dargan's fist. As Dargan aimed, Allan gathered all his strength and with an athlete's precision timing, just as Dargan's fist was on its way, kicked both his feet forward with all his might into Dargan's groin.

The pain in Allan's arms, as he swung on them and they were wrenched upwards behind him, matched the blinding pain in Dargan's groin. But whereas Allan's pain ceased immediately when the two men let him fall to the ground as they dashed to the aid of their friend, Dargan doubled up on the grass as the pain grew in his stomach, swelled and filled his whole being, until he retched spontaneously. With his three attackers occupied, Allan got up and had half-turned to run when he collided with Harry Fletcher and Sergeant Ron Evans. 'Oh no you don't, my boy,' Evans said. 'We saw that, and there's no getting away with that sort of behaviour.'

Allan put his fists up as Harry, seizing the opportunity to express the anger which had been seething inside him since Jeanna had told him half an hour earlier that Lesley had found them out, lunged at Allan yelling, 'Come on, you black bastard, I'll teach you what happens to boongs who fuck white women.'

Harry was wearing one of his large checked sports jackets. He jumped up and down in front of the much bigger man and as he finally reached out his fist, Allan simply put his forearm toward off the blow and then knocked Harry to the ground with one hit from his other fist. 'Watch I don't step on you by mistake, you fucking midget,' Allan sneered.

'OK fellow, that's enough of that sort of language,' Sergeant Evans said, and fumbling in his pocket he brought out a set of handcuffs. 'Come on, quiet now, up the station with you.'

'I'm not going anywhere with white-pig-scum like you, Evans!' Allan yelled. 'You'll have to bloody catch me first,' and he started off at a sprint.

From then on it all happened so fast that Allan was never sure of the sequence of events, except that ever since, he could only walk slightly pigeon-toed with his weight thrown forward on to the balls of his feet.

It was one of Dargan's friends who brought him down with a flying tackle. He fell face forward on to the loose gravel and putting his hands out to break the fall, exposed the pink flesh of his palms, which immediately began to bleed. Then they were all on him, pummelling, punching and kicking. He felt several ribs crack and caught his breath as he grabbed at the big, black, heavy-capped police boot. Wrenching the policeman off his feet and tearing the truncheon out of his hand, he laid about the sergeant's head with it as heavily as he could.

Someone kicked the truncheon away and then he felt him or her dragging him by his legs face downwards over the gravel. He tried digging his fingers in to resist the pull but there was nothing to clutch on to and the gravel ate away the skin on his forearms.

He could see the still form of the sergeant sprawled in the road -as he struggled to kick free, but the four of them were too powerful a combination.

They dragged him to the edge of the road, turned him over and pulled his legs up on to the pavement.

'Jump on the fucking bastard,' someone yelled.

And there, outside the Woongarra RSL Club, in the warm, silvery, northwest moonlight, as The Rockaires played, 'Love, Love Me Do', two men held Allan Foster's legs over the edge of the pavement while the other two jumped on his shins, which splintered and cracked and stuck up white and bloody out of the burst black skin.

The Woongarra Memorial Hall is an ugly stucco building, quite out of character with the rest of the architecture in the town. Built in 1927 with shire funds, the foundation stone laid by the wife of the then Shire President, it was a symbol of what the residents imagined their town represented: the triumph of man over his hostile surroundings.

It had since come down in the world. The pale green paint was peeling, several of the windows were boarded up and the lower half of the walls were defaced with misspelt obscenities. It was now used, in a desultory manner, for the art classes attended by a few of the local white housewives, and to house the Historical Society's small collection of fascinating bric-a-brac, illustrating how the white man had managed to impinge himself momentarily on this huge land. It was also used for public meetings, which were a rarity, and on this night, for the dance to raise funds for Gary Andrews's widow and her five children.

George Davies, his street service finished, crossed to the hall and threaded his way through the crowd at the door.

'Give us your dollar then,' Betty Flinders called hoarsely. He fished in his pocket and brought out a bill.

'Should make you pay double.' She put it in an old cardboard shoebox where it lay among other tired looking bills and assorted coins. 'Seeing as you're always saying how your Lord goes everywhere with you. But I guess you don't have to pay for invisible partners.' She laughed at her own joke and the soft dewlaps of flesh hanging under her neck jiggled up and down. George laughed too. He liked Betty, even though she was a hopeless alcoholic. Her family had lived in the tin humpy nearest to his own family's place down on the river and they'd played together as young children. He hadn't been in the least surprised when he'd been told about her eight-man frolic at the back of the Garra on Monday night. Nor was he shocked.Sometimes he wondered if all the experience he'd had during his life had made him unshockable, and furthermore, whether this was a good or bad thing,

'You watch you don't go having too much and getting yourself into trouble again,' he chided her.

'Nah,' a big fat woman standing beside Betty said, 'she got to behave herself tonight. Gave herself a sore throat, she did!'

Several women cackled with coarse laughter and Betty said, 'Bill's over there, why don't you go and have a word with him? He's not himself, you know.' George looked in the direction she indicated and saw Bill Flinders slouched on a metal chair.

There were almost three hundred people in the hall. All of them were part Aboriginal and most of those over fifteen had been drinking heavily. The smell of stale alcohol and body odour was very strong. The band, a piano player, an accordionist, and two guitarists, played without the benefit of microphones and the scene on the dance floor resembled nothing more closely than a bizarre parody of a corroboree, or the death dance of some once-beautiful animal.

There were a few older couples trying out half-remembered foxtrot steps, but mostly people danced alone, some opposite partners, others singly, swaying their cirrhosis-swollen stomachs, their eyes glazed and their features slack with alcohol.

Between the befuddled dancers ran the children. There were dozens of them. The older ones sliding on the filthy floor, while some of them lay on their backs, their friends pulling them along by their legs. Others were playing tag or holding races. All of them were dirty, tousle-headed, snotty-nosed and screaming with laughter and delight.

George said hello to many of them by name, but they just smiled quickly back and said nothing. They were rather scared of him because they knew he was somehow different from them and their families.

The smaller children stayed close to their parents who sat on the row of chairs down the sidewalls of the hall. They sat on adults' knees and were hugged indiscriminately by anyone who felt like hugging them. They too were dirty and unkempt and mucus ran down from their noses into their mouths, as they sucked their thumbs and gazed at their older brothers' and sisters' wild games.

In several places on the floor, in front of the chairs, thin, well-worn blankets were spread out and on these lay an assortment of tiny babies. The youngest one was three weeks old. It lay on its back, silently

staring up at the neon strip lighting, blinking occa-
sionally. Beside it were Ann Marshall's twins, yelling
as they had done more or less continuously since their
mother was taken across to Bourke prison on Tuesday
morning. Four months old and suddenly deprived of
their mother's milk, their stomachs and their emotions were having difficulty adjusting to the change.

George knelt down and wiped one twin's nose
with his handkerchief and tickled the other one's
tummy, making gooing noises at it. Mrs Marshall
stopped haranguing another woman for long enough
to give a quick smile and a 'G'day.'

'How's Ann?' George asked.

'OK. Her dad's stayed over in Bourke. She don't
come up for trial for another two weeks and the lawyer chap over there reckons she'll get a year. I don't
reckon she should get anything.Bloody Billy Saunders
deserved what he got and he'll get away with it and
she won't. 'Tisn't fair. But what can we do?' She
shrugged her shoulders.

George tickled both babies a little more and
chucked them under the chin. They were quiet for the
time, but started bawling again the minute he left
them and went on over to Bill Flinders,who sat forward with his elbows on his knees, his chin in his
hands, staring vacantly into space, mumbling to himself and humming.

'Evening, Bill.' George sat down. 'How's tricks?'
Bill made no sign he'd heard and continued to hum.
'What's up then Bill, aren't you talking to your old
mates?'

Bill blinked rapidly and, keeping one eye shut,
turned his head slowly round. He hiccupped.

'Lo mate,' he said, George realized that Bill didn't recognize him.

'Having a good time?'

Bill nodded with the whole top half of his body, slowly.

George glanced back at the entrance and saw that Betty was watching. No wonder she's worried, he thought. He tried again. 'What you been up to lately?' Bill Flinders pursed his mouth and mumbled a few inarticulate sounds. He looked sideways at George, pressed his lips together and gave what passed as a smile.

Dear Lord, George prayed silently, Dear Lord, help me to help this man.

His meditation was abruptly interrupted by Doug Foster, who appeared pushing his way through the crowd of people on the floor and fell on his knees in front of George, clutching at him. 'George, George, help me, please help me.'

There were tears streaming down Doug's face. Bill Flinders made no sign that he'd noticed this new arrival. He continued to stare into space, mumbling and humming. A little bubble of spittle, oozing out of the comer of his mouth, ran down his chin.

George was one of the few people in the hall who hadn't already heard about the new baby and he imagined that Doug was still referring to Carol and Steve. He was angry and disappointed with Doug, because it was obvious that he was drunk.

'I can't do anything more for you, Dougo,' he said. 'I've told you what I think would be best for you to do and it doesn't include getting drunk.' Then, feeling repentant at having made such a harsh judgment, he added, 'If you decide to build down on the river, I'll comedown and give you a hand and I'll bring Steve and Carol so they can be part of it. But I can't do more than that. The rest is up to you and Flo.'

At the mention of his wife's name Doug began to sob, 'Flo, Flo,' and George realized that something else had happened.

'What is it? What's up, Dougo?'

'Flo, Flo.'

'Is she all right?'

Doug nodded.

'And the baby? Has she had it?'

Doug groaned, 'It's not a baby, it's a monster. A monster. Why can't they kill it?'

George stiffened. 'Don't talk like that. What-ever else the baby is, it's still a human being, created by God.'

'Some fucking God,' Doug yelled, relieved that at last his frustration and sorrow had found someone to vent itself on in anger.

George stood up so quickly that Doug, who had been hanging on to his knees, was thrown backwards and sprawled across the dirty floor. A child, unable to stop in time, skidded into him and fell on top of his head, Doug lashed out with his hands and pushed off the child, who ran crying to find its mother.

Bob and Dave Foster came out of the crowd and helped their oldest brother back on to his feet.

'I'll fix that bloody George Davies,' Doug yelled. 'Telling me that monster is a gift from his God.' He struggled free of them and pushing through the crowd, made for the door through which George was disappearing.

'Let's get him home,' Dave said, 'before he gets into any more trouble.'

The two brothers had spent the last part of their celebration evening in the back bar of the Imperial, staying until Sergeant Evans had thrown them out at closing time. While they were weaving their way across to the hall they'd seen Doug coming down the road from the hospital and called out to him. 'Here's Old Dougo. Hey, Dougo. Come on, you old bastard.'

They'd sat in the gutter of the main street and through his tears Doug had told them about the baby.

'You poor bastard,' Dave commiserated. 'Here, have a bloody drink, mate, that'll make you feel better.' He held out a bottle.

Doug drank the port and immediately the liquor spread its warmth through his empty stomach, up his spine and into his brain and he did feel better. After a few more long pulls he felt better still, though when, a little while later when they were in the hall, he broke the news about the baby to Allan, he'd burst into tears again. Allan hadn't said much, just that they'd work things out, and then he'd left, but not before instructing Bob and Dave to takeDoug home. Doug, who was exhausted with emotion, fatigue and now liquor, was leaving quietly with them, when he'd spotted George Davies sitting beside Bill Flinders.

Now, as Doug charged off, Bob felt panicky and distressingly sober. 'We better get after him.'

Near the door, Pete Mathews barred Doug's way. He was smaller than Doug, but even so he stood his ground and said, 'OK. OK, mate. That's enough from you. We don't want any trouble,right? So now you go on home or I'll call the cops and get them to give you a ride back.'

In his blind fury Doug pushed Pete Mathews aside and sent him crashing against the table on which Betty Flinders had her shoebox till. The table collapsed, the box fell, coins rolling in every direction. Children whooping with joy as if it were a game swooped down on the floor, diving among adult legs in search of the money. Several people laughed as Betty Flinders shouted, 'Fuck off, you stupid bastard,' at Pete Mathews, knowing that it wasn't his fault but glad to have an excuse to yell at him because, in common with a large majority of Aborigines in Woongarra, she didn't like the man. She thought him too clever by half.

Angry at being made to look a fool in front of so many people, Pete Mathews brushed himself down and rushed off after Doug, who had now caught up with George Davies and was hanging onto his arm. George turned to Doug and with a compelling calm slowly said: 'Dougo, Dougo.'

Doug let go of his arm, feeling the anger subside. 'Well, why'd you say that about it being a gift of God and all that?' he said lamely. 'How can it be, a monster like that?'

'God works in mysterious ways.'

The anger started to lick up again. 'Yeh, bloody mysterious ways. He's made a bloody mess of things, that's what he's done.'

'He's not responsible. It's not his fault.'

'Whose bloody fault is it then?'

Pete Mathews raced up the street and threw himself on Doug. Caught unprepared, Doug fell heavily back against his brother's bright red Ford, parked in the street behind them.

'Right, now you've done your dash, mate,' he glowered in Doug's face. 'No one pushes me around like that. Call the station,' he shouted back at a young man who had followed him out.The youth hesitated, torn between loyalty to this man, whom he thought could lead him on to a position of power, and his natural antipathy towards white policemen. By the time he decided to move, it was too late, for he turned and saw Bob and Dave Foster running up towards him.The brothers jostled him.

'No one calls the pigs,' Dave said. And then, 'Come on, Dougo, we're going home. Let him go, Pete, before we have to help you.'

Pete Mathews reluctantly let go of Doug's shirt-front and stopped leaning on him, but just like a dog worrying a bone, Doug couldn't stop. 'I'm not going anywhere,' he said, 'until George tells me if it isn't his God's fault, then whose fault is it that I've got a monster for a son?'

Before George could answer, Pete Mathews shouted: 'Whose bloody fault d'you think it is? Flo's, of course. Whose else? What else can you expect from a whore like that? She slept with every bastard in town while you were gone. Probably got screwed so much that's what buggered up the kid. How d'you even know it's your bloody kid anyway?'

Like a faulty projector, Doug's mind did a spontaneous 'fast rewind' and came to rest on a frame in which a shiny, sweating face grinned out from the back seat of the car, as Flo slammed it shut and came towards him clutching her shoes. In a second, Doug realized that the face he'd seen was Pete Mathews and in the same instant he realized that it was Pete Mathews who had sold his kids for two hundred and

245

fifty thousand dollars and a promise that Woongarra would stay out of the headlines.

Before Doug could reach Pete Mathews, his brothers had pinned him against Allan's car.Holding his arms down against his sides, they tried to lift him bodily to take him away.

'Get lost, you bastard,' Bob shouted over his shoulder at Pete, 'Go on, piss off.'

George Davies tried to lead Pete away, but Pete shook the hand off his shoulder and stood in front of the pinioned Doug, sneering with contempt. Wishing that he'd had the courage to talk to his former boss, Allan, instead of attacking him through Doug, he spat out the words: 'The great thing is, Dougo, you'll never know, will you? Whether that monster is yours or somebody else's and you're just the fall guy who got landed with the baby.'

He laughed, and his mouth was still open when Doug felt the boner's knife tucked in Bob's belt pressing against his hand where it was held firm. In a gigantic explosion of energy, stimulated by an overwhelming white-hot anger, Doug broke free from his brothers' grip and dragged out the blade, slicing off Bob's thumb as his brother threw out his hand to try to prevent him from lunging forward.

The knife sliced right through Pete Mathews's jugular vein. His eyes bulged in surprise, but he felt no pain and his mouth still gaped in frozen laughter as the blood spurted out over George Davies, Bob and Dave Foster and Doug himself, before sluicing over the red Capri, making it appear as if the duco had suddenly begun to melt and drip.

Inside the Memorial Hall, Bill Flinders waltzed by himself with outstretched arm holding an imaginary partner. Not once colliding with the numbers of children playing tag around him, he executed perfect turns and intricate embellishments as, with his eyes closed, he went back in his memory to the night when he and Betty came fifth in the Newcastle Palais Ball-room Dancing Championship. The band played as it had then, their song, 'In Your Sweet Little Alice Blue Gown', and Bill Flinders hummed the tune. There was a bottle wrapped in brown paper tucked under his arm and every now and then, with practised ease, and without even standing still, he took a swig of his rose hip syrup and methylated spirits.

CHILDREN OF BLINDNESS

# CHAPTER TEN

## MONDAY

'**D**ouglas George Arthur Foster, it is charged that on the twenty-fifth of February 1975 in Culgoa Street, Woongarra, in the State of New South Wales you did feloniously and maliciously murder Peter Stanley Edward Mathews . . .'

Out at the old mission, Carol and Steve Foster had helped clear away after breakfast and were now rounding up the other children to attend George Davies's Sunday service. Over the railway, in his government built brick house, Gordon Wright lay in bed reading a month-old airmail edition of the London Sunday Times while his wife pretended to sleep in the other single bed. Up at the hospital, Flo Foster, in a drug-induced half-coma, dreamt happily about a house on the river with her husband and children, while in the humidicrib in the nursery her new baby succeeded in its battle to live. Over at the West, Betty Flinders slept on while her husband Bill padded down the litter-strewn street to Fred Pepper's ever-waiting mobile liquor store. Back up at the hospital, Lesley Armstrong stood at Allan's bedside waiting for the arrival of the ambulance, which would take him down to

Sydney. In another ward, only thirty feet away, Sergeant Ron Evans was recovering from severe cuts and abrasions to the head and chest. At the Imperial Hotel, Harry Fletcher retied the laces of his new golf shoes and, standing in front of their bedroom mirror, took a practice swing with an imaginary club, while his wife watched him contemptuously over the top of the sheets. In the room behind the altar at the Catholic church, Father Michael Clancy packed the sacramental wine and bread into a new suitcase, while eighty miles away to the north-west, Col Richards kept walking, following a tributary of the Barwon upstream, determined to forget Woongarra and the battered body of his dead wife. Beside him, the river flowed down into the Barwon. Past gums and coolibahs and wattles it flowed, just as it had for millions of years; long before any man, white or black, came to light fires and live on its banks, hunt for food, carve canoes from trees which overhung it, to fight each other, or to fish and swim in its waters.

And in the wooden courthouse, where the summer heat was already beginning to curl the corners of the official papers, Doug Foster wondered why Constable Ed Vickers's eyes were moist and he faltered as he asked,

'How do you plead . .

ABOUT THE AUTHOR:

**Trish**

....has been a journalist, a radio and TV producer and presenter, as well as an author, for more than forty years. She has written several fiction and non-fiction works, as well as co-authoring five non-fiction books with Iain Finlay.

A co-founder and Associate Producer of the internationally successful science programme for television, Beyond 2000, she has travelled, lived and worked on every continent. In recent years she has also worked with Iain as a volunteer with the Voice of Viet Nam radio network helping broadcasters there improve their English language programming.

The two of them have recently embarked on the challenging task of wrenching back the ownership of all their titles, written solo or together and are having a deal of enjoyment in establishing an e-publishing company, by which they hope to make all their previously published and unpublished titles available to a wider public.

She and Iain have children and grandchildren and, when not traveling, live in Australia on the far north coast of New South Wales.

# Read about other titles by Trish Clark:

*ANDREA
*AUSTRALIAN ADVENTURERS
*MOTHERHOOD
AN IMMACULATE CONCEPTION

## with **Iain Finlay**

*AFRICA OVERLAND
*SOUTH AMERICA OVERLAND
*ACROSS THE SOUTH PACIFIC
GOOD MORNING HANOI
THE SILK TRAIN

Titles marked with an asterisk were originally
published under Trish's previous name,
Trish Sheppard.

# ANDREA
## by Trish Clark

Ahead of the kiss and tell pack by several decades *Andrea* was a close intimate of European royalty and silent-screen Hollywood stars as well as Australian politicians and socialites. She also spent four character-building years in a Japanese prisoner of war camp.

At the time of its publication her no-holds-barred biography caused a legal flurry at the highest levels. Despite demands for its publication to be banned, it has gone on to become an established social history of a time when live radio was the power domain and Andrea was its Queen. 'He was up me like a rat up a rope,' is just one of her earthy comments about an Australian Prime Minister.

Now, with all her personal papers stored in their own archive at the Library of NSW its time to re-read her story and be amazed how little has changed when it comes to Sex, Money and Politics.

(Illustrated. Available 2011)

Website: www.imperium.com under construction


# MOTHERHOOD
## by Trish Clark

Fifteen women living through the various stages of motherhood from pregnancy to the anticipation of an empty nest, reveal their innermost desires and fears. While dealing with the unexpected blows of early widowhood, an offspring's physical incapacit, or even a child's death from drug addiction, they unveil the determination and courage that is at the core of their chosen lifelong role.

Strung along the thread of the author's own experiences their survival mantra, at a time when the choice for motherhood is no longer a natural given, is the feeling that there is only one thing worse than having children and that is not having them.

(Illustrated. Available 2011)

Website: www.imperium.com under construction

# AN IMMACULATE CONCEPTION
## by Trish Clark

'...just when you thought it was safe to get on
with your own life.'

Cathy Connolly is revelling in the newfound joys of being Sam's grandmother. At work she is Ms. Catherine Stuart, a high-powered, senior executive in the Education Department. She's in good health, her husband Steve, is a successful architect, she has a happy daughter, a settled son and daughter-in-law, an erratic but charmingly likable brother and a distant, but well-loved mother.

Suddenly, within the space of less than two weeks, her life plunges into disarray. A colleague at work is trying to push her out of her job, Steve wants to take off in a 4-wheel drive for the Kimberleys, her daughter has given her boyfriend the boot, her brother wants to leave his wife and two daughters for a woman twenty-five years younger, and her son is donating his sperm to a lesbian couple. But, worst of all, Cathy finds she has cervical cancer.

*'Life has taken a sudden lurch,' her voice was tremulous. 'Last week it all seemed so simple and straightforward. I feel as though I have stepped off into the deep end.'*

*'Just keep treading water and ring your Mum.' Steve told her.'*

A fascinating and witty slice of modern Australian life, *An Immaculate Conception* highlights the dramatically changing standards, morals, and attitudes, not only of the cool, modish inhabitants of Sydney's eastern beach suburbs, where it is set, but of the whole country.

(Available 2011)

Website:
www.animmaculateconception.com under construction

# AUSTRALIAN ADVENTURERS
## by Trish Clark

What drives a person to purposely place themselves beyond the comfortable, safe borders of the known; to push on further, to the risky edge and perhaps even over it?

Is there some intangible physic payment for placing yourself in physical jeopardy? Is that reward so addictive that it cannot be resisted as it grows to be a compulsion beyond family, friends, financial reward, even life itself.

Twenty *Australian Adventurers,* of all ages, share the passion that drives them to film sharks in the wild, climb Everest or become Australia's first aviatrix. To solo sail or to helicopter solo around the world. To voyage alone in the Antarctic or to recreate the 4000-kilometer open boat voyage of the Bounty mutineers. To be determined to hold the world hang gliding records for both height and distance at the same time, or to be the first to canoe right around the Australian continent. To put grandmotherhood on hold in order to become a backpacker, or to join the wartime resistance. Stories about those who dare ...to delight and challenge those who stay at home.

(Illustrated.  Available 2011)

Website:

www.highadventurepublishing.com  under construction

# TRAVELING WITH CHILDREN

You'd love to travel to remote and exotic places but...you have kids. So? Why let that stop you? You're worried about their education...think you should wait. Don't!

Iain and Trish didn't. They made three big journeys through some of the toughest territories in Africa, North and South America and the South Pacific with their two young children. Using public transport; buses, trains, trucks, trading vessls, sometimes hitching, each of them shouldering their own backpack, they spent months at a time on the road.

Spread over period of just on four years, their travels took them first from Capetown to Cairo. Eighteen months later they journeyed overland from Canada to Tierra del Fuego, at the bottom tip of South America and within another year and a half, they island hopped across the South Pacific from Chile to Australia.

Not only did they survive to write the books, which also look at the history, politics and way of life of the countries through which they traveled, but, with the passing of the years they know their travel adventures truly sealed an on-going adult friendship with their children.

(All titles illustrated and available 2011)

# AFRICA OVERLAND
## by Iain Finlay & Trish Clark

Capetown to Cairo! A magical phrase...the journey of a lifetime. Around 12,000 kilometers, nine countries, four months on the road with nothing booked or arranged in advance. With their two children; a son aged eight and daughter nine, carrying their own back-packs and often sleeping in rough circumstances (like in the back of a truck laden with copper ingots), Iain, Trish and the kids get to see: Kruger National Park, Victoria Falls and travel on the TanZam railway. They experience the vast herds of game in Serengetti, Lake Manyara, Ngorongoro and Amboseli, go to the source of the Blue Nile in Ethiopia, travel on 'Kitchener's Railway' across the Nubian Desert from Khartoum to Wadi Halfa, Aswan and the great temples of the Nile Valley... all the way down to Cairo and the Pyramids.

And the kids did travel projects the whole way!
Projects that were the envy of their classmates.

Website: www.africaoverland.net under construction

# SOUTH AMERICA OVERLAND
## by Iain Finlay & Trish Clark

This incredible journey includes much more than just *South America*. It starts in Canada as Iain, Trish, their ten-year-old son and daughter, aged eleven, set out in a blizzard that covers most of the US, to deliver a car cross-country to San Diego. Then they travel by train and bus through Mexico, Belize, Guatamala, El Salvador, Honduras, Nicaragua and Costa Rica to Panama. Along the way they visit the great Aztec and Mayan temples of Tenochtitlan, Palenque, Tikal and many others.

Then on to Ecuador and Peru, where they puzzle over the mysterious lines in the Nazca Desert and visit the fabled Lost City of the Incas at Machu Picchu. Across the Andes, on the Amazon headwaters, at Pucallpa and down-river, they find barges, ferryboats and a trading boat for a 3,000-kilometer, month-long journey down the Amazon to Iquitos and Manaus.

On through the Matto Grosso to Bazilia, Rio and Sao Paulo, Iguasu Falls, Montevideo and Buenos Aires, before hitching for much of the way south through Patagonia to the amazing glaciers of southern Argentina, the Magellan Straits and Tierra del Fuego. Here they reach the southernmost city in the world, Ushuaia,  Six months, 17 countries, 23,000 kilometers: endless school projects for the kids.

Website: www.southamericaoverland.net under construction

# ACROSS THE SOUTH PACIFIC
## by Iain Finlay & Trish Clark

Leaving Santiago, Chile after a frightening night of earth tremors, Iain, Trish and their two children, now 12 and 13 years old, fly to Easter Island, where, using their own tents, they camp out in remote corners of the island as they explore the huge, enigmatic stone monoliths. From there, its Tahiti and the stunning beauty of Bora Bora, Morea and the unbelievable Tuamotu atolls.  In the Cook Islands they board a copra trading vessel for a journey through the island chain; Aitutaki, Rakahanga and Manihiki. When it breaks down, mid-ocean, they go overboard with the crew to swim in water 3,000 metres deep. American and Western Samoa are next, in the midst of a typhoon. Then the pleasures and beauty of Tonga, the Fiji Islands, Vanuatu and New Caledonia, before finally returning to their home in Australia.  The message about travelling with your kids is: do it before  their teens. By then its too late. Ian & Trish only just made it.

Website: www.acrossthesouthpacific.com under construction

# GOOD MORNING HANOI
## by Iain Finlay & Trish Clark

When Iain Finlay and Trish Clark arrive in Hanoi on a one-year work assignment for the English language service of the communist government-run radio network, they can hardly foresee the intense and exceptional experiences that await them. Coming to Vietnam for an Australian aid agency, their intended role is to coach and instruct, or at least to share their knowledge, with a small group of young reporters. But they find that they learn more than they teach.

As friendships with their colleagues grow, Iain and Trish are involved in developing and presenting a daily radio program - the first run by Westerners on a regular basis - and they become immersed in the stimulating life of one of Asia's most enchanting cities. In the process, they gain fascinating insights into Vietnamese society and culture, as well as a greater understanding and respect for the new Vietnam.

*Good Morning Hanoi* also illuminates the lives of a group of people dwelling in crowded conditions around a small courtyard in central Hanoi where Iain and Trish find a house to rent, and who become like an extended family living in the heart of the city.

In *Good Morning Hanoi*, Iain and Trish, two of the founders and producers of the international television program *Beyond 2000,* return to a country from which they had reported during the Vietnam War. They find an extraordinarily friendly people whose resilience and irrepressible good nature enable them to put the past behind them and move into the future with confidence.

(Illustrated. Available 2010)

Website: www.goodmorninghanoi.net under construction

# THE SILK TRAIN
## by Iain Finlay & Trish Clark

*The Silk Train* is travel adventure with a geo-political backbone. Veteran journalists Iain Finlay and Trish Clark set out to travel 21,000 kilometres from Singapore to Venice, by hopping on and off trains up through South East Asia, across China, Central Asia, the Caucasus, Turkey and the Balkans. Much of their route covers territory along which the ancient Silk Road trails wound their way over the past two thousand years. They planned to use rail lines that form part of an embryonic, UN-backed Trans-Asian Railway network, that will eventually create unbroken freight and passenger corridors all the way from China's far-eastern seaboard, to Europe.

While visiting some of the great historic sites of China and Central Asia, among them: Xi'an, Dunhaung, Samarkand and Bukhara, they also become aware of the changing dynamics of Big-Power politics across the vast Central Asian steppes, once the stamping grounds of Genghis Khan and Tamerlane, which now include the newly independent countries of Kazakhstan, Kyrgyzstan and Uzbekistan. They very quickly realise that, by far the most important items of trade along the modern equivalents of the Silk Road, are now oil and natural gas. Oil is the new silk. It is the new trans-national currency of the Silk Road, with China and its voracious, seemingly insatiable appetite for energy, emerging as the most significant factor in the political and economic arena of Central and South East Asia.

Further west, Russia's increased pressure on the Caucasus, particularly Georgia, is just another indication of how vital the world's dwindling energy resources are and will remain for most of the twenty-first century. By journey's end, in Venice, they realise they have travelled a very different Silk Road than that of Marco Polo.

(Illustrated. Available 2010)

Website: www.thesilktrain.com under construction

Imperiumbooks.com
Highadventurepublishing.com
and
Highadventureproductions.com

are part of
High Adventure Productions Pty. Ltd.
PO Box 111
Tumbulgum, NSW 2490
email: iaintrish@mac.com
Australia